Blessings!

Mermaids Never Drown

Muncy Chapman

Mermaids Never Drown

ISBN: 1-928602-82-7

Published by MountainView Publishing
1284 Overlook Dr.
Sierra Vista, AZ 85635
http://www.trebleheartbooks.com

This is a work of fiction. Some of the towns and beaches named in this book are real. Weeki Wachi Spring is a real place, and people can go there to watch mermaid performances. However, the events, people, and technical information in this book are fictional. Any resemblance to any kind of technical apparatus, or any persons, living or dead, is strictly coincidental. They are simply results of the author's imagination.

Mermaids Never Drown

Muncy Chapman

MountainView Publishing
A Division of Treble Heart Books

Dedication

Dedicated to the lovely mermaids who cavort daily at Weeki Wachee Spring, to the delight of the many people who come to watch them.

PROLOGUE

The tires of her sleek blue sports car squealed as Lori rounded the S curves of the narrow black asphalt. A cold March wind raked through her thick hair, billowing it into a mass of long, dark tangles. It wasn't important. She could brush it out later. For now she only wanted to savor the excitement of being in complete control of her very first car.

In truth this was Lori's third car, but this one was special. Unlike the other two, which had been given to her by indulging parents, she'd paid for this one out of her own hard-earned wages. Independence had a sweet taste for which Lori was fast developing a hearty appetite.

The day had been exhausting. A record crowd had attended the afternoon performance of the mermaid show at Weeki Wachee Spring, and Lori had stayed late to work on a new swimming routine. Mr. Porter, director of the famous Mermaid Follies, wanted the cast to be perfect before next season. A sudden rush of air through the car brought with it an exhilaration that swept away her fatigue like feathers in the wind.

She glanced down at her watch. Six-thirty! She'd have to

rush to be ready before Ken came for her tonight. Her right foot pressed harder on the accelerator and the car responded instantly.

Rounding the next sharp curve, she cautiously braked and glanced down over the steep drop-off into Bottomless Lake. Formed overnight by a sinkhole nearly a century before, the gaping hole was a distinct contrast to the gently rolling hills of north Florida. Oddly, instead of slowing, her car seemed to gain momentum as she frantically pumped the brakes, trying to bring it under control. The sharpest curve was only a few yards ahead. It would be impossible to negotiate that curve at this speed. Panicking, she used both hands in an effort to maneuver the treacherous turn as her left foot groped for the emergency brake.

The resounding crash could undoubtedly be heard for miles around, and like clothes in a dryer, Lori felt herself tumbling over and over again, until suddenly there was no feeling at all—only blackness and silence.

Chapter One

Last night the dream returned, and with it all the fears that had surrounded her for the past few months. If Lori had thought leaving home and traveling to a beautiful vacation spot hundreds of miles away would relieve her anxieties, she was wrong. Her father had been right when he'd said, years ago, "You can never run away from your problems, Lori. Share them with the Lord, then meet them head-on."

Daddy! The wisest, most thoughtful man she'd ever known. If only he were here with her now to help her get her thoughts in proper perspective. She missed him so! Even though she often sensed his palpable presence, the two years since his death had done little to heal her grief.

Further sleep was impossible. Lori's friend, Nicole, slept peacefully in the next bed. Lori was careful not to awaken her as she slipped quietly from her own bed. She picked up her Bible and tiptoed onto the balcony.

For lo, I am with you always, she read in the final chapter of Matthew. She lifted her eyes and scanned the ocean where first dawn was breaking. She was not alone. Hadn't He protected her when her life had been threatened not once, but twice in recent weeks? No matter what happened in the days and weeks ahead, she knew she could depend upon Him to be with her forever. *Even unto the end of the world.*

Mr. Porter had been generous in allowing her to take time off from the Mermaid Follies for these two weeks in the Florida Keys, and she and Nicole planned to enjoy every minute of it.

"Lori? Where are you?"

"Out here on the balcony, Nicky. I came out here so I wouldn't disturb your sleep."

Nicole pulled her short robe around her nightie and joined Lori on the balcony. "Why are you up so early? Was it the dream again?"

Lori pulled in a deep breath. "Yes. The dream—it's always the same. The air around me seems to evaporate and I can't breathe. It's as though something is smothering me. All I can see is a burst of bright colored lights. Then I always wake up, gasping for air."

"Well, there's certainly plenty of fresh air out here," Nicole observed, inhaling deeply of the cool salty breeze. "I think this place is just what you need to get some much needed rest and relaxation."

"It's lovely," Lori agreed. "Go back to bed, Nicky. I'm sorry I disturbed your sleep."

"Are you staying up?"

"Yes. I think I'll walk down the beach to that cove where the old pier juts out into the water. I want to practice my routine among the coral reefs. Want to come?"

"No, thanks! This is one mermaid who's going to stay dry for two whole weeks. Have fun, and I'll see you when you get back."

Nicole returned to her bed and pulled the blanket over her head. Lori changed into her bathing suit and tiptoed out of the room.

The water was as clear and sparkling as fine crystal. Splashes of reds and golds flashed before Lori's eyes like a giant kaleidoscope, ever moving, ever changing. She stretched her fingers to explore the coral crevices of the renowned barrier reefs, pulled fresh oxygen from her tube, and dove still deeper. Long, dark hair trailed behind her like a silky mane as she used her long legs to propel herself downward through the seemingly bottomless sea.

The warm ocean water was a direct contrast to the cold spring water in which she usually practiced her swim routines, and the salt content gave her buoyancy that made movement easy. She turned several flips, exhilarated by this new sensation of weightlessness.

In this silent world shared with harmless creatures from the sea, Lori felt surrounded by a peace she had rarely experienced in recent months. "Thank you, Lord," she prayed, "for Your constant love and protection. Please help me leave my fears behind and regain my faith in my fellow man."

How foolish her fears must seem to her friends and coworkers. She had no known enemies. Why would she think anyone would deliberately set out to kill her?

Mr. Porter was convinced exhaustion and stress, plus a vivid imagination, all played a part in Lori's anxieties. "Take a little vacation," he had urged her. "Get away and erase all this nonsense from your head."

Lori realized the importance of getting her mind back on a rational track. In just two weeks, she would return to Weeki Wachee Spring and resume the starring role in the Mermaid Follies. Mr. Porter's patience had already been stretched to the limit. She mustn't let anything jeopardize her leading role after she had put so much effort into getting the part. There were at least ten girls who would jump at the chance to take her place, and one in particular.

Helga Larson had been quite outspoken about her desire for the lead. Her father, a prominent Florida State Senator, had reportedly even tried to pressure Mr. Porter into featuring his daughter in the show. Lori had heard rumors of a veiled threat to have the mermaid show closed—something to do with permits and state regulations—but of course, no names were mentioned. Since no action ever came of it, she refused to let herself get burdened down by the rumors. Some people thrived on stirring up gossip, but Lori had never been one of them. She had enough to do just keeping up with her own obligations.

Taking another gulp of air from her oxygen tube, she slid through the water. Mr. Porter had designed the swimsuit she wore, disguising the tubes of oxygen in the lining so they were almost invisible. In her mind he was a genius, always coming up with new ideas to add authenticity to the act. The thousands of tourists who flocked to watch his shows year after year were living proof of his expertise.

As the warm, gentle currents lifted her lithe body, Lori twisted to weave between the reefs, feeling a new surge of peace and security in this sanctuary beneath the sea.

A baby octopus brushed against her leg and scurried for cover mong the coral reefs. Lori laughed, causing a spiral of iridescent bubbles to rise above her. In spite of their ominous reputation, Lori knew these mollusks to be the shyest of all sea creatures.

But her tranquility turned abruptly to horror as she felt her neck jerk from a sudden hard tug on her hair. Unwillingly, her body was propelled through the water at an alarming rate of speed and raw panic shot through her like a jolt of electricity. She twisted to see what kind of creature held her captive, but because of the tight hold on her hair, all she could see was a pair of legs churning through the water ahead of her. Definitely human legs! Muscular, hairy, masculine legs. Her mind whirled with a thousand frantic questions that had no answers as she struggled to free herself from her assailant's grip. *Dear God, please help me!* Had the horrible nightmare followed her all the way here to the Florida Keys?

She could see strong legs scissors kick their way toward the surface, even as she fought desperately to free herself from his grasp. The length of her hair allowed him to remain a safe distance away from her kicking and struggling, yet still retain his control of her body. This was neither nerves nor imagination. This was stark and terrifying reality. Lori *had* to break free— her very life depended on it.

As the frantic struggle continued, lack of oxygen seemed to be weakening her aggressor. Taking full advantage, Lori gave one sudden, forceful lunge and broke through the surface of the water. In panic, she turned to face her attacker. He still maintained a firm grip on her wet hair as he pulled her toward the pier, releasing it only to grasp her waist with his big, strong hands and lift her onto the old wooden jetty.

Too exhausted from her struggle to speak, Lori collapsed onto the warm deck and looked up into eyes as blue and clear as the watery depths she had so recently left behind.

Strangely enough, earnest concern was written on his sun-tanned face. Lori blinked twice as she studied his ruggedly handsome features and tried to remember if she had ever seen him before. She struggled to regain her breath and raised herself to a sitting position, cautiously edging back to widen the distance between them.

"Are you okay?"

"What are you? Some kind of maniac?" Anger overpowered her fear, even as she realized there was no help in sight and probably no one within hearing distance to respond to her screams. "You just tried to kill me down there, and now you have the audacity to ask me if I'm okay? No, I'm not. What in heaven's name were you trying to do to me?" Too late, Lori realized her best bet was probably to appear calm and continue edging toward the end of the pier. If he came too close, she'd have to make a dive for it. She had a better than even chance of out-swimming him.

"Now look here, lady. I just saved your life. You're the most ungrateful creature I've ever seen. Either in *or* out of the water." A near-smile played on his lips. He seemed more amused than angry at her outburst.

"What do you mean? You almost drowned me! You call that saving my life?"

A smile spread across his face, revealing straight, white teeth and two pronounced dimples. When he didn't answer, but continued staring at her with that maddening grin, she asked the all-important question that had haunted her for weeks. "All right, just tell me. Who put you up to this?"

Lori had thought she would be safe down here in the Florida Keys where no one knew her. Yet here it was again, another attempt to snuff out her life almost before it had time to get a good start. There were just too many of these *accidents* to be considered coincidental any longer. And worst of all, she hadn't a clue why anyone would want to do such a thing. As far as she could tell, she hadn't an enemy in the world. "Why don't you tell me who's behind this? I'm just so terribly tired of it all." Lori's lips trembled as she struggled to hold back the tears that threatened to erupt at any moment.

The amazed look on his face told her he was either genuinely innocent, or else should be given an Academy Award. He certainly didn't look the part of a killer. In fact, he looked almost comical as he stood on the dock, his white duck shorts plastered to his muscular thighs and his unbuttoned shirt hanging from his shoulders like a Monday morning wash line.

Drops of salt water clung to his bronze body and glistened in the sun like chips of blue-white diamonds. Hair bleached white by the sun lay wetly pasted to his forehead and clung to the back of his neck. A gold chain hung from his neck and nestled in the blond, curly hair of his chest like a gilded serpent. Even as she feared him she was aware of a strong, almost hypnotic attraction to this unusual man.

His deep, resonant voice relayed a mixture of perplexity and amusement, with just a slight added touch of annoyance. "I saw you dive off the pier and I watched for a long time, waiting for you to surface. Do you realize how long you were down there? Frankly, I'm surprised you're still alive. At first I thought you had run into trouble— some kind of accident— and might need help, but your struggle with me proved you knew exactly what you were doing." He gentled his tone and moved closer to her. "Listen, my friend, nothing can be all that bad. Let's talk things over. I'd really like to help you."

Now it was Lori's turn to look amazed. Did he actually believe her to be suicidal? She, a devout Christian who considered herself to be the luckiest girl alive? As realization of his motives set in and her anger ebbed, her fear began to subside. Was it possible he really believed he was trying to rescue her? She laughed at the incongruity of it.

"I fail to see the humor in such a serious situation." Like the flick of a light switch, his concern turned back to anger. He threw up his hands in utter exasperation. "I have just soaked the only decent clothes I brought with me, and risked life and limb around those jagged reefs—all to save your beautiful little neck—and now all you can do is laugh at me?" His nostrils flared as he stood over her, looking down into her eyes.

"I— I'm sorry." Though she tried, she just couldn't stop laughing.

"What's so funny? Listen, lady, you can jump back in there and drown for all I care. Just don't count on me to rescue you again!"

She saw his anger rising and wondered if his intentions, even though misguided, might have been unselfishly heroic after all. Again she said, "I'm sorry, really." Her words came in little spurts, with small bubbles of stifled laughter interspersed. "It's just, I couldn't possibly drown." She rose to stand beside him now; their bodies' only inches apart. "You see, I'm a mermaid!"

The flush on his face told Lori she had pressed him too far. She saw his hands twitch and realized he was restraining an impulse to shove her back into the salty ocean depths. She tried to lessen the tension with a smile, but he was not so easily placated.

"You're no mermaid, and this is no fairy tale. Furthermore, I don't appreciate your perverted sense of humor." But even as his anger mounted, Lori could sense a softness about him as he fastened his gaze on her eyes.

Following a long, unbroken silence, he finally gave a sigh of resignation and extended his right hand. "I'm Kevin Collins. Since you almost cost me my life, may I know your name? Or do I have to call you Miss Mermaid?"

"You may call me Miss Mermaid if you like," she answered with a flip of her head, intentionally ignoring his outstretched hand. "I rather like that. But my name is Lorelei." As soon as the name left her lips, she dove back into the crystal blue waters of the Atlantic Ocean and disappeared among the twisting clusters of coral reefs.

"Lorelei? That figures!" He watched her cut through the water, clean as a knife, leaving a trail of spiraling bubbles in her wake. He dove and followed her, carefully turning to avoid the coral fingers that grabbed at him from every direction. The weight of his clothes slowed his progress, and his shorts snagged on a piece of coral. Where had she gone? Without his scuba gear, he had to resurface in seconds and he panicked when he saw no trace of her.

To an untrained ear her laughter might have been interpreted as sheer mirth, but Kevin's professional training and experience detected the inward hysteria she tried to conceal. There was some kind of deep-seated trouble here. He didn't know its source, but was certain it wasn't limited to his rescue efforts. Had she really tried to end her life? If she was that desperate, he should find some way to help her.

What was it she'd said? Mermaid? For a moment his imagination took hold and he wondered— but, no! *Good Grief! Get a grip on yourself!* Mermaid, indeed. Still, she had literally disappeared before his eyes. Where had she gone? Had he fallen asleep on the dock and dreamed the whole crazy experience? Strange things happened sometimes to people who stayed in the sun too long. No, he knew better than that. Still, there was not a ripple on the smooth, glassy surface to mark her departure. For a moment, he almost feared for his sanity. There had to be some plausible answer.

His eyes perused the shore for a glimpse of a tall, slender figure topped by a flowing mass of jet black hair, but there was not a soul in sight on this isolated stretch of tropical beach. Should he call someone and start a search party? What could he say that would sound believable? He'd best get back to his hotel. Perhaps he *had* been in the sun too long, after all.

He walked the length of the pier toward his car and lifted the lid to his trunk. Luckily, he remembered throwing in a pair of faded swim trunks in case of an emergency. Who could have predicted the kind of emergency he had just encountered? Grateful for the seclusion of the little cove, he quickly shed his sopping clothes. He threw them into the open trunk and slammed the lid. The swim-shorts he put on were faded and well worn, but at least they were dry.

He walked out onto the dock once more and shielded his eyes from the sun while he scanned the surface of the water, but a hungry gull swooping down to catch a fish was the only creature he could see. He shook his head in resignation and headed back to the shore.

Sitting in the driver's seat of his rental car, he took one last, lingering look toward the water before starting his engine. The wind had picked up, and the smooth surface had changed into soft ripples. There was absolutely no trace of a swimmer, and certainly not of a mysterious green-eyed mermaid!

When he remembered her eyes— those sparkling emerald pools of light fringed with long, sooty lashes— his heart lurched and his anger took a back seat to emotions he couldn't begin to define.

Jennifer's eyes had been green, too. But not a warm, clear, honest green. More like cold, hard slabs of dark green jade. Even when he had believed himself in love with her, he had looked upon her as a cool, self-sufficient princess on an ivory pedestal. He had even admired her icy aloofness; it seemed to set her a notch above her contemporaries.

Whenever he thought of her now, and he found himself doing so less and less, the anger and hurt were gone. In a way, he should feel grateful to her. She had opened his eyes to what today's women were really like, ridiculing his idealistic views of a Christian home and children, and a lifetime of love and loyalty between a man and his wife. She had not only refused his proposal of marriage, but had laughed at him, calling him old-fashioned and unrealistic. After their breakup, she had flitted from one affair to another like a butterfly in the garden.

Growing up on a small farm in Iowa, nurtured by loving Christian parents, Kevin had always assumed when he fell in love it would be forever. He knew beyond a shadow of a doubt this was the only kind of life he could ever settle for. But apparently that was not the way things worked any more.

He could not understand how he had ever been so gullible

and naive. But he was older and much wiser now, and he supposed he should be grateful to Jennifer after all. She had opened his eyes, and he would not be fooled again.

He reminded himself of the two promises he made he started this vacation. The first and most important one had to do with women. He vowed to keep a tight hold on his heart. No summer romances meant there would be no pain and regret to bring back home.

The second promise was to tell absolutely no one the nature of his profession. Not because he had anything to hide or be ashamed of. In fact, he was rather proud of his accomplishments. There were good numbers of people whom he had been able to help, and it always gave him a great feeling of satisfaction to know he made life better for someone. But every time he went to a social function or found himself in the midst of a group of people, he was barraged with shoptalk. He knew that sort of complaint was common among doctors and lawyers, but he failed to see why it should be so for him. Ordinarily he did not mind passing out free advice to his friends. But for these two weeks, he resolved to keep his work a secret and enjoy his first real vacation in years.

Two wonderfully relaxing weeks with no shoptalk and no summer romances! Renewing his promises, he started the engine and headed toward his hotel.

CHAPTER TWO

Lori rounded the point of the little cove before she surfaced again. Luckily she had worn the extra oxygen tube when she began her morning exercises.

In the tanks of the amphitheater at Weeki Wachee Spring, she could usually get by with only one tube because of the many auxiliary tubes strategically hidden among the artificial seaweed and underwater props. The mermaids could dart in and out, taking inconspicuous gulps of air as they performed their intricate aquatic ballet for their audiences. When a routine made it impossible to reach one of the stationary tubes in time, she could always rely on the small oxygen tube hidden inside her specially constructed swimsuit. Mr. Porter had patented the clever breathing system and taught the girls to use it. She had so much respect for him. With such an ingenious director, it was small wonder the mermaid show continued to gain in popularity each year.

When Lori was within sight of her hotel, she swam toward shore and walked along the water's edge, thinking of her strange underwater encounter. Who was Kevin Collins? Where did he come from? She walked briskly; looking over her shoulder to make sure she was not being followed. When she reached the beach in front of her hotel, she let go of her anxieties and heaved a sigh of relief. She wouldn't go alone to such a remote place again. Encounters like the one this morning did nothing to restore her peace of mind, whether the danger was real or merely a figment of her imagination.

The gaily-striped cabanas that lined the beach in front of her hotel were filled with people. Children sat at the edge of the surf, building castles in the sand and splashing happily while protective parents sat nearby and watched. Serious shell gatherers roamed the shore with downcast eyes, stooping to retrieve the treasures left behind by the early morning tide.

Spying an unoccupied cabana, Lori dropped onto the chaise and closed her eyes. She wanted to understand what had happened this morning. Was this Kevin guy on the level? He certainly seemed sincere. But how many of these accidents could she continue to dismiss as coincidental? Yet, on the other hand, if her friends were right and she was being silly and hysterical, she might be passing up opportunities to make exciting new friends. It all seemed to overwhelm her. She needed some objective person she could turn to for advice.

If only her father were still alive. He was the only person in this world who ever completely understood her. She could talk to him about anything. They had shared laughs and dreams, and an abiding faith in Christ that cemented their father-daughter bond and lifted it to a spiritual plane. His untimely death two years ago had completely shattered Lori, and now she found herself needing him more than ever.

It was true she had not always heeded his advice. When he advised against her dropping out of college in her junior year to audition for the Mermaid Follies at Weeki Wachee Spring, she followed her own heart instead. Still, he was as proud as a brand new father when she was chosen for the cast. He had come to watch her performances whenever he could. Sadly, he didn't live to know that after two years of hard work she finally earned the coveted starring role in the show.

Could there possibly be someone now who actually wanted to kill her, or was Nicole right in labeling Lori's fears simply a product of her active imagination? If her father were here, his opinion would dissolve her uncertainties and convince her one way or the other. Without him to talk to, where could she turn for advice?

She certainly couldn't discuss her fears with her mother. At one time that might have been possible—before her mother had met and married Andy Marcellona.

Andy was closer to Lori's age than to Jean's. He came along six months after her father's death, just when her mother was most vulnerable, and swept Jean off her feet. Within weeks they were married, living in the house where Lori grew up, and since then things had never been the same between Lori and her mother.

Her mother's hasty remarriage was a bitter pill for Lori to swallow. She felt her mother was disrespectful and disloyal to her father's memory.

"You don't understand what it's like to be lonely," her mother tried to explain. "Your father was such a strong person and I depended on him for everything. Now I just don't know how to cope." Then when the fresh tears would start, it was Lori who didn't know how to cope.

Eventually Lori had come to accept Andy without bitterness, but she had never been able to develop a closeness to him. It irked her to see him wearing her father's ties, his solid gold cuff links. He had created a barrier between Lori and her mother that stood like a wall between them whenever they spoke. Both were aware of it, and their conversations had developed a stiff formality far different from the warmth they had shared through all her growing-up years. Now Jean, caught up in her new life with Andy, was completely oblivious to her daughter's troubles and there was no chance Lori could turn to her mother for understanding or advice.

The situation might have been easier for Lori to accept if she thought Jean was truly happy, but she had watched her mother change from a gregarious socialite into a serious, withdrawn woman who was seldom seen without her handsome young husband at her side. She no longer invited friends into her home, and she politely declined their friendly overtures. Even to her only daughter, Jean Marcellona had become a virtual stranger, seemingly sheltering some terrible dark secret.

Completely engrossed in her own concerns, Lori didn't hear the crunch of approaching footsteps. "How was the workout?" Nicole flopped down on the chaise next to hers.

"Oh, Nicole, you won't believe this. It happened again today. Someone is definitely out to get me. What am I going to do?" Utter despair reflected in her voice.

Nicole groaned. "Lori, please don't start in on that kick again. We came down here for a change of scenery and some much needed rest."

"I know, Nicky, but—"

"We didn't tell a single soul we were coming to Marathon, so there's no possible way anyone can know we're here in the Keys. You promised to put all those bizarre thoughts out of your mind."

What was the use? No one took her seriously. Not Mr. Porter, and not Nicole. They both felt she was imagining these threats to her life. They'd almost succeeded in convincing her, until the crazy episode this morning. Thinking again of the underwater confrontation with Kevin Collins, her head reeled with a strange mixture of fear and fascination. Fascination? Now, that was a wild thought. Mr. Porter had hinted that she was watching too much television. Maybe he was right.

"Okay, so tell me about it." Nicole sounded resigned. "What happened this time?"

"What's the use? You won't believe it anyway."

"Try me."

"Okay. But you have to promise not to laugh."

"Oh, Lori, I *never* laugh at you. I only try to give you an objective perspective."

"I know. I'm sorry. You're such a good friend, Nicole. I don't know what I'd do without you. You'll just have to put up with me until I get my head on straight. I'm not quite myself yet, but I'm working on it."

"I know you are, honey. It's okay. Just tell me what happened this morning."

"Well, you know that cove just north of our beach here?"

"Yes, where the old wooden pier juts out into the water."

"That's the one. I went there to practice my routine early this morning. The water there is so clear, and it seems isolated. I felt I could practice there without being disturbed. Oh, Nicky, you can't believe how beautiful the reefs are down there. You have to come with me next time."

"Lori, I'm sure the reefs are spectacular. But even before we left home, I told you this is supposed to be a vacation. Here's one mermaid who plans to stay dry for two whole weeks. So go ahead. What happened at the cove this morning?"

"I was having such a great time exploring those incredibly beautiful coral reefs. I saw fish that looked like neon signs, and I even saw a baby octopus. It was so much fun I forgot every care I ever had. Honestly, Nicky, I resolved to forget all my worries and settle down for two weeks of uncomplicated fun. I was at peace with the world and completely relaxed. Then, right out of nowhere, something grabbed my hair with an iron grip and I couldn't break free. I could see the legs of a man, and I tried every way I could to get loose. I was kicking and struggling, but he wouldn't let go. Honestly, I felt like my hair was coming right out of my head. Then finally, though I'm still not sure how, I managed to get to the pier." Just thinking about it made Lori's heart pound like a hammer.

"Did he get away?" Nicole sat bolt upright. Her wide eyes told Lori that at last she had made a believer of her.

"He didn't even try. He just put on this Mr. Innocent act, and pretended he thought I was drowning. He claimed he was trying to save my life."

Nicole eased her body back onto the chaise. "Obviously, there is more here than you've chosen to tell me. Any chance he really thought he was doing just that? Coming to your rescue, I mean?"

Lori was forced to admit Nicky was echoing her own uncertainty. "I suppose it might be a possibility," she admitted. Actually, it was a possibility she would like to find revealed as truth. There was a certain sweet innocence about the man that belied any thoughts of foul play. Still, in view of her recent problems, this morning's episode had been a terrifying addition to her growing collection of mystifying experiences. She needed time to put everything into proper perspective.

"Let's don't talk about it right now, Nicky. I have to sort it all out in my mind."

"What did he look like?" Nicole persisted.

Lori paused thoughtfully, taking a long time to answer. Finally, looking out over the distant waves, she took a deep breath and said dreamily, "Like a bronze god."

"You mean he was a real hunk?" Nicole's interest immediately escalated, and her eyebrows arched into two half moons.

"A real hunk." Lori had to smile at Nicole's sudden snap to attention. "He said his name was Kevin Collins, but I wouldn't bet on it."

"And how did you manage to break away from this real hunk who told you his name, and who you think is out to murder you?" Nicole made no effort to conceal the sarcasm in her voice.

"Oh, Nicky, I knew you wouldn't take me seriously. I said I don't want to talk about it any more. Okay?"

"Okay, but you obviously got away without any serious injuries. At least tell me how you accomplished that."

"I just swam away. Oh, I guess you're right. It does sound rather foolish when I tell you about it. I have to quit looking for trouble and concentrate on having fun."

"Listen, Lorelei. I'm your best friend. I'm the last person in the world who wants anything bad to happen to you. But you absolutely must get a grip on your nerves. Mr. Porter was right when he said he'd been working you too hard. In a way this is really his fault, but that won't stop him from replacing you if he feels you can't handle the pressure of the leading role. And we both know at least two girls who would do anything to get your part. Now that he's given us this great vacation, let's make the most of it."

Lori *was* trying. "But how can you expect me to forget that so-called accident when the brakes on my new car failed?"

"That accident would never have happened if they hadn't sold you a car with defective brakes in the first place. I still get mad every time of think of it. It's truly a miracle you came out of that wreck without serious injuries. You could have been killed!"

"The mechanic told me it looked like someone had tampered with the brakes."

"Well, what did you expect him to say, for goodness sakes? After all, he works for the dealership where you bought the car. He's not going to stick his neck out and say they sold you a lemon. He knows you could slap them with a big law suit."

"Well they worked it all out with the insurance company, and I did get a brand new car, so I quit worrying about it until the next thing happened. But how can you explain that hit-and-run driver who jumped the curb and tried to run me down with his car before he sped away?"

"Like the police said, it was probably some drunk who never even realized you were there. Those things happen all the time. I'm just glad you were able to jump out of his path in time."

"That was my lucky day, I guess." She had never told anyone about the mental flash of warning that saved her life that day. "Look out!" her father screamed, and although Lori knew the familiar voice was cached inside her head, the words were as clear as if they had been shouted from the rooftop.

"I guess that's one way you could look at it. But it was too bad you didn't get his tag number," Nicole lamented.

"Everything happened so fast, I couldn't even give the police a good description of the car." Lori couldn't remember the car, but she would never forget the ugly, leering face of its determined driver. She shuddered, just thinking of it. The warning words emanating from the depths of her mind that day had caused her to turn at the precise moment the car jumped the curb and veered toward her. Two seconds later and it would have been too late. And if she hadn't jumped out of its path...

"Well, just quit thinking about it. It's over now. And so is our work, for two whole weeks. Helga was only too glad to have the chance to fill in for you while you're gone. I don't think she feels it's very exciting to be an understudy for someone who never gets sick or just plain goofs off. This is the chance she's been waiting for."

"You're right. She even acted downright friendly toward me before we left. I was really surprised when she volunteered to feed Fluffy while we're gone."

The big yellow cat that reigned supreme over their small apartment had never been left alone for more than a day or two. "I'm afraid we've spoiled him rotten," Nicole mused. "I hope Helga takes time to talk to him and pet him when she goes in to feed him. I'm sure he's indignant at being left behind."

"Yes, he's bound to miss us," Lori agreed. "And I miss him, too. Don't you? Anyway, I was glad Helga seemed to be extending the olive branch. I've tried every way I know to get her to like me.

All the other girls in our group are so friendly. I've never understood her snobbery."

"Helga's okay. It's just that she suffered a terrible disappointment when she didn't get the lead after Julie left to have her baby. After all, she's been there longer than the rest of us. It was only natural for her to expect to be the next leading lady."

"I know. I felt a little sad for her. But I'll have to admit being chosen for the lead was the most exciting thing to ever happen to me." Lori smiled, remembering her delight on the day of the surprising announcement.

"Hey! I thought we were going to forget mermaids for two whole weeks. I have just the thing to get your mind off your worries." Nicole held up two slips of paper she pulled from the pocket of her denim shorts.

"What's that?"

"These are two tickets for a day on the *Mattie B*."

"Why am I having to pry all this information from you piece by piece? What's the *Mattie B*?"

"It just happens to be the greatest deep-sea party boat in the Keys. Captain Charlie leaves his dock every morning at seven, and stays out on the water all day. When he comes back in the late afternoon, his passengers almost always have a big catch to brag about. Now does that sound like fun, or what?"

Lori grinned. "That sounds like fun, all right. Just where do we go to meet up with this Captain Charlie and his *Mattie B*?"

"It's only about a mile from the hotel, and the nice part is that everything we need is furnished. Captain Charlie supplies the bait, the lines, everything. All we have to do is present these." Nicole waved the little slips of paper in her hand.

"Nicky, you're great. I'm sorry I've been such a worrywart. I don't want to spoil your vacation. I'll try to change my attitude. You'll see." How foolish she had been. She always made friends easily, and inherently trusted everyone. Now suddenly everyone she met became suspect. Well, no more. From here on out she would be the old fun-loving Lorelei who liked and trusted everyone. She owed that much to her friends.

"I'm starved." Lori stood and stretched. "I haven't had any breakfast except for a glass of fresh orange juice from the fridge in our room, and that swim has made my stomach sound like a bear."

"Get dressed then, and let's eat brunch in the dining room. It's lovely and cool in there, and maybe we can meet some of the other guests in the hotel."

Lori suspected what her friend had in mind. Nicky loved to socialize, and her vacation wouldn't be labeled a success unless she met at least one handsome bachelor during her stay.

"I'll just run up and get out of this damp suit. Suppose I meet you in the dining room in half an hour?"

She left Nicky sitting in the cabana, eyeing the crowds on the beach. Undoubtedly she was looking for Mr. Right among all those tanned bodies. And the funny thing about Nicky was, she always managed to find at least one acceptable candidate everywhere they went!

Not that Lori herself disliked men. Far from it. But she was not at all interested in a casual relationship just for the sake of male company. Ever since she'd ended her long running relationship with Ken Talbot, she hadn't been attracted to anyone enough to remain interested beyond one or two dates.

Breaking up with Ken had been her own decision, but a tough one. He was a great guy, and she truly liked him. But she wasn't in love with him, and the best years of her life were rolling by. She had finally decided to end it and take her life in a new direction.

The extent of Ken's bitterness had surprised her. It also reinforced her convictions that she'd made the right decision about ending their relationship. His angry reactions had revealed a side of him she hadn't realized existed. She hadn't seen or heard from him now in over four months, so that part of her life was over. End of chapter.

Nicky had told her this trip could be the real springboard for a new beginning. She was ready for a new beginning all right. But not before she settled the troubling things that kept clouding her mind, and most assuredly not with some stranger she might meet during a two-week holiday. No, Nicky could look for romance in the tropics if she chose to, but Lori just wanted to rest, relax, and recapture her peace of mind — and the beautiful Florida Keys seemed like the perfect place.

Helga stood below the marquee and watched while Gerry removed each letter that spelled the name of Lorelei Cramer. She had waited a long time for this day. Too long.

Gerry, unaware of her presence, stretched the pole to position the new letters directly under the word, *starring*.

She smiled as she watched him place the *H*. She didn't need to stay until he spelled her entire name. She already knew just what it would look like. In her mind's eye, she had seen it a thousand times. *Starring: Helga Larson.*

Of course, it was only for two weeks. Unless ... But she must not even think about that now. There was a lot of work to be done during the next two weeks, and no room for errors.

Helga turned toward the bus stop. Of course, the real *star* of the show had her own new car. On her salary, she could afford it. Lori Cramer never rode the bus. Sometimes life wasn't fair.

When she reached the corner, she dropped her canvas gym bag onto the bench and turned around. The marquee stretched above the treetops and was plainly visible from two blocks away. *Starring: Helga Larson.* Just the way she had always visualized it. Her skin tingled, and her breath came more rapidly. Those letters were the ones that belonged up there, and she'd do *anything* to keep them in their proper place. Reluctantly, she lowered her eyes and turned toward the approaching bus.

CHAPTER THREE

Lori ignored the whistles and admiring glances that followed her as she hurried over the sugary sand toward the hotel. If Nicole hoped to find male companionship during their brief visit to the Keys, they had obviously chosen the right place.

The exterior of the expansive resort was swirled in pink stucco, and its shiny red-tiled roof reflected the sun's noonday rays like a mirror. *La Hacienda* was aptly named. Although modern in all its comforts and amenities, an aura of yesterday extended from the hibiscus-filled patios to the spacious marble lobby. Dark, heavy furnishings were elaborately carved and elegantly appointed with old pewter and silver accessories at every turn. Ornate crystal chandeliers hung from the high ceilings, their tear drops acting as prisms to catch the artificial light in shimmering rainbows of color.

Lori entered through the side patio to avoid walking through the lobby in her bathing suit. Using the back elevator provided for pool and beach patrons, she slipped unnoticed into her room on the sixth floor.

In her absence the room had been tidied and the heavy drapes drawn aside, allowing the midday sunlight to flood the elegant surroundings. French doors opened onto a wrought iron balcony facing the Atlantic Ocean and the colorful cabana-laden beach.

In less than fifteen minutes, Lori emerged fresh from the shower. She pulled on a pair of crisp white shorts, a sailor blouse, and white leather sandals. A built-in hair dryer conveniently located beside the lavatory helped her regain control of the long, thick hair that fell in soft waves around her face and down her back.

The smiling face of Kevin Collins kept playing across her mind like instant video replay, but she forced herself to reject the disturbing picture. She refused to allow her thoughts to linger on the strange events of the morning. There was no time for that now. Nicky was waiting in the dining room, and Lori's stomach was growling like an angry bear.

She rinsed the salt water from her bathing suit and draped it over the nylon clothesline that unwound and stretched across the length of the tub and attached to the wall.

A quick splash of summer cologne and a touch of red lipstick completed her toiletry. She grabbed her new straw handbag and headed for the elevators.

This time she used the main elevator to return to the lobby on the ground floor. Swimming always made her hungry. Spicy smells floated from the kitchen into the downstairs hall and inspired her to quicken her steps.

Pausing in the dining room doorway, her eyes scanned the tables. "May I seat you, Señorita?" The hostess who stood at the doorway was a typical Spanish beauty in gaily ruffled, brightly colored costume. Heavy bracelets jangled on both arms when she lifted a stack of menus.

"I'm looking for my friend, a small blond lady seated alone."

The hostess looked puzzled. "Perhaps she has not yet arrived," she offered.

"That's possible, but unlikely. Still, I don't see her. Why don't I just take a table for two, and when she comes, you can direct her my way."

"Sí! Right this way, Señorita."

She followed the hostess across the room and onto a small sunlit porch facing the water.

"Lori! It's about time you got here." Nicole rose to meet her.

Surprised, Lori could only stare. No wonder the hostess hadn't recognized Lori's description. Nicky certainly was not a lady dining alone! The proverbial tall, dark, and handsome man stood beside her, dwarfing Nicole's petite frame by contrast. Smiling, he extended his hand and waited for introductions.

"Lori, this is George. He's a scuba diving instructor, and guess what? He's giving me my first lesson this afternoon. George, meet my dearest friend in the whole world, Lorelei Cramer."

Lori gasped in astonishment. She must have misunderstood. "Scuba lessons?"

"I can't wait to learn!" Nicky interrupted her quickly and gave Lori a chance to regain her composure. There was no misunderstanding the glare Nicky aimed her way. So Nicole was already up to her old games! Lori tried hard not to snicker.

Lori held out her hand and George shook it vigorously. "Happy to meet you, Lorelei."

"I hope you won't mind my leaving you alone, Lori. I simply couldn't pass up an invitation for a free scuba lesson, now could I? But it's only for a few hours. Besides, you and I will have the whole day together tomorrow on the *Mattie B*."

George responded just as Nicole must have hoped he would. "You're going out on the *Mattie B* tomorrow? Now, there's a coincidence. I was just thinking I hadn't been fishing for quite a spell. Yes sir, I think tomorrow would be a perfect day for fishing."

Lori rolled her eyes at her friend. What a schemer! By now she was so accustomed to Nicole's tactics that it just seemed par for the course. "Of course, I don't mind being alone for the afternoon." With a sly smile, she couldn't resist the temptation to add, "But please be careful, Nicky dear. I wouldn't want you to drown out there in all that deep water."

The waitress brought frosty glasses of water with lemon slices and took their orders. Nicole and Lorelei chose crab salad plates, but George ordered a jumbo hamburger with French fries and onion rings on the side.

All through lunch, Nicole kept up a lively chatter. She nibbled at her salad and coyly rolled her eyes toward George, who looked completely mesmerized while wolfing down his hefty burger and fries.

As soon as she finished her salad, Lori excused herself, tactfully leaving Nicky and George alone to become better acquainted. Poor George, he didn't stand a chance against Nicky and her wiles. On the other hand, he could do a lot worse. To her casual friends, Nicky was a cute, petite blond, flighty and fickle as a hummingbird, but to Lori who knew her best, she was a kind and loyal friend, generous to a fault. George would be a lucky man if he could claim Nicole's heart, but Lori wouldn't want to lay bets on that possibility.

Glad for a few hours alone to organize her thoughts, Lori wandered out to the beach and sat on a chaise lounge under the shade of the coconut palm trees. She never tired of watching the whitecaps roll into shore. Sometimes the foamy swells rolled in with a pulsation akin to a heartbeat, and other times like today, they gently lapped the blue surface with a soothing, hypnotic melody all their own. Far from shore, a porpoise arched and flipped high into the air, and then another and another, as though they were in competition to see who could jump the highest.

A cool breeze broke the midday heat as Lori lay back and allowed her heavy eyelids to close. The morning had been exhausting. Physical exhaustion she could handle; she was trained for it. But mental exhaustion was something else. Did one ever become conditioned for stress?

Willing herself to concentrate on the steady sounds of the sea, she dozed. But a few moments later, she awoke with a start to an unexplained feeling of unease. Strangely, it reminded her of the day she narrowly missed death by sensing the approaching hit-and-run driver— the day she so vividly felt her father's presence. She now had the distinct sensation of being watched.

When she opened her eyes and looked up, she saw only the familiar sights of innocent children at play and relaxed adults attending them. Her imagination must be in gear again. She had promised Nicole she'd get a grip on her nerves and enjoy this vacation. She lowered her eyelids and tried to resume her nap, yet the disturbing feeling persisted. Warily, she turned her head to the right.

There he stood, at the water's edge, boldly staring at her across the sand!

The stranger who called himself Kevin Collins was staring at her as though he saw a ghost.

Lori's emotions defied description. She wasn't sure whether the sudden racing of her pulse was due to fright or anger or something else she couldn't yet define. Just when she managed to convince herself she could forget all about Kevin Collins and his strange behavior, he popped up again like a cork in water. Who was this man, and why did the sight of him make her heart pound and her knees feel like wet cardboard? Perhaps her trembling and palpitations were some kind of premonition. At least she was on safe ground here in view of so many people. She was entitled to know his intentions, and this time she intended to find out!

Kevin was experiencing his own emotional turbulence. He had spent the last few hours agonizing over whether his unusual experience this morning had been some kind of hallucination, or whether he had allowed the most beautiful creature in all the world to disappear and perish without so much as reporting it to the authorities. Seeing her now on the beach, apparently without a care in the world, angered him. She had intentionally caused him hours of anxiety. But his anger was diluted with such tremendous relief at having found her alive and well that his impulse was to rush over and hold her securely in his arms.

He remembered the warm, euphoric feeling of holding her when he lifted her onto the pier this morning, but he also remembered her volatile reaction to his efforts to save her life. He couldn't put all the pieces together.

And then, there was that strange conversation about mermaids. She seemed to be playing some kind of game with him, and something in his brain warned him he should distance himself from this unusual girl. She had a mystical charm about her that could captivate a man and make him forget the painful lessons he had already learned about modern women and the games they played. Something told him he should turn on his heels and run before it was too late.

But instead, as though driven by some invisible magnetic force, he felt himself drawn by slow, steady steps to her side.

Much later, thinking back on this moment, he never could find a rational explanation for his actions, although they were to alter the course of his entire life. Even as his mind was shouting "*Run,*" his feet carried him straight to her side.

Looking down into her enormous emerald eyes, he read complete bewilderment. In an effort to lighten the moment, he quipped, "We have to stop meeting like this!" Then dropping to his knees in the sand, he reached for her hand. "We got off to a bad start this morning, didn't we?"

Lori made no effort to pull her hand away. Encouraging such familiarity from a complete stranger wasn't permissible in her own personal code of conduct, and in view of the unexplainable events of this morning, could be downright dangerous. But Kevin didn't seem a stranger at all; indeed, it seemed she had known him all her life. The warmth of his hand holding hers sent a pleasant current through her whole body.

Lori lowered her eyes. She didn't want to look at him. Every time she did, it seemed to rob her of her normal intelligence. This was absolutely the most outrageous thing she had ever allowed herself to be a part of. She must put a stop to it at once, before she found herself in deeper trouble than she was already.

"Kevin, that is your name, right?"

"Yes."

Lori groped for words. She couldn't explain her own behavior, much less his. Clearly, this was a situation that could quickly get out of hand. "I— well, I just don't know who you are, or where you came from, or why you're here. I've had some very frightening experiences lately, and I'm trying to get my thinking back on a rational tract. I must say, you aren't helping much."

"Look, I'm sorry if I startled you. I'm just so thankful to see you here, alive and well. When you disappeared this morning, I almost called out a search party. Where did you go?"

She was faintly amused, remembering he had no way of knowing about her extra supply of oxygen. He must surely have thought she drowned. In spite of her firm resolutions, she smiled at him. It wasn't her fault he had worried; she told him mermaids never drown. "You didn't listen to me, did you? I told you I'm a mermaid."

He didn't answer, and his stern, piercing look brought Lori to her senses. She pulled her hand from his. What was she thinking, anyway? Even giving Kevin Collins the full benefit of the doubt, she was not some girl to be picked up on the beach.

"There doesn't seem to be any polite way to say this, Kevin, but I think the best thing you can do for me now is to go away. Please don't come anywhere near me again."

"Do you really mean that?" he asked her.

She wasn't at all sure she did. Part of her wanted him to stay, even though she knew it was wrong. She felt as though she was locked on a merry-go-round that kept going faster instead of stopping to let her off.

It had to be more than coincidence that this man kept turning up whenever she was alone. She came to this place to put her fears at rest, but she could never do that as long as he kept turning up wherever she went. Attracted as she was to him— and yes, she had to admit to a compelling attraction— she knew nothing at all about him. She didn't know where he came from or his purpose in following her around.

She remembered the warm sensation of his hand holding hers. A repeat of that and her will power would go down the drain like so much dishwater. She couldn't risk it. Kevin Collins simply had to go.

She couldn't trust herself to speak, so merely nodded at him. Looking into his clear blue eyes, she could not doubt the sincerity of the hurt and disappointment she read in them as he rose in the sand and slowly walked away.

Her eyes followed him far down the beach until he became lost in the crowds. Her heart felt heavy with the realization she would probably never see him again. But of course, that's what she wanted. Wasn't it?

CHAPTER FOUR

The day had barely begun when Lori and Nicky arrived at the landing where the *Mattie B* was docked. Already people were lined up at the ticket window. With tickets in hand, Lori and Nicky decided to wait in the coffee shop until the boarding call.

The crowd of vacationing novice fishermen spilled over into the small restaurant, forcing Lori and Nicole to find seats at the counter.

Over mugs of hot coffee, Nicky held out her hand and offered Lori two pills. "George says we should take these half an hour before boarding, so we won't get seasick."

"Thanks, but no thanks. I'll just take my chances."

"Don't be silly, Lori. Why take a chance on feeling sick?" Nicky pushed the pills toward her.

"You can label it paranoia if you want, Nicole, but I'm not taking any pills given to me by someone I don't even know. Especially after all the things that have happened to me recently."

"Not that again!" Nicole rolled her eyes skyward. "Lori, what's happening to you? You used to trust people. How do you think your wary attitude makes them feel?" Nicole made no attempt to hide her annoyance.

"Please, Nicky. Just drop it. I don't plan to get seasick, okay?"

"No, I won't drop it. I don't care if you take the pills or not. It's your stomach. But I do resent the implications you're aiming at my George."

"*Your* George? And all this in less than twenty-four hours!"

Nicole was not amused. "George has become very important to me, Lori. Sometimes it doesn't take long to know a person is right for you."

Lori chuckled. "It seems to me I heard those very words when you met Jerry, and again when you met Trent."

Small spats were not unusual between the two of them when tempers flared like small candles, but their friendship was too strong to sustain lengthy animosity and the flames were always extinguished before any lasting burns occurred.

With a begrudging shrug, Nicole conceded. "Well, no one said we have a lifetime commitment or anything. But I like George, and my instincts tell me I can trust him." "Nicky, I'm glad. I was only teasing. But seriously, I've never been seasick. So I'll just think positively and hope for the best. Now, finish your coffee. I think they're beginning to board the boat."

"May we have our check, please?" Nicole pushed her coins toward Lori and walked outside. Lori settled the bill at the cash register and followed.

George was waiting for them just outside the door. "Come on, ladies. Let's go catch a big one." Nicky grabbed his thick, muscular arm, and Lori walked close behind as they pushed along with the crowds toward the end of the dock.

The boat was larger than Lori expected, and she was surprised at the number of people boarding. She found a seat on one of the benches surrounding the deck and dropped her canvas bag to the floor. Looking up, she expected Nicky and George to take their places beside her. But they were off in a world of their own. Walking arm in arm, absorbed in animated conversation, they circled the deck and disappeared from her view.

An elderly couple sat down beside her, the woman nervously fidgeting with her handbag.

"Is this your first time out?" Lori asked her.

"Yes, it is, dear. I'm only doing this to please Edward. He did so want to come, and wouldn't do it without me." She looked at her husband and smiled, and he patted her hand affectionately.

"Ruth's a little nervous," he said. "But once she gets the feel of a fish on the end of her line, I know she's gonna love it."

"Well, this is my first time too," Lori admitted. "I'm certainly looking forward to catching a big fish. The only fish I've ever caught were small lake trout. My father used to take me fishing when I was a little girl."

The engines roared to a start, making further conversation difficult. The big boat began to move, slowly at first, but soon accelerated to a speed that surprised her.

Lori leaned her head against the backrest and relaxed. How good it felt to get away from the crowds on the beaches. Out here, she knew no one except Nicky and George. They were so absorbed in each other, they hardly knew she was around. Unlike Nicky, Lori enjoyed being alone once in a while. The salt breeze blew through her hair and seemed to carry away all her worries like puffs of dandelion caught in the wind. Today promised to be a glorious day, fish or no fish, and Lori resolved not to let any fears or apprehensions cast a cloud over it.

They were completely out of sight of land now. Lori's eyelids slid shut, and as her mind drifted, it began to replay that crazy scene on the beach yesterday. What kind of man would just walk up to a strange girl on the beach and try such an offbeat line? For that matter, what kind of girl would encourage him by prolonging the conversation and even allowing him to hold her hand? And to be completely honest with herself, she had to admit she'd enjoyed it. Thankfully, she had regained her senses and set the record straight before he formed any mistaken ideas. Her response to his strong physical attraction was more in character with flirtatious Nicole than sensible Lorelei Cramer.

She'd always heard the tropics could cast a mysterious romantic spell. Was it really true? For someone determined to be extremely careful, she'd surely made a fantastic start!

Nicole was a firm believer in love at first sight, but Lori's definition of love was quite different. Whenever Lori thought of falling in love, she remembered the kind of relationship her parents shared before her father's death. Added to the strong physical attraction they obviously enjoyed, there were intangibles like consideration and respect and honesty. Some day Lori knew she, too, would find that special person whom God had created to fulfill all her lofty dreams. But she didn't think it likely she'd bump into him along a tropical beach on a two-week vacation.

And neither did she think her mother that fortunate on her second time around. Andy and her father were about as opposite as two men could possibly be. But of course Andy was not her father, and maybe her comparison was unfair. For her mother's sake, and with God's help, she must work harder to develop a friendlier attitude toward him.

Her thoughts were interrupted by a coarse, grating noise. Her body swayed involuntarily as the ship ground to a slow halt, causing her to fall against Ruth. "I'm sorry," she apologized, righting herself.

"Oh, mercy! What was that? Is something wrong with the ship?"

"No, Ruth," Ed assured her. "We're here, that's all. This is where the fun begins."

Lori felt anticipation in the air as Captain Charlie's voice sounded over the loud speaker. "Ladies and gentlemen, we're gonna drop anchor here and try our luck. We're using the latest electronic equipment to measure the depths of the water and spot the most likely places to catch fish. So if you don't get a bite right away, don't get discouraged. There's plenty more places out here to try, and enough fish for everyone. We'll keep trying 'til we find a place where you can catch some. My mates are circling the decks now with drop-lines and bait. If you have any questions, they'll be glad to try and help you."

The young boy who approached Lori with lines and a bait bucket looked like a teenager. According to the embroidered logo on his pocket, his name was Tony. "Here's your line, miss. Just put your bait on the hook and drop it over the side. When you feel a tug, give a little sideward jerk to set the hook, then reel him in. That's all there is to it."

Lori was surprised at the size of the hook. It looked big enough to catch a whale! And that line! It looked almost like clothesline. What were they expecting her to catch? Then her eyes fell upon the bait bucket. "Ugh! Squid? Why?"

"It makes great bait. Just reach in and grab some."

Maybe she should have taken those pills after all! Her stomach did a flip-flop as she retrieved one of the slimy pieces from the bucket. Now, if she could just get it on the hook. She looked around to see if Tony could help her, but he was down the line doling out his dubious treasures to others.

"Yuck!" She finally managed to spear the slippery bait with the big silver hook. She was only too glad to release it over the side of the boat and into the waves. She held fast to the hefty rod and let the line slip gradually into the water, carrying the obnoxious bait out of sight.

She didn't have to wait long. In only a matter of moments she felt her first hit, and it almost pulled the rod from her hands. She tried to set the hook the way Tony had taught her, and watched the spool whir as the nylon line slipped rapidly through the water. If her pole hadn't been anchored into one of the rod holders on the side of the boat, she might have been pulled into the water herself. Almost all her line was out now, and she set herself to the task of pulling in her catch.

Tony raced to her side. "Looks like you hooked a big one, lady. Just let him play with the line for a while until he gets tired, then we can pull him in. Want me to take it for you?"

"No way! This is what I came for." With all the strength she could muster, Lori began to reel in her line. Sometimes it seemed to move easily, then suddenly balk and pull back the other way. She fought with it for thirty minutes, almost ready to admit defeat from sheer fatigue. Where was Tony when she needed him? As if in answer to her silent plea, she saw him running toward her.

"Ma'am, I think we may have a little problem here. Would you let me have your line for a minute?"

This time she didn't protest. Glad to relinquish her rod, she flexed her fingers in relief. "Don't let him get loose, Tony. I want to be able to brag to my friends back home about this."

She watched him play with the line a few minutes, jerking it this way and that. Finally he said, "Just what I was afraid of." Taking a pair of clippers from his belt, he cut the line and a shocked Lori watched the iridescent cord slide into the dark, choppy water and disappear from sight.

"Tony! How dare you cut my fish loose! And after I worked so hard and so long to pull it in!"

"Come with me, ma'am, and I'll show you why I did that."

Reluctantly, Lori left her pole in the rod holder and followed Tony around the deck. Looking back, she noted that the people who'd been standing beside her cheering her performance seemed as puzzled and disappointed as she was. This boy had some nerve! She'd make certain his actions were reported to the captain. She had plenty of witnesses, too!

Rounding the bow of the boat, they approached a gathering of people who were watching a young woman reel in her catch. Nicky. At least one of them would have a catch to brag about. She couldn't wait to tell Nicky about her big one that got away.

Lori stood beside her when Nicky's catch came up. She reeled it in with no resistance. The poor fish must be worn out.

The first thing Lori saw was the giant hook, devoid of bait, and worse yet, devoid of fish. The only thing attached to the hook was another hook of equal size, trailed by a seemingly infinite fishing line.

At first no one understood what had happened. Nicky looked crestfallen, and Lori shared her friend's disappointment until Tony explained.

"Don't you ladies see what happened? Your lines drifted beneath the boat and the hooks got tangled together. You've both been fighting each other for nearly an hour."

A roar of laughter rose from the crowd who had watched Nicky's battle with her "fish." Tony tried to suppress his laugh, but couldn't resist a grin. But there were two who did not laugh—two very solemn young women who exchanged looks of disappointment and embarrassment. But in the end, the comedy of the situation was too much even for them. As their laughter bubbled up and spilled over, they fell into each other's arms with good-natured grins and hugs. "So much for our big catch of the day!"

George, standing by, had watched with amused but sympathetic interest. "Come on, ladies. I'll buy you both a cold drink, and we'll sit on the bench for a rest. I think you deserve it."

"No thanks, George. You and Nicky can rest. I'm going back to the other side to reclaim my rod. I think I just found my second wind. I know there's a big one down there somewhere, just waiting for me to catch him." Lori suspected her two friends would be just as happy without her company for a while. Besides, she really did get her appetite whetted to catch a fish.

Resuming her place along the port side of the boat, she tried to explain to the curious bystanders what happened. "My friend and I caught each other instead of a fish."

In her absence the catches had mounted, and Tony was busy collecting the fish and putting them into the holding tank. Lori eyed the enviable catches and determined to catch one of her own—a real one this time.

Minutes later she felt a tug again—different this time. This bumpy, fluttery sensation must surely mean she had a fish on the end of her line. She hadn't experienced anything like that last time. She reeled and pumped, giving her fish a little line from time to time, but bringing him closer and closer until she could see his yellow body break the surface of the water.

"Pull him in," people around her shouted. Excitement charged the air like electricity. She flipped him onto the deck and appraised her yield. How disappointing. He was only about ten inches long, and the ugliest fish she had ever seen. Big eyes bulged from his spotted head, and his back was spiny like a porcupine. Then he seemed to grow before her eyes. He was puffing up like a balloon! She'd caught a blowfish!

Before she could comment, Tony appeared. "You caught a blowfish, ma'am. It's non-edible, and he won't even make good bait. We'll just toss him back and let him go home to his family."

The crowd laughed as they watched the funny fish huff and puff and blow himself up to nearly double his original size. True to his name, he looked like a big, ugly balloon.

Tony released the hook from his mouth and flipped him over the side. "Here, ma'am, help yourself to some fresh bait." He proffered the disgusting-looking contents of the bait bucket toward Lori.

"Tony, I wish you'd stop calling me 'ma'am'," she told him. "You make me feel like I'm a hundred years old. My name is Lorelei, but you can just call me Lori."

"Okay, ma...er... Lori. I'll try to remember."

Lori went through the agonizing procedure of getting her hook rebaited, and once more dropped her line over the edge.

This time, it was nearly ten minutes before she felt any resistance to her line, but when it hit, she knew this was a real fish. "This is sure no little weasel," she declared. She remembered how Tony had taught her to set the hook, and once more her battle began. For minutes that seemed like an hour, she reeled and pumped with all her strength, and still her fish refused to yield.

Tony appeared by her side again. "Don't let him have any slack, or he'll shake that hook right out of his mouth!"

Perspiration ran down her face and into her eyes, but she didn't have a free hand to wipe them. "I'd better not be fighting with someone on the other side this time, Tony," she said, gasping for breath.

People on either side of her reeled in their lines, giving Lori plenty of room for the big fight. Bystanders seemed almost as excited as she when a shimmering gleam of silver gave a mighty flip, breaking the surface of the steely blue ocean and sending an iridescent spray of saltwater onto the deck of the *Mattie B*.

Lori didn't mind that her clothes were drenched. The sight of the beautiful creature filled her with renewed determination, and a sudden surge of energy drove out any thought of fatigue.

Now it was all over but the shouting. Although lifting him into the boat required every ounce of her strength, she refused all offers of help. She wanted this catch to be totally a result of her own efforts. With a mighty heave, she hoisted her beautiful prize onto the deck.

Applause surrounded her. "Look at that!" "What a beauty!" "He must be part whale!" The compliments floated around her like sunshine.

Wild exhilaration quickly made her forget all about her exhaustion, as she proudly accepted the congratulations of her fellow fishermen. Even George and Nicole appeared from out of nowhere.

"Gosh, he must weigh fifty pounds!" George declared.

"What kind is he?" Nicky asked.

"That's a big grouper. One of the tastiest fish you'll ever sink your teeth into." George spoke with the knowledge of one who'd been saltwater fishing many times before.

"Tasty? No one is going to eat *my* fish. I'm going to have him mounted, or else no one will ever believe me back home."

With the excitement over, most of the crowd went back to work, encouraged by Lori's success.

"Where have you guys been?" Lori asked, watching Tony put her awesome catch into the holding tank.

"We've been fishing over on the other side. It's not quite as crowded. Why don't you come over there?" Nicky kept one arm linked with George's as she spoke.

"Okay. I might as well. I can't fish anymore now anyway. My arms are aching. I need to walk around a bit." Lori followed them around the stern of the boat to the spot where they had left their fishing gear.

As she rounded the corner, she glanced toward a group of people gathered several yards ahead. No, it couldn't be! *"Kevin!"* As she spewed out his name in disbelief, he looked up in surprise, then darted from the group and was lost in the crowds of people.

"What did you say, Lori?" Nicky heard her startled outcry, and turned to see her suddenly ashen face. "Lori! What is it?"

"It was him, Nicky! Kevin Collins! He's right here on this boat, spying on me. And you thought I was imagining things." Lori began to tremble, and suddenly she felt chilled to the bone, although the temperature must have registered ninety degrees. "I knew from the first he's been up to something. What am I going to do?"

"Now, Lori, you're perfectly safe here with George and me. It was probably just someone who looked like Kevin." She put her arm around Lori's shoulder and gave George a look that seemed to say *See what I've been telling you?*

George edged closer to Lori and, standing between the two of them, she did feel momentarily safe. But her body continued to tremble, and tears pushed hard against the back of her eyelids. "No, I'm sure it was Kevin. He was watching me, but when he saw me spot him, he ran away."

George drew himself up to his full height and put himself in charge of the situation. "I'm going to find that wise guy and see what he's up to. Come on, Lori, you'll have to point him out to me."

The three of them circled the deck, pausing to study each group of passengers, but there was no sign of anyone who even remotely resembled Kevin Collins. "He's staying out of sight, but I know he's here somewhere," Lori stated emphatically.

"You two sit right here on the bench," George ordered. "I'm going around the deck again. Tell me once more what he looks like, and what he was wearing, Lori."

"It all happened so fast. But I think he had on a green striped shirt." Lori searched her memory and remembered those sky-blue eyes, but decided not to mention those now. "His hair is so blond it looks like cotton, and he's big and tall and—"

"I think I'll know him if I see him. Now, don't either of you move from this spot until I come back." George hurried away and was soon lost from their view on the crowded deck.

"Listen, Lori, I don't know quite how to put this," Nicole said gently, groping for words. "But you *must* get this idea out of your mind. You're ruining our vacation, and you're not letting yourself get the rest and recuperation you need."

"*Recuperation? From what?*" Lori was quick to take umbrage at the implications. That just confirmed what she suspected they were all thinking about her.

"From, um, well, just from overwork." Nicole must have realized she had hit a sore spot, because she tried immediately to smooth things over. "Let's have a cool drink and calm down. Just think, your catch probably set the record for the day. You should be celebrating instead of worrying."

Clearly, Nicky didn't believe she had really seen Kevin. Well, no matter what anyone said, no matter what everyone else might believe, Lori knew what her eyes had seen. This man, whose unexplained actions were highly suspicious to say the least, was evidently stalking her, just waiting for another opportunity to—what? She didn't have a clue what, or even why!

And, no matter what anyone said, she knew the hit-and-run driver who tried to run over her back at Weeki Wachee Spring had been no accident either. She had seen the look of determination and hatred on his face in that brief moment before she managed to jump to safety.

She felt less certain about the first accident when her brakes failed. She was so shaken by her brush with death, and so grateful to have survived with only minor injuries, she was quick to accept the less ominous conclusions. Fortunately, she'd been wearing her seat belt. The thick brush that stopped her car just short of the bottomless sinkhole had probably saved her life.

Lori was surprised when the mechanic who worked on her car thought someone had tampered with the brakes. Mr. Porter and Nicole both felt sure he was trying to protect his employer who had sold her the car. That did sound reasonable, so when her car was replaced at no cost to her, she had been happy enough not to pursue the matter. But in retrospect, she felt that might have been a mistake.

She couldn't talk about these feelings to anyone, though. People were already labeling her demented. She'd just have to continue being cautious while working out her own solutions.

Lori and Nicky were sitting on the bench sipping colas from cans when George returned. There, walking sheepishly behind him, was none other than Kevin Collins!

"Lori, I met Kevin on the other side of the boat and I think you should listen to what he told me."

Kevin stood in front of her with a less-than-happy expression on his tan face. She could read his stress even before he spoke. "Lorelei, I just don't know what's with you. Somehow you've decided I'm an evil demon, but I don't know what I've ever done to give that impression. Just tell me what's bothering you, and I'll try to make things right between us."

Lori realized all three of them were casting doubts on her sanity. "Are you trying to tell me it's mere coincidence that you're here on this boat today?"

"This is not a private charter, Miss Mermaid."

"Sarcasm will not get you off the hook, Kevin Collins. You can't deny you were jumping around trying to stay out of my sight a few minutes ago."

Kevin rolled his blue eyes upward in a sign of complete frustration. "But that's what you told me to do."

With a jolt, Lori suddenly remembered. It was true. She really had asked him to stay out of her sight. Oh, he just came up with an excuse for everything!

"Look here, lady," Kevin continued, clearly angry. "You're not making my vacation any picnic. I worked hard all year to earn a vacation, and I came down here for some rest and fun, but everywhere I turn, you're right there making trouble for me! Why don't you explain why you singled me out to pick on?"

Their conversation grew steadily louder and began attracting the attention of those around them. Nicky decided to put a halt to it. "Lori, did you really tell this man to stay out of your sight?"

"Well, yes, but that was—"

"Then I think that explains his elusive behavior, and just maybe we all owe him an apology."

Lori felt like a chastised child, as all three of them watched to see what her next move would be. Clearly they all thought her in the wrong, and perhaps she was. She drew in a deep breath and swallowed her pride.

"I'm sorry, Kevin. I told you I've been under a strain lately, and I seem to have let some things slip out of perspective. I'll try not to cause you any further inconvenience." She spoke primly, carefully avoiding contact with his eyes.

George spoke to break the uncomfortable silence. "Tell you what, Kevin. Nicky and I are going out for dinner and a little dancing tonight. Why don't you and Lori come along and make it a foursome?"

"No, really, I don't—" Lori's refusal was cut short by Kevin's quick reply.

"Sounds like a fine idea to me. Just tell me where to meet you."

Lori started to protest once more, but Nicky silenced her with a quick jab of an elbow to her ribs and smiled sweetly. "Then it's all settled. You guys figure out how to get together, and meet us in the lobby of *La Hacienda* at seven. We'll be ready."

Captain Charlie ordered all the lines pulled in, and he revved the engines once more. Lori began to wish she had taken the seasick remedy after all. The sea had grown much more active, with waves so high that some of them were washing over the sides of the boat. All the strange happenings of the day had left her head in a whirl. She'd have to convince them later that she was simply not up to partying tonight.

Kevin had disappeared, and George and Nicky sat holding hands, trying to talk above the din of the engines. Lori sat quietly holding her head in her hands, wondering if the trip to shore would ever end.

At last, Captain Charlie maneuvered his big boat up to the landing and passengers crowded forward toward the catwalk. Lori tested her legs. They were a bit wobbly, but she felt she could make it ashore.

"Stand over there, ma'am, by that big framework, and we'll fix you up with a souvenir picture to take home." Lori looked up to see Tony standing beside her, holding her beautiful fish on a stout line. "Folks back home'll be mighty proud of you when you show 'em this!"

He hung the grouper from a hook at the top of the frame and positioned Lori beside it. Large letters across the top of the framework proclaimed, "CAUGHT ON THE MATTIE B".

Lori gave him her name and the name of her hotel, and he promised to have the picture sent there the following day. "Now, what do you want to do with your fish? We can have it cleaned and filleted for you."

"No, thanks. I don't want to see or smell any more fish today." Lori could still feel the sway of the ocean, even though she was now standing securely on dry land. "You can keep it, or give it to someone who can use it," she offered.

Her one and only catch weighed in at just over forty-seven pounds and claimed the jackpot prize of the day. Captain Charlie presented her with five crisp twenty-dollar bills. "Congratulations, little lady." Another picture was snapped with Captain Charlie beside her, the beautiful fish hanging in the background.

Lori didn't see Kevin anywhere. She should be happy about that, shouldn't she? Then why did she feel a twinge of disappointment as her eyes scanned the crowds?

Lori and George had caught nothing. In truth, although they had hardly dampened their lines, neither of them complained about the day.

"Back to the hotel, girls! You'll have time to do whatever it is y'all do to keep yourselves looking so beautiful. I've made arrangements to pick up Kevin at his hotel, and we'll be waiting for you in your lobby by seven." George steered them toward the parking lot.

Lori felt too woozy to protest. She kept feeling the roll of the waves as she walked toward the car. There would be time later to tell them she intended to stay in her room this evening. She could have a tray sent up if she decided she wanted something. Right now, she felt certain she wouldn't want to think about food ever again, or at least not for a very long time.

Nicky's voice broke into her thoughts. "You're right. He is a real hunk!"

"Who?" Lori tried to feign innocence.

"You know who. And did you see the way he looked at you? He's already smitten!"

"Don't be silly, Nicky. It's quite obvious Kevin and I don't get along. We're about as compatible as water and oil." Lori realized the words she spoke were all too true, and that realization filled her with a bittersweet sadness she could not begin to explain.

Kevin Collins left the marina parking lot in his rented car. In spite of today's disturbing events, he actually looked forward to tonight. This haughty girl who called herself a mermaid was the perfect example of modern womanhood. Still, he knew how to play that game now, too. And it just might be interesting to see what made her tick. He had to admit Lori Cramer was different.

CHAPTER FIVE

Harry pulled the compact car into the parking lot of the *Lazy Days Motel*. Checking his rear view mirror to make certain he was not being followed, he parked behind the office building in the darkest corner of the lot and killed the motor.

His hands shook as he snubbed out the short butt of his cigarette in the ashtray, slid out of the car and locked it.

Room 220. That's what his instructions said. Avoiding the elevator, he took the concrete steps of the fire escape.

He wished he knew of some way to avoid this confrontation. Yes, a confrontation is what it would be. But he might as well go inside and face the music. There was no other way out of it.

He drew in a deep breath. He must appear confident and capable, without any suggestion of being on the defensive. Drawing himself up to his pudgy height of five-feet-seven, he raised his rough knuckles and rapped sharply on the door.

"Come in," said the familiar voice.

A lamp on the bedside table cast a dim glow across the worn carpet, and the sparse furnishings of the cheap room gave him little choice of where to sit. He sank down on the straight chair near the door.

The air was heavy with smoke. He pulled his own pack of cigarettes from his shirt pocket and held it out in a friendly gesture.

"No, thanks. Let's get right down to business."

"Okay. Now, look. I know what you're thinking. You think I failed to get the job done. But things are not as bad as they might seem." Where was the confidence he meant to project? He was already on the defensive, and the conversation hadn't even begun. A knot had been growing in his stomach all morning and now it tightened its grip, causing him to grimace.

A stream of obscenities spouted across the room. "You were paid to do a job, and the job still isn't done. And now you're here to tell me things aren't as bad as they might seem? Well, tell me, Harry, just how bad are things?"

"Okay, boss. First of all, I did the job on the brakes just like you told me. I didn't want to do it that way, remember? I told you if you tried to create an accident, it just might accidentally not work. Sometimes those things can backfire. A bomb would've been much surer. Quicker. The whole mess would all be over by now." Bombs were more in Harry's area of expertise. He knew how to make 'em, and he knew how to use 'em. They didn't leave any fingerprints, either.

"You knew from the get-go that a bomb was unacceptable to me. I told you from the first, it had to look like an accident. So go ahead; tell me about the second time. You had a golden opportunity, and you muffed it. What happened there?"

Harry flinched. He hated this kind of work. She was such a pretty kid, too. If only he didn't need the money so desperately. But where else was he going to lay his hands on that kind of dough? Those loan sharks were breathing down his neck, and he knew they couldn't be put off much longer. His time was running out.

"Well, Harry, I'm waiting to hear your explanation."

"I had it all set up, boss. Perfect planning. I studied her schedule, and I knew just where she'd be. My timing was perfect.

I watched her leave the theater, and I got up my speed and everything. I still can't understand how she got out of the way so fast. I was coming from behind. It was like she had eyes in the back of her head." Perspiration popped out on his narrow forehead as he recalled that horrible experience. "Like I said, when you insist on making it look like an accident, it complicates the picture."

"I paid you for complications. Well, now I'm telling you to forget the whole thing. We're calling it quits. And there's the matter of the five grand advance. I'll expect that back."

Harry thought he was going to faint. His stomach contracted painfully. He couldn't give it back. He didn't have it. He had already given it to the loan sharks in a stall attempt. If he didn't get the rest of it soon, folks would be finding him at the bottom of some river with a brick tied to his feet.

"Look, boss. All I need is one more chance. I'll come through for you this time. Just give me two more weeks."

"Why two weeks? I thought you said you could get the job done quickly."

"Yeah, but she's gone off somewhere and nobody seems to know exactly where."

"Yes, of course, I know about that. She was given a short vacation because this is the slow season for the show. But if you were worth your grits, you'd make it your business to find out where she went."

"Believe me, I've tried. She didn't tell *nobody.* Just up and left with that girlfriend of hers. But she'll be back in a couple of weeks, and I only need one more chance. I promise I'll do it right next time. I've got a foolproof plan." Harry was desperate now. He was pleading. "Just let me tell you about this new idea."

Evil eyes glared at him across the room. "Read my lips, Harry. I said you are *out* as of this very moment. I should have taken care of things myself in the first place. Then they would have been handled right, and we wouldn't be sitting here having this conversation. You haven't done one single thing right. All you've done is sound an alarm that's gotten everyone's guard up. It'll be much harder to do now. And another thing; I want every penny of the advance money back. Today. Do you understand?"

Harry squirmed uncomfortably on the hard little chair. "I had to spend some of it doing the things to her car. And I had to rent a car for the other accident. You didn't think I could do the job with my own car, did you?"

The sinister mind that perpetrated the assassination attempt began to plan ahead. You could never depend on someone else to do things the way you wanted them done. You just had to do them yourself. All right, that's the way it would have to be.

But there was no use making Harry mad. When the crime was successfully completed, Harry would be the only one who could blow the whistle. No, better not make an enemy of Harry. Anyway, what was five grand? Chicken feed!

"Okay, Harry. Forget the five grand. But we'll have to forget the rest of the deal, too."

"Why, boss? I told you I had a new plan. Don't you even want to hear about it?" Part of him was relieved about the five grand, but where could he get his hands on the kind of money he needed to pay the loan sharks if this deal fell through?

"Use your head, Harry. You've aroused so much suspicion now, anything we do will be like waving a red flag. We'll just have to back off and forget it." No need to let Harry know any of the plans for the future. Best to just get rid of him, and the sooner the better. "No hard feelings. Just chalk this one up to one that didn't work out."

Harry had no choice but to shake the hand that was extended to him. "If you have any other jobs come up, I hope you'll remember me." It was obviously one last attempt to get his hands on some money.

"Oh, you can bet I'll do that, Harry. Yes, sir, I'll remember you, all right." That sinister smile was the last thing Harry saw before he turned to leave the room.

"I'll have filet mignon, medium please." Lori knew this restaurant specialized in seafood, but after seeing squid on the menu, she decided to have a reliable beefsteak.

She still could not believe she had let herself come here after all her resolutions to stay in the hotel room by herself tonight. Yet here she sat, beside this strange man who seemed to possess some unfathomable attraction that caused her to take leave of her usually reliable senses.

And Nicky hadn't helped matters. She had threatened to stay in the room and have supper with Lori unless they all went out together, using her guilt trip technique to make it almost impossible for Lori to refuse.

Sitting beside Kevin, feeling the pressure of his arm against her own, Lori felt annoyed at herself for allowing her emotions to overpower her cool reserve.

Music from the band filled the air with a romantic song from the fifties, and George led Nicky toward the dance floor. This was the first time Lori had been alone with Kevin since their antagonistic encounter on the beach.

"What kind of work do you do, Kevin?" She made a deliberate effort to keep the conversation friendly and casual.

"Nothing at all this week, Lorelei. I'm on vacation, and I'm determined not to mention or even think about my work for two wonderful weeks." He smiled at her, and the soft lights of his blue eyes were disarming. Was he being purposely evasive? She tried again.

"Me too. But I'd still like to know what you do when you're working."

"Tell me about your job first. It sounds much more interesting than mine. You know, you had me convinced for a while that you were really a mermaid. I thought I was losing my sanity. Then George explained to me what you and Nicole do, and it sounds like a job too good to be true."

"It's fun," she admitted. "But there's a lot of hard work involved, too." So George had pulled the truth from Nicole, had he? The last Lori heard, Nicky was taking scuba lessons and playing the part of a novice.

"What happens to the performances when you're away? I'm sure 'The show must go on!'"

"Yes, every day of the year. But there are plenty of girls who rotate in the cast. My particular spot is filled this week by a friend named Helga." *Friend?* Yes, she considered Helga a friend even though she'd been giving Lori the cold-shoulder treatment lately. Still, she had volunteered to feed Fluffy. "Helga's not only swimming for me this week; she's even feeding our cat while we're away."

"Sounds like a true friend."

Kevin still hadn't answered her question. In fact, he seemed to be purposely directing the conversation in other directions. "What line of work did you say you're in?" No one ever accused her of being irresolute.

With a low chuckle and a mischievous grin, he rose and stood beside the table. "I didn't say, did I? Well, as a matter of fact, I'm in business for myself, in Jacksonville. Sort of a public servant, you might say. Would you like to dance?"

He held out his hand, and she stood to join him. He had not given her a real answer, and she wasn't ready to drop the matter. But for now, she surrendered to the rhythm of the band and the sweet feeling of his arms around her as he led her across the small dance floor in graceful steps matched to the beat of the band.

Lori felt herself floating as they circled the floor, their bodies swaying in perfect harmony. Was this dizzy, delightful feeling a carry-over from her day on the rolling ocean? Or was it something more? She couldn't afford to let herself get personally involved with anyone right now. There were too many uncertainties in her life already. Too many blanks to be filled in. The timing was all wrong.

His head was bent over hers, and he softly crooned the lyrics against the thickness of her hair. No one had ever affected her like this unusual man. What was there about him that pulled at her like a magnet? Was this just the romantic mystique of the tropics? She couldn't give in to it now, no matter how enticing it seemed. She'd have to put all her romantic inclinations on hold until she found some answers. New encounters could spell danger, and she couldn't risk that right now.

She felt his embrace tighten as the beat of the music changed, and she heard him whisper into her hair, "Lorelei, you're something special."

"I think they're serving our dinner," she told him, easing from his tight hold. "Probably we should get back to the table."

Kevin sighed. He released her reluctantly, keeping hold of her hand as she led the way back to the table. Nicole and George were waiting for them. "Doesn't this look delicious?" Nicky had ordered broiled grouper. George and Kevin had chosen surf and turf platters. Only Lori had refused the house specialties.

"Normally I love seafood," she confessed. "By tomorrow, I'll be ready to abandon this landlubber kick."

"Speaking of tomorrow," Kevin began.

Oh, my! Did he think she was hinting about making plans together for tomorrow? "I have a lot of things to catch up on tomorrow," Lori ventured quickly, coloring as she spoke.

"Like what?" Nicky asked. "I thought we were on vacation."

Thanks, Nicky! "Well, of course we are. But I have to get some postcards, and— She struggled for words to make her stand plausible. "I need to call my mother, too. I haven't talked to her lately, and I didn't even tell her where I'd be, in case she needs to contact me for anything."

"Oh, for goodness sakes, Lori. Your mother is probably off on some holiday herself with that good-looking husband of hers. She's not worrying about you."

That was probably true. Jean and Andy might be on another cruise, or up in the mountains, or no telling where. Wherever they were, it was a cinch they weren't worrying about her. The only time she ever heard from either of them was when she placed the call herself, and even then she was seldom able to find them at home.

"Anyway, Lori, you can't call anyone while we're here. It was your own idea not to tell anyone where we were going. Remember?"

"What I had in mind," Kevin continued, as though he had not heard a word of interference. "Was for the four of us to get up early and drive down to Key West. You can't come to the Keys without visiting Key West. That's one of the unwritten laws."

"Great idea," George boomed enthusiastically.

"George, don't you have to work?" Lori grasped at straws. Part of her longed to go on what was sure to be a fun adventure, while another part of her was flashing a yellow caution light that said, "G*et off this merry-go-round before it's too late!"*

"No, I think I deserve to take a little break. I've put off taking a vacation for a long time. There are two other instructors at the school who can fill in for me this week. They'll be happy for me to get away now, so I'll be ready to give it my undivided attention next week when school is out and all the kids descend on us. Anyway," he continued with a conspiratorial wink at Nicky, "my star pupil just graduated with honors after just one lesson."

"I think it's a lovely idea," Nicky chirped, ignoring the icy glances Lori was sending her way.

"Then it's settled," Kevin said with satisfaction. "I'll drive my car this time. I'll pick you up at six o'clock tomorrow morning. If you're ready when I get there, we can get over to *La Hacienda* in about ten minutes from your place."

"I'll be ready and waiting at the door."

"Just call us on the house phone when you get to our hotel, and we'll come right down." Nicole was elated. "What kind of clothes shall we wear?"

"Everything in the Keys is casual. Just be comfortable." Kevin looked pleased with himself. "Lori, you can get plenty of postcards down there. We can even find a place for you to call you mother, if you decide you want to."

Again Lori felt maneuvered. If she refused to go now, she would be the wet blanket that spoiled the day for the whole group. And Nicky wouldn't let her soon forget it. All right, she'd go, but she'd warn Nicky not to wander off and leave her alone with Kevin tomorrow. She could feel herself growing more and more vulnerable to his charming ways, yet there was an air of mysticism about him that worried her.

Standing over them, the waiter offered dessert menus. "Mango meringue pie is our house specialty. The tropical fruit ice cream is quite nice, too. We make it right here in our own kitchens from fresh cream and native island fruits."

Though the offerings sounded deliciously tempting, the dinner had more than satiated their appetites.

"But I'd love a cup of espresso," Lori said.

"Make that two, please."

"Three."

"Four!"

Over coffee, they made plans for the day ahead. "Be sure to wear comfortable shoes. We'll be doing lots of walking."

"I've wanted to see Key West ever since I was a little girl," Lori confessed. "How long will it take us to get there?"

"Less than two hours, if the traffic's not too heavy," George told her. "You'll love the scenic drive down, especially in the early morning hours."

In spite of her earlier reluctance, Lori was beginning to catch the excitement. "Let's find a nice Key West souvenir for Helga, Nicky."

"Maybe we can find a pretty shirt that says 'Key West'. It would be a nice way to thank her for taking care of Fluffy," Nicole agreed. "Helga was dying to know where we were going, and she seemed a little miffed when I wouldn't tell her. Maybe a souvenir would help salve her wounds."

When the waiter appeared again, he offered the check on a small black tray. As Kevin reached for the bill, Lori dug into her purse and pulled out a long white envelope. "I've been waiting for the opportune moment to do this." She handed the envelope to Kevin.

"What's this, Lori?" Kevin opened the flap and shook the contents over the table. Five twenty-dollar bills floated out onto the white linen cloth.

"Why, Lori, that's your fish prize money," Nicky exclaimed.

"Wrong. That's *our* fish prize money. You bought the tickets, Nicky, and George, well, he and Kevin both helped to make the day interesting." She grinned sheepishly, remembering the trouble she had caused them all. "It's my way of saying thanks."

Kevin was reluctant to accept, but both women insisted. "I think it's a lovely idea," Nicole chirped. "Thank you, Lori."

"But only if it's understood that tomorrow is our treat." Kevin picked up the money and the waiter's check.

As they started for the door, Lori heard Nicole behind her crooning happily, *"Tomorrow, tomorrow, I'll love ya' tomorrow—"*

Yes, Lori thought as the catchy lyrics played through her mind, and *"you're only a day away!"*

* * *

Walking to the car, Kevin resisted an impulse to sing along with Nicole. Spending tomorrow in the company of Lorelei Cramer was indeed an exciting prospect. Her physical attraction was undeniable, and as long as he remembered to label it that, her presence could be a pleasant vacation diversion.

Now that he had learned the new rules of the game, he could better understand how to play by them without getting hurt. Of course, he would never compromise his own ethics and standards of living, but as long as he held firm to his beliefs and principles, he might as well enjoy a day in the company of a beautiful mermaid.

CHAPTER SIX

Although the day had scarcely begun, traffic on the famous Overseas Highway was already heavy. Kevin was a smooth, confident driver, and Lori relaxed on the seat beside him, enjoying the ever-changing panorama as they passed from one Key to the next.

Through her right window she could look out over the sparkling whitecaps of the Gulf of Mexico, where people were already congregating along pristine beaches. On the Atlantic side, the emerging sun hung low in the morning sky. Like a big, fluorescent balloon, its rays bounced off the billowy white clouds and painted a medley of gold, orange, pink, and silver against a canvas of soft blue horizon.

"This is the new Seven Mile Bridge," George said from the back seat. "You can still see the old one right down there." He pointed to the pedestrian bridge beneath them. "That's where Henry Flagler built the first overseas railroad you read about in history books." Early morning anglers were already staking claims for choice fishing spots along the preserved remnants of the famous old landmark.

The antiquated bridge had long since been abandoned for transportation purposes, but was obviously still a popular spot for the tourists and locals as a fishing pier and observation deck. Lori watched a young girl struggle to reel in a fish and remembered the excitement of her own recent success.

She twisted her head toward the back seat. "I suppose you've made this trip many times, George. Have you always lived down here?"

"Yep! I was born in Key West. That's the southernmost city in the continental United States." He spoke with pride. "My folks moved up to Marathon, though, when I was only about four years old, and I've lived there ever since. Don't think I'd care to live anywhere else, to tell the truth."

"I can see why," Nicky gushed. "This place is heavenly." She was laying it on a bit heavy, Lori thought. But maybe Nicky had the right idea about life after all. She lived for the moment, confident tomorrow would take care of itself. What was that old proverb? *Sufficient unto the day are the troubles therein.* Whoever said that surely knew what he was talking about.

But Lori was sure today would be a good day. She could already feel it. Nicky had talked to her late into the night last evening, forcing her to face up to all the ridiculous fears she'd been harboring these past weeks, convincing her she should lighten up and enjoy this great vacation before it was all just a memory. Now in the daylight hours, Lori began to see the wisdom of Nicole's advice and realize how foolish she had been to waste so much time worrying. She renewed her resolve to put all negative thoughts behind her and make the most of the remaining days of their glorious holiday.

She stole a sideward glance at Kevin. Just sitting here beside him sent delightful shivers up and down her spine, and this time she did not try to subdue them. She would talk to him today, discover where he was from and what he did, and settle some of the mystique about him. Then who could know where fate might lead them?

As though he could read her thoughts, Kevin glanced down at her and smiled. His right hand reached for hers and gave it a gentle squeeze. "Are we having fun?"

"We're having fun," she confirmed, returning his smile. Refusing to allow her day to be marred by the ridiculous suspicions that had clouded her recent thoughts, she remembered Mr. Porter's words, and Nicole's, too. They were both right. This holiday was just what she needed.

Kevin drove across one bridge after another as they covered key after key. None had been as impressive as the Seven-Mile Bridge, yet each was a doorway into a different world. To Lori, the stretch of bridge-connected islands seemed endless.

"We're now in what the natives refer to as the Lower Keys," George said. "Just a whole cluster of small Keys that form a chain leading right into Key West."

"It wouldn't do to be in a hurry, would it?"

"For people in a hurry, there's air service into Key West," George explained. "The only two major airports are the one in Marathon where y'all landed, and in Key West where you're going today."

How could this possibly be the same state where Lori was born and had spent most of her life? In northern Florida, she had grown up among spreading oaks and rolling hills, interspersed with cool, bubbling springs like the one where she performed her water ballet. Here the land was as flat as the western prairies, only wetter. Water in every direction, as far as the eye could see, dotted with bits of land like jewels in a priceless regal crown. It wasn't hard to understand why George loved this area so much.

Lori was pulled from her reverie by a sign that read, "Welcome to Key West, Doorway to the Past and the Future."

In the driver's seat, Kevin slowed to get directions. "Where do we go first?"

As unofficial tour director, George decided they should find a place for brunch. "Let's drive into the Old Town area. After we eat, we can ride the Old Town Trolley, or the Conch Tour Train. Either one will give us a good look at the city." He guided Kevin through the narrow streets toward the town's much-publicized historic district. "There's too much to see and do here to crowd it all into one day, but we'll do the best we can."

Kevin pulled into the parking lot of a tin-roofed building constructed entirely of pink and white sea shells. Judging from the crowded parking area, *The Conch House* was a popular place.

We can walk to most of the things we want to see," George told them. "In fact, we can stay right here on Duval Street and walk from the Gulf of Mexico to the Atlantic Ocean. Bet you've never done that before."

Kevin held the restaurant door open for Lori, and as she brushed against his arm she felt something akin to an electric current pass between them. Was this what people meant when they talked about summer love, or was it something deeper and more important than that? She didn't know; she only knew this man affected her in a way no one ever had before. It was unnerving to say the least, but she had to admit it was not altogether unpleasant. It was something like reading an exciting book, not knowing what the next chapter would reveal, and not an inkling of how it would all end. She'd just have to take things one chapter at a time, being careful not to get carried away on the tide of tropical illusions.

In the powder room, Nicky was fairly bubbling. "Isn't he just wonderful, Lori? George knows all these interesting facts about the Keys. I've never been very interested in history before, but I think it's just fascinating to hear him tell about it." Her face was flushed with excitement. "Oh, Lori, I think I'm really in love at last."

Lori could not suppress her skeptical smile. How many times had she heard those words pour from Nicky's mouth? Dear, sweet Nicole. Was there ever a friend in the world like her? "I'm happy for you, Nicky. Just don't get too carried away. Remember, we're only going to be here for two weeks, and then we'll be returning to the real world."

Nicky's bubble was not that easy to burst. "Marathon isn't really all that far away. Anyway, we aren't going to be mermaids forever. Don't forget there's a life above sea level, too."

"Of course." Why spoil Nicole's carefree mood? "George does seem awfully nice," Lori agreed, splashing fresh color onto her lips and running a comb through her hair. "Now let's get back to the dining room before those handsome guys find two other girls to take our place."

The buffet table was sumptuous and inviting, especially since there had been no time for breakfast before leaving Marathon. In addition to the usual assortment of meat and egg dishes, there were various delicacies from the sea along with light, flaky pastries and sweet, juicy tropical fruits.

The waiter kept their glasses filled with fresh-squeezed orange juice and their cups with rich, strong coffee.

Lori and Kevin returned after their second trip to the buffet table. "I had to have another bowl of that fruit," Lori declared, spooning a bite from the medley of guavas, mangoes, star fruit, papayas and pineapple. "I've never seen such an array."

"You're in for a lot of surprises before this day is over," George told her, without realizing how prophetic that statement was to become.

Outside in the sunshine, the four of them plotted their course. "How would you like to take a trip on the Old Town Trolley?" George asked them.

"I'm game."

"Me, too."

"Where do we board?"

"The Trolley Car Barn is on North Roosevelt. We can leave our car in their parking lot until we're ready to go home. The trolley'll take us completely around the town. We can get off whenever we come to a place we want to see, and whenever we want to move on, we just catch the next trolley."

"How often do they run?" Kevin asked him.

"Every thirty minutes, so you never have to wait very long at any of the stops."

"You can't beat that." Kevin unlocked the passenger door and opened it for Lori. "Just point us in the right direction."

"Oh, look, George. There's one now." Nicole pointed to a passing trolley car. "It looks just like the ones in San Francisco."

They were close enough to hear the tour director's voice vibrating over his loud speaker, pointing out the highlights of the area.

"Turn here, Kevin, and then right on North Roosevelt Boulevard. Just across First Street, you'll see the Trolley Barn."

The next trolley was waiting to depart. The men bought tickets while the women found seats near the rear. "It'll be easy to get off from here," Nicole decided.

The sides of the little orange and green car were open air with vinyl flaps that could be lowered in case of rain. With a ring of the bell, they were off.

The driver introduced himself as Clarence, then proceeded to entertain them with bits of local history and anecdotes about some of the past and present residents of Key West.

They traveled north, along the shores of the Gulf of Mexico. Hotels and motels peppered the coastline, partially blocking their view of the water.

Their bodies swayed in unison as the trolley began turning in a giant curve, past a large shopping plaza and a community welcome center. Rounding the loop, they proceeded down South Roosevelt Boulevard, following the shoreline of the Atlantic Ocean. Clarence pointed out the Key West International Airport, the East Martello Museum, and the city beaches. Passengers got off, and new ones boarded to take their places at each stop.

"All of these are great stops," George told them. "The museum is especially interesting. But since we have only one day, I think we should concentrate on the Old Town area."

"If we get to come again, we'll plan to see all the places we miss today," Kevin suggested.

He's probably thinking about the next time, with the next girl, too, Lori speculated.

"After we pass the county beaches, we'll come to the Southernmost Point," George told them. "Let's plan to get off there."

When the county beaches came into view, a family with several small children picked up their picnic basket, towels, and beach toys, and climbed over their feet to get off.

Lori stole a sideways glance at Kevin. He was listening intently to Clarence, soaking up the area history like a sponge. She detected an air of intelligence about him that she admired. If only their personalities were a little more compatible. They had gotten off to a bad start, but maybe it wasn't too late to change.

"The monument here is designated as the Southernmost Point," Clarence explained.

Kevin was the first one off, and extended his hand to help Lori down the little step. As she stepped down, her right foot landed on a half-eaten lollipop, probably dropped by one of the children who disembarked at the beach. The step was low, making her slide swift and short, right into Kevin's waiting arms.

"Steady." He held her a few moments longer than necessary, but she pretended not to notice, and stumbled again to add a small delay of her own. His sturdy arms felt strong and reassuring.

"Are you okay?"

Those words brought back memories of their first unpleasant meeting. His voice expressed concern now, as it had that day on the old wooden pier, but today his words neither irritated nor frightened her.

"I'm fine," she assured him, scraping the sticky candy from her shoe onto the damp grass beneath her feet.

Clarence hustled around the side of the car to check on her. "What happened?" he asked. "Are you hurt?"

"No, really. I'm fine. Kevin kept me from falling."

"Glad I could help." Kevin grinned at her and winked.

Lori returned his smile. "What's next on our agenda?"

"From here we can walk to Fort Zachary Taylor, if you're sure you're okay, Lori," George suggested.

"Better than just okay. I'm rarin' to go."

The day was like a journey back in time as they relived history, feeling the presence of the Spanish conquistadors, pirates and salvagers, New England seafarers, European royalty, and more.

Kevin's favorite stop was the centuries old fort, and they spent nearly an hour exploring it.

Lori loved the old Hemingway home and the museum that eulogized her favorite author. "Here among his personal belongings, you almost expect him to walk through the door," she mused. "I see now where he received his inspirations for *The Old Man and the Sea*."

They climbed the steps of the ancient lighthouse and studied relics of mariners of the past in the lighthouse museum.

"We'll save Mallory Market and Mallory Square until last," George told them. "You have to be there for the Sunset Celebration. That's where everyone meets to rate the sunset. You'll love it, Nicky. Then after the sun goes down, the whole city suddenly changes beat, and it's like a big street carnival."

"I love it already! Oh, George, I'm so happy you brought us here today."

George beamed. "Let's just wander along some of these side streets. No telling what we'll see." He led them into one of the many narrow streets that emptied into Duval.

Quaint shops lined both sides of the cobblestone street. No wonder the sign had called this a city of the past.

"Oh, look over there!" Nicky started across the narrow street, pointing to a storefront whose windows were heavily draped in deep red velvet.

"Madame Zenobia," the sign proclaimed. "Palm Readings, Tarot Cards, Tea Leaves."

"Come on," Nicky urged. "Let's all go in and see what the future holds in store for us." George ran to catch up with her and, like eager children, they joined hands and headed for the door.

"Thanks, but I think I'll just wait to be surprised." Lori lagged behind, and Kevin stayed by her side.

"Well, at least come in and give us moral support. No telling what kind of news we're going to hear." Nicky's grin let everyone know she considered this nothing more than an enchanting game.

Kevin looked at Lori to pick up his cue, and when she hesitated, he took her arm and led her toward the door. "Come on, Lori. We might as well see what Nicole is going to learn about her future."

A tinkling bell announced their entry. Warily, they found seats on the dark, heavy upholstery. The small waiting room was dimly lit and oppressive, the velvet drapes blotting out most of the light from the late afternoon sun. Glass beads strung in a narrow doorway obscured the view beyond.

An ominous silence was finally broken by a gravelly voice calling out in monotone. "Enter my parlor and drink of the tree of truth."

After an exchange of glances, George shrugged and led the way through the beaded curtain.

Madame Zenobia was seated at a small round table, swathed in colorful flowing robes, a gold turban hiding her hair. Only her wrinkled face and gnarled hands were visible as she gazed into an eerily iridescent crystal ball. Large gold loops fell from her leathery earlobes and glistened as they caught the reflection of a solitary candle burning in one corner of the room.

Lifting one arm, she beckoned toward Nicky, indicating the

chair opposite her own. "Sit here, my child, and I will give you the answers you seek."

How did she perceive this visit was Nicole's idea? A vague sense of unease washed over Lori, and she wished she'd remained firm in her refusal to come in. Well, it was too late for that now. Since the three of them were being completely ignored, Lori found a chair in the opposite corner of the room and George and Kevin quietly followed. All eyes were riveted to the table.

"What is your choice?" the old crone asked.

"What do you mean?"

"The crystal ball is twenty dollars. It is the most reliable and complete. Palms, cards, or tea leaves are ten dollars, or any two for fifteen dollars." She passed Nicole a small silver tray and waited to see the cash.

While Nicky was plowing into her purse, George stepped forward with two bills. "Get the works, honey. We want to know everything."

"No, I think I'll just have the palm reading." She returned one of the bills to George. Her flippant attitude was gone as she offered her trembling hand across the table.

Madame Zenobia bent her head over the proffered palm and studied it intently. "Mmm. Mmm." She seemed to be receiving a message from some outer source. "Water. I see lots of water. Water all around you."

Nicky's eyes grew round with wonder. "Why, that's amazing! Yes, yes. I do work in the water."

In the corner, Lori snickered. "Hardly an astounding revelation to people visiting the Florida Keys," she whispered to Kevin. "Nicky is so gullible."

The monotone droned on. "I see romance. Strong, powerful men. Your love line is very pronounced."

"You see a strong, powerful man?" Nicole prompted eagerly.

"Men. I see men in your life."

Now Lori couldn't stifle a giggle. "She's better than I thought."

Madame Zenobia was silent for a few moments, but when she spoke, her tone was sternly severe. "You will ask your friends to wait in the next room. There is too much interference with the spiritual vibrations in this parlor. If you are to hear the truth, it must be heard with receptive ears. Otherwise, the signs become unreliable."

Chastised, the three onlookers quietly tiptoed from the parlor and reclaimed their seats in the front room.

Ten minutes later, a starry-eyed Nicole joined them. "Lori, you simply must have your palm read. That woman is wonderful! She knows more about me than my own mother."

"There are lots of things about you that your own mother doesn't suspect," Lori quipped.

"Please, Lori. I know you don't think this is real, but you'll change your mind in a hurry if you just talk to her."

"It's my treat," Kevin volunteered. "This should be fun."

"No!" Lori was adamant. She had lots of unanswered questions, but that old phony couldn't help her.

"Come on, Lori. It'll give us something to laugh about all the way home." Kevin urged her toward the curtain. "I'll go in with you, and I promise not to disturb your spiritual vibrations." He didn't realize it, Lori mused, but he was already sending her plenty of his own vibrations and they had nothing to do with Madam Zenobia! Reluctantly, she moved forward. "It's just such a foolish waste of your money, Kevin."

"Shh. You're disturbing the vibrations," Kevin whispered, giving her a playful shove through the beaded curtain.

Lori sat before Madame Zenobia and tried to maintain an air of solemnity. This was all so stupid!

Kevin discreetly laid a bill on the silver tray, as Lori extended her fingers and revealed her palm to Madame Zenobia.

"Mmm. Mmm." This seemed to be a part of her ritual. This time the silence lasted longer, broken only by the monotone humming of the old soothsayer. One of her wrinkled hands supported Lori's, turning it this way and that, while the other used its bony fingers to trace the creases in Lori's open palm. Still she spoke not a word. The humming took on a more intense tone, more like an agonizing groan. Finally, she turned Lori's hand palm-down and placed it on the table. She raised her eyes and looked directly at the startled young woman before her. Coal black eyes seemed to pierce like arrows into Lori's questioning gaze.

Suddenly Madame Zenobia's voice lost its mystical tone and became apologetic. "I'm very sorry, miss. I cannot continue with this reading." Picking up the bill from her tray, she held it toward Kevin. "Go now. Go in peace."

Lori sat in stunned silence. Kevin bounded from his chair. "Now, you listen here. We came in here and paid for a service. You can't just quit before you've even started. I'll have you reported to the Better Business Bureau."

"I'm sorry, sir. I have refunded your money. My establishment is closed for the day."

"Your sign says you're open until nine o'clock tonight. You're not closed." Seeing Lori so visibly shaken seemed to fan the flames of Kevin's anger. "Finish your job."

Lori stood up. "Never mind, Kevin. I didn't want to come here in the first place. Madame Zenobia probably knew that, and she feels offended. Let's go."

Kevin had to hurry to catch up with her as she stumbled out the door and into the street. Nicole and George stood on the sidewalk waiting for her. "What did she say, Lori? It sure didn't take very long. Isn't she great?" Nicky continued to rattle on, completely oblivious of her friend's timorous state.

Kevin gave silent hand signals to George, who picked up on his cue and led Nicky across the street to look at something in one of the shop windows.

Kevin placed a protective arm around Lori's shoulder. "Just like you thought, the old woman is a complete charlatan. They shouldn't allow quacks like that to practice within the city limits."

Lori tried to laugh it off and forget it. She had no faith in the so-called art of fortune telling. But nevertheless, the experience had been unnerving. She willed her body to quit trembling.

Farther down the street, Lori saw Nicky and George reboarding the Old Town Trolley. "Hurry, Kevin. We mustn't get separated."

"It's okay. We'll all end up at Mallory Dock by sunset. They're just as happy to get away by themselves. And frankly, I don't mind it myself."

With his arm around her shoulder, they sauntered down the sidewalk. They looked in store windows at the displays of priceless antiques mingled with cheap souvenirs, then stopped to watch a mime perform in the cobblestone street. Boutiques and art galleries beckoned invitingly to the passersby, and vendors hawked their wares of such delicacies as boiled shrimp and fresh, hot peanuts. It was impossible to remain tense in such an atmosphere, and in the midst of her unique surroundings with Kevin beside her, Lori soon forgot the problems with Madame Zenobia.

"The old adage about time passing fast when you're having fun is certainly true, Lori. I can hardly believe this day is almost over."

"I feel the same way, Kevin. I'm glad you let me change my mind about coming. But shouldn't we be getting over to Mallory Dock for that Sunset Celebration George told us about?"

"Seems like the perfect way to end a wonderful day."

The famous dock was already crowded with people by the time they arrived. Surely George and Nicky were among them, but it was doubtful they would all find each other in the crowd. Lori was pressed close against Kevin's side as the sun crept lower in the sky.

"I'd have to vote for you as the girl I'd most like to share my sunsets with." Kevin gave her arm an affectionate squeeze. They pushed through the crowds, edging near the end of the weathered old pier.

"At least if you fall in, I won't have to worry about your drowning," Kevin quipped. "And I refuse to ruin any more clothes coming to your rescue. You're on your own today."

The sky looked like a piece of tie-dyed silk, its shades of pink and gold subtly bleeding into the snowy clouds adrift on an azure sea. A soft summer breeze cooled the salty air and tousled the long dark waves of Lori's hair.

"There's one brief moment," a seasoned onlooker told them, "when the sun first meets the water, and it seems to spread like butter on the horizon just seconds before it drops from view. It can't be adequately described; you have to experience it, so watch closely."

Ten minutes later, Lori and Kevin understood the meaning of his words. Lori and Kevin had to agree it was a breathtaking experience, like orange butter melted against the gulf for a brief flash before it dissolved into the sea.

For a moment, the whole crowd stood in awed silence. Then everyone seemed to shout at once. "Beautiful!" "Awesome!" "Each one seems more beautiful than the last!"

Rating the sunset on a scale of one to ten was a time-honored daily ritual on Mallory Dock. Seldom, unless there was a storm, did the appraisal drop below eight, and most often it was a unanimous ten, as it was on this unforgettable evening.

"What a lovely custom," Lori remarked as they moved with the crowd toward the shore. Holding hands, they walked across the sand and into the street leading toward the trolley stop.

As if by cue, Nicole and George were waiting for them. Nicky was sporting a new wide-brimmed straw hat and carried a shopping bag that boasted *Belinda's Boutique*. George had been doing some shopping of his own. His wrapped package was long and slender, and appeared to be some kind of a fishing rod. They were grinning like two school children sharing a private prank.

"We're starved," Nicky declared. "George knows lots of good places that serve the native cuisine."

"Barnacle Bill's is just down the road from the Old Town Barn. That's where a lot of the locals eat. It's not fancy, but the food is great and the price is right. No one ever leaves hungry, either."

"Sounds like my kind of place, George. Here comes the trolley now."

Barnacle Bill's was on the waterfront. The weather-beaten clapboard exterior of the building gave little clue to the casual elegance of the restaurant itself. The dining room was surrounded by aquarium walls behind which swam colorful fish of every description. Bubbles from the aerators rose and crystallized as they swirled through intricate seaweed patterns, forming an exquisite backdrop for guppies, neons, eels, and other aquatic life that claimed their habitat.

"I thought you said it wasn't fancy," Lori said, her eyes scanning the decor. "I think it's spellbinding!"

Waitresses wore bright, tropical printed sarongs and flowers in their hair.

Supper consisted of turtle soup, broiled dolphin, and of course, key lime pie. "They must bake about a million of these every day," George guessed.

"No wonder they're famous for it." Lori wiped whipped cream from her lips. "I've ordered it in other restaurants, but it never tasted this good. Are you sure this isn't lemon? If it's lime, wouldn't it be green instead of pale yellow?"

"They use a special lime that's grown down here," George explained. "It's called a key lime. It's just a little thing— not nearly as big as a regular lemon or lime. But it has a flavor distinctly its own. The limes themselves are yellowish green, but the juice is the light yellow color you see here. Any time you get a piece of pie with green filling, you can be sure it's not genuine key lime pie, unless they've added food coloring to change its appearance."

George had certainly spoken the truth about no one leaving hungry. Standing outside under the huge, spreading Banyan tree, everyone groaned from pleasant overindulgence.

The night air was clear and alive with the flickering of fireflies and overhead stars, and island music drifted on the breeze.

George offered to relieve Kevin of the driving on the return trip, but Kevin refused. "I'm wide awake after all that coffee I drank. The coffee down here rates right up there with the key lime pie and the sunsets. All tens."

Bright red, Kevin's rented sports car was easy to spot in the parking lot. Nicky and George snuggled in the back seat, and Kevin pulled Lori close beside him as he began the long drive home.

"Kevin, this day will live in my memory forever. I enjoyed every minute." Maybe not *every* minute. Lori had a hard time getting Madame Zenobia off her mind. Of course she didn't believe the old woman could foretell her future, but yet she wondered what it was that had turned her off so abruptly. Even a fraud would try to say *something,* just to get her hands on the money. Madame Zenobia had turned down an easy chance for a ten-dollar bill—most unusual for such a crafty con artist.

Kevin switched on the radio, and the stereo system surrounded them with a soft, romantic melody. The nearly full moon made a path across the water and crowded out the darkness of the night. Lorelei let her head rest against Kevin's sturdy shoulder. It felt so right there. She closed her eyes and let the music seep through her like a tranquilizing balm.

A surge of lovely warmth swept through her veins and seemed to permeate her whole body. What kind of spell had this man cast upon her? She had never felt this way before. Not about Ken, and not about anyone she had ever known. Why, if her good senses did not tell her differently, she would swear she was falling in love!

CHAPTER SEVEN

On Thursday morning a gentle rain fell steadily from a dismal sky, and without sunlight streaming through the windows, both Lorelei and Nicole slept late.

"What a dreary day. If this keeps up, I won't be able to go home sporting the tan I've dreamed about," Nicky complained.

"It may clear by afternoon," Lori consoled her. "Besides, we've been on the go for the last two days. I need a few hours to get my clothes organized. Let's indulge ourselves this morning by having breakfast sent up here to our room."

"Oh, yes, let's," Nicole agreed, reaching for her peignoir. "There's not much we can do for fun while it's raining. I can't even write letters or postcards home, since you made me promise to keep our whereabouts a secret." She shot Lori an accusatory glance.

Momentarily ignoring her friend's jab, Lori called the dining room and placed their order. She listed all their favorite breakfast items. "And be sure to send a big carafe of coffee," she added. "No, I think that will be all, thank you."

Then turning back to Nicky to address her earlier complaint,

Lori said, "I suppose that was a foolish idea on my part, not letting our friends and family know where we'd be. But you must admit it's been rather nice not having the phone ring all the time."

"That's a matter of opinion," Nicky replied tersely. "Personally, I've never been annoyed by telephone calls from my friends."

Before the words died in her throat, the phone on the bedside table sounded a sharp ring and Nicole sprang across the room to grab the receiver. "Hello," she purred into the telephone. Not surprisingly, it was George. Lori picked up her short terry robe and slippers and headed for the shower, glad for the interruption that was sure to have a soothing effect on Nicky's rainy day disposition.

Fifteen minutes later, when Lori emerged from the bathroom smelling of soap and spearmint toothpaste, Nicky was still whispering into the phone. "Yes, George. Oh, yes, I do, too. Of course, love."

Lori held her stomach and pantomimed an attack of nausea, and Nicky giggled. Then she hastened to explain, "Oh, no, George, I wasn't laughing at you. No, it— it was Lori." She stuck out her tongue at Lori, who was now acting the part of a doting, star-struck lover. "Oh, she's just, well, I don't know what she's doing. Don't even ask. I guess this rain has us both feeling a little crazy. I'd better go now, love. I think I hear our breakfast arriving at the door. What? Well, yes, I know it's nearly lunchtime, but we haven't had our breakfast yet. Call me later, darling. In the meantime, I'll try to get rid of this clown." Replacing the receiver, she grabbed her pillow and, with all the strength she could muster, threw it at Lori, who now lay on her bed convulsed with laughter.

Since it was nearly noon, Lori had ordered a substantial Spanish omelet with sausage and grits and biscuits. The bellboy pushed his cart through the doorway and spread a white cloth on the small table by their window before arranging their food and utensils on it. Deliciously tempting smells rose from the table. "Will there be anything else, ladies?"

"Not this morning, thank you," Lori said, smiling as she gave him a generous tip. He bowed and thanked them before he left the room, closing the door behind himself.

"Mmm! This was a marvelous idea," Nicky cooed, spreading a thick coating of honey butter on a fluffy hot biscuit.

"And would you look at this! They sent *two* pots of coffee." Lori filled both their cups with the steaming brew. "I could get used to this kind of life in a hurry."

"Look, Lori," Nicole squealed. "It's beginning to clear a little." Although the sun seemed to be making a determined effort to crack through the clouds, a light drizzle persisted. "I guess we could take in a movie this afternoon, but George and I are planning to see one tonight. I don't think I could sit through two movies in the same day. Are you sure you don't mind my going out and leaving you alone tonight?"

"Of course not, silly. I thought we already agreed we should each feel free to do whatever we choose on this trip. Besides, I brought along that new Jared Jones mystery I've been dying to read. I don't need a baby-sitter, Nicky. I'll be fine," Lori assured her.

Nicole looked relieved, but then her expression changed. "I wish you'd quit reading those murder mysteries. Sometimes I think that's where you get all those weird ideas."

Lori felt slightly offended, but in order to avoid a further confrontation, she covered her pique with a laugh. "Just go on and have a good time. Quit worrying about me. I'll be fine."

"Maybe Kevin will call, and then maybe you'll go out tonight, too."

"You can scratch that idea. In the first place, I doubt Kevin will call, but even if he does ask me out, I've already decided to decline."

"Why on earth would you do that? Lori, I wish you'd just

relax and have a little fun. Besides, I thought you and Kevin were finally beginning to like each other."

"For goodness sakes, Nicky, quit trying to manage me. Can't a girl just enjoy a quiet evening alone once in a while without getting the third degree?"

"Then why are you blushing?"

"You're imagining it. I don't blush. But okay, I'll tell you this much. It's true. I really do like Kevin. I didn't say I'd *never* see him again, but I want to cool it a bit to be sure things don't get out of hand."

"What do you mean by that?"

"Well, you know how easy it is to get carried away by the romance of the tropics. You of all people should know that."

"And what's that supposed to mean?" Nicole bristled, crossing her arms and glaring at Lori.

"Strike that last remark. Sorry. I didn't mean to get personal. All I really meant to say was I'm not cut out for these typical little summer romances that begin and end all in one breath. You know very well once we leave this place these fellows we've met down here will find two more girls to take our place. In a few weeks, they won't even remember our names."

"Speak for yourself, Lorelei. Just leave George and me out of your categorizing." She looked more than a little piqued as she picked up her clean clothes and headed for the shower. "I'm going to get dressed and go downstairs to the game room where the atmosphere is sure to be more sociable."

Lori was straightening her bed when Nicole came out of the bathroom fresh from her shower. Without a word of goodbye, Nicky flounced out of the room, letting the door slam behind her.

Lori immediately felt repentant. She hadn't meant to offend her best friend, but all the same, what she said was true. After yesterday and last night, she knew Kevin was beginning to be much more important to her than she'd ever intended. She didn't want to go home with a broken heart to add to all the other problems she still had to work out. There was only one more week of vacation left, and if she could just manage to keep busy without seeing too much of Kevin Collins, she could avoid adding him to her list of worries.

She fully expected him to call. She silently rehearsed her demure refusal. She would be courteous and friendly, of course. But no matter how insistent he became, she would be adamant in her refusal to go out with him tonight.

The rain had stopped now, although the sky remained overcast with pearly gray clouds. She decided to go down to the game room to find Nicky, make her peace, and suggest a set of tennis to work off their tensions.

She passed the front desk just as the shift was changing and the day clerk was leaving. "Oh, Miss Cramer," he called to her. "Did your brother get in touch with you?"

"My brother? No, I'm afraid you have the wrong party, Chuck." She'd never had a brother, but with so many people staying at the hotel, it was easy to understand how the desk clerk could get the residents confused.

"No, Miss Cramer. There was a call for you this afternoon. He said he was your brother and wanted to confirm that you were staying here. When I told him you were a registered guest, he asked for your room number. But you know we're not allowed to pass out that kind of information, Miss Cramer. I offered to ring your room for him, but he said he had to run and would call you later."

Lori blanched, and he hastened to apologize. "I'm sorry about not giving him your room number, but it's strictly against the hotel policy to give them out. I hope I didn't cause you too much inconvenience."

"No, Chuck. You did the right thing." Absolutely no one knew she was here unless it had been Mr. Porter. But he would have accepted the offer to ring her room if he needed to get in touch with her. Besides, he surely wouldn't have claimed to be her brother.

Chuck could have been mistaken. The front desk probably received dozens of calls every day. They couldn't possibly keep all the messages in their heads. That had to be the answer. Still, it gave her an uneasy feeling.

She nearly bumped into Nicole as she rounded the corner on her way to the game room. "I was just coming back upstairs to see you," Nicole confessed. "I hate it when we quarrel."

"So do I, and I do understand George is special to you, Nicky. He's awfully nice, too." Lori turned to follow Nicole back to their room. "Change into your tennis clothes, and let's see if the courts are dry."

"You're on!"

La Hacienda had four tennis courts, and three of them were occupied. In the pro shop, Nicky and Lori reserved the fourth court for an hour.

"Look over there, Lori."

"Where? I don't see anything."

"Those four guys playing doubles on Court Two. Aren't they fantastic?"

Lori watched the fast paced doubles match for a few moments. "Yes, they do seem to be good tennis players," she agreed.

"Well, yes. That, too. But I mean, aren't they gorgeous? Look at that one with the dark, curly hair. He looks like he's been weight lifting or something. Have you ever seen a more perfect physique?"

Lori laughed in spite of her best efforts. She didn't want to raise Nicole's ire again so soon after their last little spat, but she couldn't resist. "What about special old George?"

"Just serve the ball, Lori. I can see you're not in a very understanding mood today. Go ahead. Let's play tennis."

After ten minutes of a warm up rally, the two friends played hard and competitively, and the intense exercise served to work off any differences they might have felt earlier in the day. Lori was even able to push aside thoughts of the strange conversation with the desk clerk, but she decided not to mention any of it to Nicky. She knew what Nicky would say, and she was growing tired of being labeled paranoid.

When they finished their game, they entered the side door of the hotel in good spirits. "You can have the first shower, Nicky, so you can get ready for your date tonight."

Nicole didn't argue but headed straight for the bath, and Lori could hear her singing happily as she took her second shower of the day.

Even though Lori planned to spend the evening alone, she groomed herself carefully. After all, one never knew who might turn up in the hotel dining room.

When the telephone rang, Nicole was quick to answer. Not surprisingly, it was George calling from the lobby. Nicky picked up her purse and hurried down to meet him.

Lori waited until she was sure they had plenty of time to leave before she rode the elevator down to the ground floor. She didn't want to put George on the spot by making him think he should invite her to tag along.

Entering the dining room, she asked Carmelita for a table facing the water. After a careful study of the menu, she ordered stuffed flounder with a big Caesar salad and a baked potato.

While she leisurely ate her dinner and sipped iced tea, she focused her eyes on the people strolling along the beachfront. Several times she thought she caught a glimpse of Kevin, but each time, when the figure came closer, she realized she was mistaken. She wondered where he was at this precise moment and what he was doing. Not that it mattered, really. She was merely curious.

A waiter pushed the dessert cart up to her table. "Care for something sweet? All our desserts are made fresh right here in our own kitchen." He pointed to several delicacies in an effort to tempt her taste buds. "May I recommend this double chocolate killer-cake?"

She hesitated for just a moment before deciding. "Thank you, but no. Perhaps I'll come down a little later this evening for a piece of that pecan pie and a cup of coffee." Actually, it wouldn't hurt anything if, when Kevin called, she invited him to come over for dessert. It wouldn't be a date. More like a friendly matter of common courtesy.

Back in her room she checked to see if the message light was on, but apparently no one had called while she was out.

She picked up her new book and opened it to the first page. She would not undress for bed just yet— it wasn't even completely dark outside. She opened the drapes and sat where she could keep an eye on the beach.

She finished the first chapter and got up to pour herself a glass of water. Why was she so restless tonight? Had she become so addicted to Nicole's constant chatter that she could no longer enjoy a quiet evening alone? She stepped onto her balcony and looked out over the water. The moon cast a silvery sheen over the cobalt ripples, and a clear sky was spangled with a thousand stars. It brought to mind one of her favorite Psalms, Psalm 8:3,4: *When I consider Thy heavens, the work of Thy fingers, the moon and the stars which Thou hast ordained; what is man that Thou art mindful of him?*

What was Kevin doing tonight? Was he standing on his balcony looking at the same moon? Was he thinking about her, or of someone waiting for him back in his own hometown? She realized then how very little she knew about him. Just one more reason to strengthen her resolve not to get romantically involved with a virtual stranger.

She turned back to her room and checked her message light again. Sometimes those electronic devices didn't work properly. Perhaps hers was out of order. She rang the front desk to make sure. "This is Lorelei Cramer in Room 641. Have there been any calls for me tonight?"

A voice on the other end of the line replied, "Just a moment, Miss Cramer. I'll check." Then after a short pause, the response came back. "No, ma'am. I don't find a record of any messages for you. Was your message light flashing?"

"No, and thank you for checking." She replaced the receiver and picked up her mystery novel again. She had been so anxious to start this new book, but so far it hadn't really captured her interest. Sometimes it took a few chapters to get into a good book. She'd start the next chapter and see if the plot got more intriguing.

When the phone finally rang, she jumped up and was ready to answer it on the first ring. Then she caught herself. She didn't want to sound over-eager. And remember, she reminded herself, decline anything other than simply dessert and coffee in her own dining room. She absolutely would not leave the hotel tonight. After three rings, she answered in her most professional voice. "Hello?"

She was surprised to hear the long distance operator. "Miss Lorelei Cramer, please. I have a long distance call for Miss Lorelei Cramer."

So it wasn't Kevin after all. That was puzzling, especially in light of the fact that no one knew she was here in Marathon except for her few local friends. "This is Lorelei. Go ahead."

"Your party is on the line." After thanking them for using their services, the operator rang off and Lori waited for her caller to speak.

There was complete silence on the line. "Hello. Hello. This is Lorelei. Can you hear me?" We must have been disconnected, she thought. She dialed the hotel operator.

"I had a long distance call, but we seem to have become disconnected. Can you see about connecting me with the caller again?"

"I'm sorry, miss. We have no way of tracing the call. Probably the party who called will get operator assistance from the other end where the call originated."

"Oh, yes, of course. Thank you. I'll just wait." While she sat by the phone waiting for it to ring, the same thoughts continued to circle through her mind. Who could be calling her here in Marathon? It couldn't have been a wrong number, because the party had asked for her by name.

After a time, she turned back to her book. By the time she finished Chapter Four, she realized Kevin wasn't going to call her tonight, and neither was whoever had called earlier. She might as well get ready for bed.

She was glad Kevin hadn't called. It would be a lot easier than she thought to make sure he kept his distance. Probably he hadn't given her a thought since yesterday. Probably he would never call her again. And that was what she truly wanted, wasn't it?

Actually, Kevin had thought of little else since he left Lori at her hotel last night. Was it only last night? It seemed like days had elapsed since he last saw her. Lorelei! An unusual name for an unusual woman. A woman who was fast becoming far too important to him.

He must be crazy. He knew so little about her. In fact, he really didn't know her at all. She seemed to be only half human and half— what? Angel? No, more like half mermaid. Yes, he must certainly be getting a little crazy. Just when he thought he understood modern women and their games, along came this beautiful creature who blended her chic, classic style with a charm as old-fashioned as a piece of Victorian lace.

There was everything wrong and absolutely nothing right about furthering a relationship with Lorelei Cramer. She was like an itch he couldn't scratch. The more he tried to put her out of his mind, the more vividly her image invaded his thoughts.

And every time he looked into her clear emerald eyes, he felt mesmerized. But he had been mesmerized by green eyes before, and he knew the dangers they could conceal.

It was quite clear this whole thing was just a lark for her. She was playing a real cat-and-mouse game with him. *Come. No, go away. No, come back.* She must be in her hotel room laughing about it right now. True, she had seemed to relax with her head on his shoulder last night on the long drive home, and he had experienced the warm sensation of feeling it belonged there. But for Lori, it must have been only a matter of convenience because she was sleepy and wanted to make herself comfortable. It seemed obvious to Kevin that every time he tried to make any kind of plans with her, she managed to find some feeble excuse to decline.

He'd better slow things down a little. He hated to admit his feelings ran much deeper than he wanted them to, especially when he held her close. He had come down here to the Keys to relax, and the last thing he wanted was a romantic involvement.

He'd left his detective agency in capable hands, with two very good investigators on his staff to keep things rolling, and there were no vital cases pending. He recognized his tendency to become too personally involved where his clients were concerned. So far, he had kept the promise he made to himself about not revealing his profession to anyone he met during these two short weeks. It had seemed such a sensible idea at the time.

But he found it increasingly difficult to remain evasive under Lori's probing questions. He sensed she had problems of her own, and he didn't want to get embroiled in them. He didn't intend to take a busman's holiday, and in this particular case, what he *didn't* know couldn't hurt him.

If he kept out of her sight for a day or two, maybe he could sort out his conflicting feelings. In a few days, they'd all be leaving this place, and he'd be back to business as usual, working on dry land with no mermaids to cloud his thinking.

CHAPTER EIGHT

Nicole must have come in very late last night. Lorelei had stayed awake for hours reading her mystery novel, but she hadn't heard her come in. No wonder she was sleeping so late this morning. Soft snores sounded rhythmically from the next bed.

Even with the drapes drawn, Lori could tell that outside the sun was shining. The bright new day tempted her. She slipped quietly into her bathing suit, popped on her terry cover-up, and headed for the beach.

The wind was up, and wind surfers were out in large numbers to take advantage of the brisk ocean breezes. Lori didn't have a wind surfing board, but she took vicarious pleasure in watching them fight their way into the ocean to ride the frothy breakers back to shore. Sitting in the gaily-striped canvas cabana, she was impressed with the level of skill some of them displayed. It would take a lot of practice to get that good, but she could relate to that. She was no stranger to hard practice.

Her mind drifted back to Weeki Wachee Spring, where she was sure Mr. Porter was putting the girls through rigorous daily workouts between each show. She never minded the practices, though. Instead, she considered herself fortunate to be able to support herself by doing something that was so much fun.

The day would come when she would need to decide on another vocation. Most of the girls in the follies cast were still in their twenties—that meant she had at least five more years. But after that, then what?

In college she had majored in journalism, but when the chance came to join the cast at Weeki Wachee Spring, she had dropped out half way through her junior year. Her parents tried to persuade her to finish college first, but she refused to listen, knowing this chance might never come her way again.

She'd never been sorry about her decision. She loved the water, and she was fond of all the people who worked with her in the cast.

At school she had performed on the synchronized swimming team, but their coach only held practices three times a week. It was while she was on tour with her school team that Mr. Porter had spotted her and offered her a job with the mermaid show. She had a lot to thank Mr. Porter for. He had always been very good to her.

Her thoughts were interrupted by a volleyball that landed right in the middle of her lap, startling her out of her daydreams.

"Oh, sorry. I hope you're not hurt."

Both the voice and the face were familiar. Of course. One of the guys from the tennis court yesterday— the one Nicole had found so attractive.

"I'm fine." She tossed the ball in his direction with a force that seemed to surprise him.

"Say, why don't you come join our game? Right now our sides are uneven, and my side could really use an extra player."

"I've only played the game a few times. I'm not an expert by any means."

"Neither are we. We're just having fun." He held out his hand and pulled her up from the chaise.

"I'm Mike," he told her as they joined the group. "And you are...?"

"Lorelei. But just call me Lori."

"Okay, Lori. These are my friends." He named the players on his side of the net. "Herb, Lee, Bob, Ginger and Michelle. Now we're even with seven on each side."

Lori quickly realized he had spoken the truth when he said they weren't experts. Except for a couple of the men on each side, all were rank amateurs struggling to keep the ball in play.

"Can I play too?" Nicky, wearing a bikini that looked like it was painted on, crunched across the sand. Without waiting for an invitation, she joined the game on Lori's side.

"Hey, no fair!" joked one of the opposing players. "How come Mike always gets the new girls?"

"Cause I'm so sweet and irresistible," Mike replied with a grin.

Lori laughed. "Folks, this is my friend, Nicole. Come on, Nicky. Our side is losing. Maybe you can help us out."

Keeping score didn't seem important as they batted the ball from side to side, laughing and kicking up the sugary sand. When the noonday heat finally became uncomfortable, they headed for a swim in the cool ocean water.

"Say!" Mike came up to Lori and Nicky as they stood shaking off surplus salty water. "Would you girls like to come to a beach party tonight?"

"Oooh! That sounds like fun." Nicky never turned down a party invitation if she could help it.

Lori gave her a little jab in the rib cage. "Yes, it sounds like fun, and we'd love to if we hadn't already made other plans."

"What pla—"

"But perhaps some other time. Thanks anyway, Mike."

"Well, listen," Mike persisted. "I know you just met us, but it's real informal. Everyone you met today will be there. We're going to go surf crabbing and have a crab boil on the beach. If you already have dates, bring them along. The more the merrier."

"Where will it be?" Clearly, Nicole had already made up her mind to go.

"We're going to meet down on the south end of the beach about seven o'clock. Bring flashlights if you have 'em. We'll have plenty of nets."

Walking toward the hotel to change clothes for lunch, Lori asked, "Nicole, what got into you? We don't even know those people."

"Oh, lighten up, Lori. We're just here to have a good time. It's not like a date, anyway. And if George and Kevin come over, we'll just invite them along. Mike said we could."

Lori had to admit it did sound like fun. She'd never been surf crabbing, and she had never been to a crab boil.

In the room, the message light was blinking. "That may be for me, Nicky. Someone tried to call me last night, but the call never came through."

Nicole gave her a puzzled look as she reached for the phone. "You have a message for Room 641?" Lori looked over her shoulder as Nicole wrote the message on the hotel memo pad. *Please call me ASAP. 229-4302. George.*

While Nicole dialed the number, Lori headed for the shower. When she came out, Nicky was just hanging up. "George is coming over this evening. I told him about the party, and he says it sounds like fun. He said he'd give Kevin a call and bring him along too, if he's not doing anything."

"I don't need you and George fixing me up with dates, Nicole. Please just let me handle my own social life."

"Sorry, Lori. I seem to have hit a raw nerve." Nicole picked up her clean clothes and started toward the bathroom. "After I get cleaned up, we can have some lunch together. That is, if you don't think I'm making too many of your plans for you."

"No, and I'm the one who should be apologizing. I didn't mean to sound so snappy. Go get dressed so we can find some lunch. I'm always hungry here."

Although it was nearly one o'clock, the dining room was full. "Things always begin to get busy around here on Friday," the waitress told them. "It's the beginning of the weekend. But I'll be able to seat you just as soon as we get a table cleared."

"We'd prefer to sit by the window, but I suppose we can't be choosy today, Carmelita."

"No problema. They are clearing your favorite table right now."

In spite of the crowds, service was quick. Lori was halfway through her seafood quiche when she heard her name.

"Lorelei Cramer, as I live and breathe!"

"Ken! Where did you come from?" It was Nicole who asked the question, because Lori was too stunned to speak.

Without waiting for an invitation, he pulled up an extra chair and positioned his bulky frame upon it. Lori didn't remember his being that heavy. It had been months since she'd seen him, and he certainly had changed.

"I was down this way on business and decided to stay down for the weekend to relax a little." He turned to Lori. "Are you staying here?"

Lori hesitated briefly. "Yes, we are, Ken. It's nice to see you again. We were just finishing lunch, so if you'll excuse us—" She started to rise, but Ken reached out and laid his hand on her arm.

"Stay for just a moment. Please, Lori. I know I acted like a jerk the last time we were together, and I just want a chance to apologize properly."

"Three's generally a crowd," Nicole observed, "so I'll wait for you in the lobby, Lori."

"No, stay—" But Nicole was already making her way across the crowded room.

"Relax, Lori. I don't bite. I just want to talk to you."

"All right, Ken. I'm all ears."

"First of all, I want to ask you to forgive me for all those mean and unkind things I said. I was mad and hurt, and I wanted to get back at you for my pain and suffering. Now that I've had time to think about it, I see I was wrong, and I'm trying to make it right. Can we be friends again?"

They had been close for a very long time. She looked at him across the table, and the only emotion he stirred in her now was pity. She held out her hand. "Of course, Ken. That's how I wanted it all along, remember? I told you long ago I hoped we'd always be friends."

"I remember, Lori. And I abused that friendship. I've regretted it so many times since."

"Well, now that we've settled that issue, I really must go. Nicole is waiting for me."

"I'd like to see you this evening, just for old times' sake. Would you join me for dinner, just between two old friends?" He reached for her hand and held it.

She smiled at him. "No, Ken, I'm afraid I can't tonight. Nicky and I are invited to a party. But it was sweet of you to ask." She pulled her hand free from his grasp. "Goodbye, Ken, and good luck."

"Wait, Lori. Tomorrow is my last day here. I'll be going back to Chicago next week, and our paths may never cross again. Let's get together for a couple of hours tomorrow afternoon so I can tell you about my new job, and you can bring me up to date on yours."

Lori hesitated. She really didn't want to see him again, but if he was leaving the state, perhaps she should talk to him just out of courtesy. If they were going to remain friends, she'd have to do her part. "All right, Ken. Tomorrow afternoon I'll meet you in the lobby. But only for an hour, okay?"

"That's great, hon. Shall we say three o'clock?"

When she walked away, she didn't look back, although she could feel his eyes follow her out of the room.

True to her promise, Nicole was waiting just outside the door. "Well?"

"Well, nothing. We made our peace. We're friends again."

"Any chance you two might rekindle the torch?"

"None whatsoever. It's a good thing you're not a cat, Nicky, or your curiosity would have killed you by now."

"But you said you made up."

"I said we were friends again. I'm glad, too. I never did understand why he harbored so much bitterness after our breakup. It seemed out of character for him, but I guess I didn't know him as well as I thought. Anyway, I'm glad we're friends again, but believe me when I tell you friendship is all it will ever be."

"So you aren't going out with him?"

"Not *out*, no. Actually, I'm staying *in* with him. I'm meeting him in the lobby at three tomorrow afternoon, just for a final chat before he goes north to work."

Nicole lost interest in the conversation that must have sounded boring and unromantic to her, because she changed the subject abruptly. "Lori, how tall would you say Mike is?"

"Mike who?"

Nicole gave an exasperated sigh. "Mike, the tennis and volleyball player. Who else?"

"I have no idea how tall he is. I haven't even thought of it. How would I know, and why would I even care?"

"I think he must be six-four if he's an inch. Isn't he handsome?"

"Nicky, will you get off it? You told me you're in love with George."

"Yes, but I never said I was *blind*. Honestly, Lori, you don't think I'm going to walk around with my eyes closed just because I'm in love, do you?"

Lori laughed. Nicole would never change. "Let's walk into town and look through the shops."

"You know how to hit me where I'm most vulnerable. Let's go."

At quarter till seven, Lori and Nicole were waiting in the lobby when George and Kevin arrived.

"Are you sure it's okay for me to come to this party?" Kevin asked. "I don't think I was really invited, was I?"

"Of course you were. They told us to bring our own dates, didn't they Lori?"

Lori nodded. *Be still, my heart!* Just the sight of Kevin turned her knees into wet cardboard and caused her heart to palpitate at an alarming rate. She mustn't let it show. George probably had to drag Kevin over here, and she wasn't going to let anyone think she was over-eager about seeing him again. If he could be indifferent about their relationship, so could she.

George had brought flashlights for everyone, and he carried two poles with peculiar nets on the end. "I know they said they'd furnish the nets," he said, "but I have a couple of special ones I like to use."

They walked southward along the beach, past the strip of hotels to a remote, partially isolated area. Rounding a point that jutted out into the water, they saw the cheerful group of crab hunters.

"Heave ho, mates. Come join us in a round of merriment before the hunt begins." Mike lifted a can of cola in his hand and welcomed the four newcomers. Blankets were spread around a roaring bonfire, and tubs of ice held a variety of soft drinks. Higher on the beach, a long narrow table was covered with newspaper and clear plastic, weighted down at each corner by heavy aluminum kettles. Plastic containers held pretzels, chips, and assorted munchies.

It was that enchanting hour of twilight between the setting of the sun and the fall of the dark curtain of night. What was there about nightfall in the tropics that gave it a special mystique?

After a few brief informal introductions, Mike began handing out nets similar to the ones George brought, but unlike any Lori had ever seen before. The handles were longer than an ordinary fishing net, and inside the net itself was a crudely constructed scoop made of chicken wire.

"Why the wire lining in the net?" Lori asked Mike.

"That's because the crabs grab the net with their pinchers, and it's a real tough job to get them loose sometimes. With the wire insets, they can't get a good grip, and it's easier to release them. It cuts down on the danger of getting your fingers snapped, too."

"That makes sense. But now, tell me what *that* contraption is for." Lori pointed to a large washtub being pulled along the edge of the surf by a rope tied to each handle.

"That's where we deposit our catch. You'll see the little surf crabs start crowding into the surf now that dark is falling. Use your flashlight to spot 'em, and just scoop 'em up and put 'em into the tub."

"Sounds like fun." Lori's eyes scanned the shallow waters.

"Since this is your first time, I need to tell you one or two things. First, look at your crab and identify it. If you're lucky, you might get a blue, but most likely you'll have a speckled crab. They're tan with a mottling of small spots. They're quite a bit smaller than the blues, but they're every bit as tasty.

"Then why do I need to identify them?"

"What you need to look for is the sex. We only keep males and non-pregnant females."

"How kind of you. And you expect me to know the difference?" Lori looked up at Mike and grinned mischievously.

Mike returned the grin. "When you catch one, bring it to me, and I'll show you how to tell."

While Lori was talking, Kevin was busily scooping up his

first catch. "This doesn't look like it would satisfy a very hungry appetite," he noted.

"That's pretty small," Mike agreed. "It's probably a female." He took the net from Kevin and held it up to reveal the underside of the small crustacean. "See that little flap that looks like an apron?"

"Yep."

"In the males, it's narrower and spire shaped. The wider apron denotes a female, and if she's pregnant, you can see spongy looking yellow eggs protruding from underneath. Or sometimes the eggs turn dark and purplish as it gets nearer to spawning time." He shook the net over the wash tub and released the captive crab, returning the net to Kevin. "You were in luck that time. There weren't any eggs."

"Is it illegal to catch the ones with eggs?" Lori was very interested in the fate of the feisty little mothers-to-be.

"No, not illegal. But it's just good sportsmanship to release them, and most people follow that unwritten law. It just gives us hope we can come back and find more crabs next year."

"I'm glad I'm not a crab," Lori muttered, scooping up a crab so large it must surely be a male.

All up and down the shore, flashlights danced in the water, and nets dipped and dived in happy pursuit of the elusive little targets. Cries of "I got one," and "That big one got away," rang out on the evening air. It was a happy party and Lori was glad Nicky had persuaded her to come.

In less than an hour, the tub was so full that the more adventurous of the crabs were climbing to the top of the heap, trying to make their escape over the sides.

Someone had already suspended two of the large kettles over the fire, and the water was beginning to boil. The fellow named Herb seemed to be the designated chef, and Lori watched him add a squeeze of lemon juice and assorted spices to the steaming pots. He poured in salt with a free hand and added some leaves Lori couldn't identify. Last, he added a handful of cayenne pepper to spice up each pot. "Bring on the crabs," Herb told them. "The pots are ready."

It took two men to drag the heavy washtub over to the fire. They used the crab nets to scoop up the unwilling creatures and drop them into the bubbling brew.

After about ten minutes, the crabs were retrieved from the pot and carried to the table on foil lined trays. As they left the pot, others took their place, until the entire catch had been properly cooked.

When the crabs had cooled enough to handle, Mike showed those who were new to the sport how to remove the claws, crack them, and extract the tender delicacy cached inside.

"Mmm. Delicious!"

Next he showed them how to pry off the apron from the underside of the body and push a thumb under the shell itself. He removed the entrails and discarded them into a dishpan to be buried later. The remaining meat he split down the middle and washed in a pail of water before putting the snowy-white crab halves on the waiting serving platter.

Everyone worked on cleaning the crabs, eating the delicious claw meat as they worked and sipped their drinks. When the last crab had been cleaned, Mike brought out nut picks and showed them how to separate the white meat that was such a delicacy from the cartilage and remaining shell.

"This is the pay-off for a job well done," he told them.

Lori thought it the most delicious meat she had ever tasted, and Kevin agreed. "I wondered if it would be worth all that trouble, but now I know it is."

It took longer to cook, clean, and eat the crabs than it did to catch them. Now everyone joined in the clean-up. Someone provided a shovel to dig a garbage pit high above the tide line. Empty cans and reusable utensils were gathered into plastic bags. When the last traces of supper had been cleared away, the group gathered around the fire and sang songs.

Lori sat on one of the blankets with Kevin close beside her. Listening to his clear, deep voice, she wondered how she could ever make herself forget him. She was sure she never would. She had to quit seeing him. At least that would keep her from making a complete fool of herself.

The party began to break up much too soon for Lori, and guests were complimenting Mike and thanking him for a wonderful evening.

"Are you staying at *La Hacienda*?" Nicole asked him.

"No, I live here in Marathon. Three of my old service buddies are down here on a holiday, and they're staying there. That's why you see me hanging around the hotel so much."

George shook his hand and thanked him. "I live here on the island, too. We should get together some time. Come over to the scuba school by the bridge, and we'll go diving together."

"Great! I'll take you up on that, George."

"Goodnight."

"Thanks."

"Great party."

The sounds carried far down the beach as the happy, well-fed guests parted. Lori and Kevin started toward the hotel. Nicky and George lagged behind, deep in their own private conversation.

"Lori, tomorrow afternoon I plan to explore Crane Point Hammock. They're doing some archaeological digs there that reveal relics of this key that are seven centuries old. I was reading about it in my guidebook and I want to see what it's all about. Would you like to go with me?"

It sounded so interesting. Lori almost agreed to go before she remembered her promise to meet Ken. "I can't Kevin. An old friend turned up here today, and I've promised to meet him tomorrow afternoon. But maybe another time," she suggested hopefully. So much for her resolve to stop seeing him.

"Sure. Okay." He left her at the steps of the hotel with nothing but a handshake. The edge in his voice was as sharp as a knife. "Thanks for a lovely evening, Lorelei."

She was unprepared for his icy response, and it stunned her. "Thanks to you, too, Kevin," she mumbled. She turned from him and hurried inside before he could see the tears welling up and burning her eyes.

Kevin headed to the parking lot where he'd left his little red bullet. Anger welled up in him like a tidal wave. He could recognize a brush-off when he heard one. It was the same thing every time he invited Lori to go anywhere. Without Nicole there to insist, she refused to accept an invitation from him. He might as well realize it and accept it. He wouldn't make the mistake of asking her again. It must be embarrassing for her to have to keep dredging up excuses.

Pulling out of the parking lot, Kevin saw George going toward the beach. "Give you a lift, George?"

"Thanks." George swung his long legs into the passenger side of the sports car. "That was a great party," he stated enthusiastically.

"Yes," Kevin agreed. "It was fun and educational as well. I learned a lot more about crabs than just how good they taste."

"I guess any place with Nicky would be fun for me. I'm seriously attracted to that girl. But that little friend of hers is strange."

"You mean Lori? How so?"

"Well, Nicky says she has some kind of phobia about somebody out to kill her."

"Who does she think would want to do that?" Kevin was careful to make his interest appear casual.

George told him in detail each of the incidents Nicky had related to him about Lori's accidents, even down to the strange phone call the night before. "What do you make of all that, Kevin? Is Lori just paranoid, or do you think she could really be in some kind of danger?"

"I don't know, George, but I'm glad you told me about it. It helps explain some of her recent behavior."

"This is my corner here, Kevin. Just drop me at the curb. And thanks for the lift, buddy."

"See you, George."

So that was the way the wind blew! That sure explained a lot of things. No wonder Lori seemed so unstable and suspicious of everyone. She was as fragile and vulnerable as a piece of fine crystal, and just as lovely. George had asked if he believed her to be in real danger. Well, he didn't know yet, but he certainly had the resources to find out, and a few well-placed phone calls tonight would at least be a start toward getting some answers.

So he *was* going to have a busman's holiday after all. And so he *was* old-fashioned and unrealistic, just as Jennifer had said. The way he was beginning to see it, there were a few things in life worth taking a risk for, and unless he was badly mistaken, Lorelei Cramer might very well be one of them.

CHAPTER NINE

Lori was surprised to find the lobby of *La Hacienda* nearly deserted. Everyone, it seemed, was outside enjoying the bright, beautiful day. This was the kind of weather the Chamber of Commerce described in promotional brochures. Not a dark cloud in the sky, just a cool ocean breeze floating across the warm sands, carrying the essence of early summer.

Lori's canvas shoes made soft taps against the tile floor as she crossed the lobby to where Ken stood waiting with arms outstretched.

"Isn't this great, hon? Just like old times."

She drew back as he gave her a chaste kiss on the cheek. "Don't worry, Lori. Today I'm just an old friend you used to know, remember?"

She remembered, and hoped he would too. She had promised him an hour. Now she wondered what neutral ground they could find for sixty minutes of conversation.

"I thought the lobby here was kind of cold and, well, you know, so public."

Recognizing that Ken was leading up to something, Lori

tensed as he continued. "So I rented a little boat so we could go for a spin on the gulf. It's too nice a day to waste inside. The water's calm, and hey, this is what we all come to the Keys for, right?"

Boating sounded better than talking, but Lori still felt reluctant. "I didn't know you knew how to handle a boat, Ken. I don't remember that being one of your hobbies."

"You're right. I'm sure no expert, but actually, there's not much to it. The man at the marina gave me a few quick instructions and said I should be okay as long as I didn't try to go out too far."

Outside, Ken hailed a taxi and directed the driver across the island to the gulfside dock where he had anchored a small skiff.

"We could have walked," she told him. "It's not very far from ocean to gulf."

"I didn't want to waste any of our short time together." He helped her into the boat and showed her where he had stocked a cooler with sandwiches and drinks.

She softened when she realized how hard he was trying to make this outing enjoyable for her. Suddenly she was glad she had come, glad she and Ken were going to be friends again. Glad, too, for an opportunity to keep Kevin Collins out of sight and out of mind for an hour at least.

The blue waters of the Gulf of Mexico were calm and smooth, unlike the rolling surf on the Atlantic side. This was a typical Saturday, with weekend boaters as thick as ants at a picnic. Lori sat in the bow of the boat, and Ken started the engine.

She raised her head and let the wind lift her long, loose hair from her neck. This was altogether different from riding on the *Mattie B*. Wasn't Ken going a little too fast for an amateur skipper? She tried to ask him, but her words were lost in the wind. They were heading out pretty far, she thought, but she could still see the shoreline and the outline of the marina next to the boat docks.

Motioning with her hand, she signaled for Ken to turn around.

His expression was that of a small boy with a new toy, but he responded to her request and arced the boat in a giant curve. The wake circled around them like a wreath.

Ken killed the engine and let the boat drift. "Refreshment time," he announced, opening the Styrofoam icebox and drawing out its contents.

The salt air had its usual effect on Lori's appetite, and she happily accepted a ham and cheese on rye and a cold can of root beer. "Don't you think we'd better drop anchor so we don't drift out too far?"

"No, I'll start the engine in just a minute. There won't be time for us to drift very far." Ken bypassed the sandwiches and sipped a can of cold beer. He gave Lori a sly sidewise glance as though expecting her to comment, but she said nothing. He already knew how she felt about drinking, especially since he was at the controls of the boat. But Lori had long ago expressed herself on the subject. She had nothing further to add. She was only glad she had set a time limit on this excursion. Soon she would be back on familiar ground, and she could put this day behind her.

A sleek blue and silver motor boat roared by, causing their little skiff to rock precariously in its wake. For an instant, Lori thought the skipper looked like Kevin. Lately every blond man she encountered reminded her in some way of Kevin. She must stop thinking of him so much. Deliberately, she focused her attention on Ken.

"So tell me about your new job."

"I'm still in construction work. Our company just received a contract for a big new shopping mall just outside Chicago. The recession's been tough on the construction business, so this is big news for all the guys in my company."

"I'm glad things are going well for you, Ken." She was sincere. She did wish him well. She hoped his business flourished, and she especially hoped he would find a new love interest who could give him love in return.

"And tell me about yours. I heard you're the star performer now."

"It's fun, and it's hard work, and I love it. That's about all there is to tell."

"Ever think about life beyond mermaids?"

She laughed. "I told a friend recently that mermaids never drown. I guess I'll always be one at heart. But of course, I'll have to join the real world someday. I have plenty of time to worry about that, though. Right now I'm just concentrating on perfecting my routine and giving the tourists their money's worth."

"I'm sure you do that, hon."

"Seriously, people pay a lot of money just to watch us perform in that big glass tank. I do take the responsibility quite seriously."

"I wish I could get you to take *me* seriously."

"Now Ken, you promised. Isn't it time we started back?"

"I hate to admit it, but you're right, Lori. Now, if I can just get this baby started again."

Ken gave two tugs on the starter rope, and the engine groaned and died. "Don't worry. It takes several tries sometimes." He tried again without success.

"Maybe I can help." Lori stepped gingerly over the center seat and stood directly over the motor. Ken gave one mighty tug, and the boat lurched forward as the engine roared into action. Lori, standing in the stern, catapulted over the motor and into the swirling ocean path churned out by the concentrically rotating blades of the engine.

After the initial shock of hitting the water, Lori was calm as she broke the choppy surface and waved toward Ken to let him know she okay. No novice to deep water, she treaded to keep herself afloat as she watched him turn the small craft around and come back to rescue her.

"Over here," she called, knowing he couldn't hear her over the noise of the engine, but he could see her waving hand and sped right toward her. *Right* toward her. If he didn't kill the engine now, those steel blades would pass directly over her! Without waiting to be sure, she tucked and dove, straight down, her body piercing the deep water like an arrow.

When she surfaced, she could see that he was turning the boat around and circling back from the other direction. Poor Ken. It must have scared him as much as it did her. He was new at boating and didn't know quite how to maneuver it. If he would just cut the motor, she could swim to him and climb into the boat. He was headed her way again, and it almost seemed like his speed had increased. Again, she was directly in his path. What was he trying to do? An all too familiar panic seized her as she plunged down again, her heart racing wildly. Looking up, she could see the big steel blades passing over her head. How long was it going to take him to get control of the boat? Or was he even trying? Was it possible this was yet another deliberate, evil attempt to harm her? But surely not *Ken*—and yet ... She struggled to shed her waterlogged shoes and lighten the burden of staying afloat. She was thankful now for those long hours of workouts Mr. Porter had insisted upon. Her healthy endurance and her swimming expertise were welcome assets at this moment. Indeed, they were lifesaving assets!

As her head broke the surface once more, she saw a second boat speeding toward her. What was happening here? Was she going to have to dodge two boats now instead of one? This was like her worst nightmare! But just as she prepared to dive again, miraculously, both boats cut their motors and drifted toward her at a lazy pace. Now both were within easy swimming distance for her. She paused just long enough to catch her breath and then swam toward Ken's boat.

"Having some kind of trouble out here?" There was no mistaking that voice! It couldn't be coincidental again. How did he manage to be *everywhere* she went? "Kevin." She called his name even as Ken was reaching over the side and pulling her into his own boat, frantically crushing her body against his own.

"Oh, Lori, you could've drowned or worse." A contrite Ken was almost crying as he held her out from him and looked up and down her dripping body, assuring himself she was still in one piece. "I kept trying to get the boat up close to you and stop, so I could pull you in, and every time I got near, you disappeared from view. I really panicked, Lori, and when I tried to slow the boat, I pushed the speed control in the wrong direction, and it went even faster. If anything had happened to you, baby, I'd never have forgiven myself." He sank down on the seat and put his head in his hands.

"I'm okay, Ken." Seeing the pain in his face, she was ashamed to have doubted him only moments before. She didn't approve of a lot of the things Ken did, but she was quite sure he was incapable of murder.

Forcing herself to sound more calm than she actually felt, she turned to face Kevin, who stood in a sleek blue and silver motor boat, not more than six feet from the side of theirs. So it *had* been Kevin who passed them earlier. Now, that had to be more than coincidental. What was he up to?

"Kevin, what on earth brings you out here?"

"We've got to stop meeting this way," he quipped.

The sun shining on his cottony hair gave a halo effect to his bronze body as he stood with arms folded, his stance casual, and smiled at her. "Just out for a little relaxing afternoon ride, when I thought I detected some trouble. Can I be of help?"

"No." Ken answered before Lori could speak. "Thanks just the same. We're on our way in now."

"Okay. I'll just hang around to make sure you get started okay. Seems like that boat is a little temperamental today, doesn't it?"

Ken's glare was less than friendly, but Lori shot Kevin a gratefulglance. Coincidence or not, what might have happened if he hadn't shown up when he did?

The motor started with the first pull of the cord, and Ken steered the boat toward shore at a subdued speed. Lori, seated again in the bow, shivered as the wind blew against her wet clothes and body. She could hardly wait to get into a warm shower. How grand it would feel to be dry and warm again. She realized she had just survived another life-threatening experience, but she wasn't going to dwell on it. Poor Ken felt bad enough about it already. Was the trembling within her due entirely to the chill, or was it partly her nerves? She crossed her arms across her chest and tried to quell the shaking.

"As soon as I tie up this boat, I'll get us a taxi and get you right back over to your hotel," Ken promised.

"Don't bother to hail a taxi." Kevin was tying up at the slip just across from theirs. *Was he everywhere?* Lori still melted every time she heard his voice. "I have a car here, and I'll be only too happy to drop you off. *The Hacienda*, isn't it?" He grinned wickedly.

"Do you know this guy?" Ken asked Lori.

"We've met."

There was little way Ken could refuse Kevin's offer. While Ken went to the office to settle his account with the dock master, Lori hurried into the car to escape the cold wind whipping against her wet body. Kevin eased into the driver's seat beside her, and the warmth of his body beside hers felt as welcome and comforting as one of her grandmother's quilts. She looked to make sure Ken was still in the office before she poured her frosty words on Kevin.

"It's more than coincidence that you turn up everywhere I go. Why are you following me?"

"Ah, once again I come to the rescue, but sense a lack of gratitude on your part. Weren't you glad I came along?" His question seemed all the more irritating because he continued to grin as he spoke.

"I'm sure Ken, left on his own, would soon have had things under control. Your boat coming so close was probably the distraction that threw him off course. And don't change the subject, please. Are you watching me out of your own interest, or has someone asked you to follow me?"

"I wasn't aware there were private property lines in the gulf. Was I out of bounds?" He continued to look at her with that maddening grin. "Here comes your friend," he told her.

Ken opened the door and squeezed into the front seat of Kevin's small car. It hadn't seemed crowded when they drove it to Key West, but Ken's large frame pushed her tightly against the driver.

"Cute little car," Ken muttered. He didn't offer to ride in the back.

"I got it from the local rental agency," Kevin explained. "Just thought it would be nice to have something to knock around in while I'm down here."

"And the boat?" Lori queried. "Is that something you rented to knock around in too?"

"Yep. Just rented it for the day. Couldn't pass up a beautiful day like this, now could I?"

He stopped in front of the hotel and waited while Ken held the door open for Lori. "If I can give you a lift elsewhere, I'd be most happy to oblige." His smile added credence to his words, but Lori was not so easily taken in by them.

"Thanks for the ride, Kevin." Lori's teeth were chattering, and water puddled around her bare feet. "I'm need to run in and get dry now, Ken, so if you need a ride back to your hotel, why don't you let Kevin drive you?"

"Thanks anyway. It's not far. I can walk." He closed the car door. "Listen, Lori, I'm awfully sorry about the accident. Why don't you go up and get dressed, and I'll take you out to some nice place for dinner."

"Not tonight, Ken. Thanks anyway. Remember, I told you we'd only have an hour. It's been at least two already. I really do have to run now, because I'm freezing."

She turned on her bare heels and ran toward the hotel at the precise moment the little red car squealed away from the curb, leaving a forlorn Ken standing on the sidewalk alone.

CHAPTER TEN

Lori stood beneath the shower and tilted her head, allowing steamy water to slide through her long, thick hair. As the warm, wet bubbles washed over her chilled body, her tension gradually melted away and disappeared like the suds in the drain. What a surprising afternoon this had turned out to be.

She ran the events back through her mind. First there was the outing with Ken and the traumatic events that occurred. *Another life-threatening accident!* But seeing Ken's distraught face afterwards, she could not believe the mishap had been anything other than that— an accident, pure and simple.

Then the coincidence of Kevin's showing up. She didn't believe for one minute that his arrival was merely by chance. This was happening too often for happenstance. Maybe it was fate. Or maybe it was planned. She intended to get some answers next time she saw him.

Nicole had thoughtfully left a note on the table by the phone: *Gone to play tennis with Mike. Back by six.* That girl! Honestly!

Toweling her damp hair, Lori walked out on the balcony and watched the people below. The beach was more crowded than it had been all week. There were so many sailboats it looked like a regatta. The cabanas were full, and the sand was crawling with children. The surfers were missing, probably because the waters were so calm today, but there was plenty of other activity.

She heard Nicole's key in the lock and called to her. "I'm out here on the balcony, Nicky. How was your game?"

"Divine. Mike was gentlemanly and let me win a couple of games. He's really a great player. In fact, he's a great guy."

"And where does George fit into all this?" Lori tried to conceal her amusement.

"George is Numero Uno. I already told you I'm in love with George. Mike is just a good friend."

"Well, where was Numero Uno today?"

"He had a private scuba lesson at three. We're going out for dinner tonight, though." She gave Lori an apologetic look. "I'm sorry I keep leaving you on your own. Did you have a terribly dull afternoon?"

Lori laughed. "Believe me, Nicky, the afternoon was anything but dull."

"Tell me about it." Nicole's interest shot up along with her eyebrows.

Lori caste a wistful gaze over the water. Her thoughts were deep but still not clearly defined, and there was nothing she felt ready to share just yet, even if Nicky was her best friend. "Oh, we went boating and had sort of a little picnic on the water."

That was enough to reveal for now. Better get the conversation headed in a different direction before Nicky began picking her brain the way she was prone to do. "And don't give a second thought to leaving me to my own devices. I'm still hoping to finish that book while I'm here. I'm getting into the good parts now."

Nicole looked unconvinced, so Lori added, "Anyway, next week your Numero Uno has to get back to work, and I'll have you all to myself. No telling what we'll find to do in our final days in the tropics."

Nicole looked uncomfortable. "Yes. Well, there is one thing I've been meaning to tell you, Lori." She turned away so Lori couldn't see her face.

Lori had heard that tone before and knew something was up. "What is it, Nicky? Out with it."

"Well, you know how George told us school would be out next week?"

"Yes, go on." She could tell Nicole was struggling to say what was on her mind.

"Lori, they get so busy at that scuba school, you would not believe it. They just don't have enough instructors to go around."

Lori thought she was beginning to catch the drift.

"Well, I thought since poor George has been so nice to us all week, and since he is going to have such a stressful week coming up, well..."

"So you thought you would go over and help poor old George relieve some of his stress next week?"

"Yes, well, that's sort of what it is. George said I could take one of the beginner classes, and since I'd be on the staff, I'd earn some extra money. If you come up with something fun for us to do before we go home, then it'll be my treat with the money I earn."

"Nicky, you don't have to offer me incentives, and you don't have to apologize either. I don't have to be entertained, you know. There's plenty to do around here." Then an amusing thought occurred to her, and Lori couldn't resist. "I seem to remember some resolution you made earlier this week about a certain mermaid staying dry for two weeks. Won't this be a terrible drag, having to work in the water on your vacation?" Lori was glad Nicky had turned her back to her. She couldn't keep from laughing.

"Oh, yes—well this is different." Nicole stammered and grasped for words that would make it all seem reasonable. "After all the nice things George has done for us, I'm just glad I can be of help. Well, I'd better shower and get out of this sweaty tennis dress. It was so hot on the court, my clothes are soaked." She made a hasty escape toward the shower.

The telephone jingled on the bedside table. "If that's George, tell him to give me fifteen minutes in the shower and call me later."

"Hello." Lori pressed the receiver to her ear, and the deep resonance of Kevin's voice fell like the melody of a favorite song. "You had quite an afternoon, didn't you, little mermaid?"

"Yes, I must admit it was, um, pretty exciting."

"Are you okay, then?"

"Yes. Now that I've had a warm shower and put on dry clothes, my teeth have quit chattering, and I feel like a human being once again. I did lose a perfectly good pair of tennis shoes, though. They're somewhere in the bottom of the Gulf of Mexico, where I decided on impulse to shed them and go barefoot."

"Maybe they'll wash in on the tide. Why don't we walk on the beach tonight and see if we can find them?"

Now came the moment of truth. Was she going to remain firm in her resolve not to see him alone again? Her brain was telling her to decline, but her heart refused to listen. If she accepted now, she knew the whole battle was lost.

"Lorelei? Are you still there?"

"Yes, Kevin. I'm here. What was that you were saying?" She was stalling, trying to gain the courage of her convictions.

"I just suggested a moonlight walk on the beach. We could go some place and eat first, if you'd like. I still have the little red bullet."

Lori wasn't the only one breaking a resolution. Kevin, too, had promised himself he would not give her another chance to turn him down, but that was before his informative talk with George, and the conversation with his Jacksonville office this morning.

On top of that, she had scared him out of his wits on the water this afternoon. It was bad enough watching her being charmed by that big-city guy from Chicago, or wherever it was he came from. But when it became a dangerous flirt with death, he'd been forced to come out from his cover and make a fool of himself. Now he felt he had to see her at least one more time, if only to explain.

"Kevin? Did you hear me? I think we have a faulty connection. I said dinner would be nice, and we'll talk about the walk on the beach over dinner."

His heart skipped a beat. He tried to keep a steady voice. "I'll ring your room from the lobby. Is seven o'clock okay?"

"Seven is fine. I'll see you then."

Nicole emerged fresh from her bath. "Was that George on the phone?"

"No, that wasn't George on the phone. It was for me."

"Oh." Nicole didn't disguise her disappointment very well. "Was it Ken again?"

"No, it wasn't Ken. There you go again, Miss Kitty Cat. What if I told you it was Mike?"

"Mike?"

Lori's laughter brought tears to her eyes. "I didn't say it *was* Mike. I only asked 'what if.' Actually, it was Kevin."

"Oh, good. Well, of course I wouldn't care if Mike called you. I was just surprised, because you haven't seemed very interested in Mike, that's all." It was several minutes before she thought to ask, "What did Kevin want?"

"We're going out for dinner tonight." Lori was careful not to mention anything about a moonlight walk on the beach. Nicky had far too much curiosity for her own good already.

Lori was glad Nicole planned to leave early. She wanted some time alone to sort through her thoughts. She sat by the window looking out, while Nicky put the finishing touches on her make-up.

"I told George I'd be sitting in the lobby when he came, Lori, so I'm going on down. Have a nice time tonight, and don't do anything I wouldn't do."

"I'm not likely to, unless it's to say no."

Nicole chuckled as she picked up her purse and gave her hair a final pat. "See you later tonight. We can compare notes."

As soon as the door closed behind Nicole, Lori went to the closet to select something to wear. She pulled out the new dress she had bought especially for this trip, just in case some special occasion arose. Of course this wasn't a special occasion, but she might as well get some use out of the dress. After all, she *had* bought it for her vacation.

The soft cotton sundress was emerald green, with wide straps that crossed low in the back. The fitted bodice ended in a circular swirl at the hemline. Lori twirled in front of the mirror and was satisfied she had chosen the right dress for tonight.

She applied her make-up with a careful hand and brushed her hair until it shone. She dabbed a spot of perfume behind each ear, and she was almost ready. She stood back and looked into the mirror with a critical eye. "Passable," she decided, slipping her bare feet into white high-heeled sandals. Admittedly they were not designed for beach walking, but they were more flattering to her long, tan legs than her flats, and she wanted to look her best tonight.

She was standing beside one of the marble pillars when Kevin entered the lobby, and he hurried across the room to meet her. "The hotel should keep you standing there just for room decoration," he said. His eyes traveled up and down in unqualified approval. "You're wearing my favorite color."

"Green? That's your favorite color?"

"Yes, as of this week, that particular shade of green is definitely my favorite color." He looked deep into her eyes, and she could not mistake his meaning.

"Where are you taking me?"

"To the Green Room, of course." He looked about as pleased as a small boy landing his first fish.

"Kevin, you're kidding me."

"No, I'm not. Really. The Green Room is on the top floor of the *Islander Hotel*, right down the beach from here. I've heard the food and the music are both good, and you can't beat the name of the place."

She placed her hand in the crook of his arm. He led her outside into the cool evening air. The now familiar red car was waiting in the parking lot, and he unlocked the passenger door and opened it for her.

It was a short drive to the hotel. They could have walked. Kevin pulled up to the front entrance of the *Islander Hotel* and gave his keys to the parking valet.

The two of them made a striking couple and heads turned as they walked across the lobby toward the elevators.

The elevator was crowded and stopped at nearly every floor. Finally it ground to a stop at the top, and the metal doors slid open.

Just as Kevin had promised, the dining room was called The Green Room, and true to its name, the décor was almost entirely in various shades of green.

"Follow me please, Mr. Collins." The hostess led them to the table Kevin had reserved earlier. "Your waiter will be with you in a moment."

Lori's usually healthy appetite seemed to disappear as she looked at Kevin seated across from her. In fact, her stomach was suddenly filled with a bevy of butterflies. She hadn't meant to fall in love. She had fought it from the moment she first laid eyes on him. But looking at him now, she realized she'd been fighting a losing battle from the start.

"You order for me, Kevin. You always seem to know what's good."

His eyes didn't leave her face. "You're right, Lori. I do know what's good." He winked at her and turned his attention to the menu.

Thinking back on this night much later, Lori could never remember what she ate. She only remembered floating around the dance floor in his arms, wishing the music would never stop and that the night could last forever. In some ways she envied Nicole, who could fall in and out of love at the drop of a hat. But Lori had always known that when love hit her, it would not be a fleeting thing; it would be forever. And it had never occurred to her that she might fall in love with someone who did not love her in return.

They sat sipping their after-dinner espresso when Kevin reminded her of their plan to walk on the beach. "We don't have many days left, Lori, and there are some things we need to say to each other before we part."

Lori wanted to hear every word this man had to say, but she didn't trust herself to speak, lest she reveal the undeniable truth hidden deep within her heart. She'd have to be very careful for the next few days if she expected to go home with her pride intact.

On the way outside, as they passed the reception desk, Lori picked up a book of matches whose glimmering green and gold letters advertised *The Green Room.*

Kevin gave her a questioning glance. "You don't smoke, do you? Are you a souvenir collector?"

"Not really. That is, I never have been. I'll use these to light my candles when my birthday comes around." Actually, she just wanted a tangible reminder of this night. As if she could ever forget.

When the parking valet delivered their car under the portico, Kevin claimed the wheel and drove down the beach past the cove where they had caught and ate crabs. Could that have been only one night before? So much seemed to be happening, so fast.

Kevin pulled off the road next to a small picnic area with a sheltered table and concrete benches. "Slip off those heels and leave them here," he suggested. "You might ruin them in the sand."

"Only if you will, too."

"What? Slip off my heels?" His grin reminded her of a mischievous schoolboy.

Barefoot, they stood hand in hand under the shelter of the trees and looked toward the sea. She was awed by the loveliness of the balmy summer night. Graceful gray moss floated from the branches of tall pine trees, casting ethereal shadows across the silver sand. The soft fragrance of the delicate frangipani floated on the evening air.

Suddenly and without warning, she was in his arms and his tender kiss touched her lips. The soft sweetness of his kiss was like a gentle summer breeze that changed swiftly into a full-blown hurricane. "Lorelei." When he spoke her name it was like a song, and Lori was lost in its melody. But something deep within her was flashing a warning signal. With great effort, she put her hands on his shoulders and pushed him away.

"Don't, Kevin. Don't spoil the magic of this night."

"Lori, what are you afraid of? Don't you feel you can trust me? I promise I'd never intentionally hurt you."

"Kevin, there's something you have to understand. I'm not like Nicole. I need roots to a relationship before I make any commitments. I've never given myself completely to any man, and when I do, it will be for keeps. I'm a devout Christian, Kevin, and you might as well know from the beginning that my faith and the code I live by are very important to me."

Lori tried to read the incredulous look on his face. His arms were still around her, but he stared at her as though she had come from outer space. He didn't speak for several minutes, but when he did, his voice was husky when he asked, "What is it you think I want from you, Lori? Just a one-night stand? What kind of guy do you take me for?"

She didn't know how to answer him. Indeed, she had asked herself that same question and had come up without an answer.

"Lori, I don't know where our relationship is headed— it's too early to tell— but I do know that you've suddenly become very important to me. I don't seem to be able to think of anything else. You're like no other girl in the world. I guess I've been hoping perhaps you shared some of those same feelings."

"I— I haven't been very good at analyzing my own feelings lately. At the moment, those feelings are complicated by occurrences in my personal life that I'd rather not go into right now. Things I want to forget at least for the two weeks of my vacation."

With all her heart she wanted to trust this man, but if he really cared for her as he said, then why was he so elusive about his own personal life? What was he trying to conceal?

"Kevin, we hardly know each other. Do you realize you've never even told me what you do for a living?"

"I know I've been evasive about that, but there's been good reason. I need to ask you to trust me, and I promise to tell you everything you want to know very soon. Are you willing to go along with me on that?"

"Kevin, are you into something illegal?"

"No, of course not. Nothing like that. It's, well, I just have my reasons, that's all."

Lori drew away from him. There was something very wrong here. Kevin wanted her to blindly trust him, but how about a mutual trust? How could she think of sharing a relationship with a man who refused to confide in her over the simplest of matters? What kind of secret was he hiding, and why? "Let's go back to the hotel, Kevin."

"You're angry with me, aren't you?"

"No, not angry. Just confused. I need some time to think. It's easy to get carried away in the moonlight. We need to put this on hold until the daylight hours."

Kevin didn't try to hide his hurt and disappointment. He had believed it a miracle that an old fashioned, unrealistic guy like himself had finally met a girl who shared his values— a Christian girl who was honest and sincere and believed in keeping the promises she made. He had begun to realize just how much this woman really meant to him, and he had harbored a faint hope her feelings for him were growing, too. But that hope was dimmed for now. He just couldn't tell her about the investigation yet. When he could supply more of the answers she wanted, maybe then she'd be willing to trust him, and that would be the time to speak of love. He could be patient, and if he could just keep her safe from harm, there might still be some hope for their future together.

They were silent on the drive back to the hotel. Lori sat close to the window. She wanted to believe Kevin cared for her. When he decided to open up to her, maybe then they could begin to build a meaningful relationship, but until he was ready to trust her, she was going to tread very carefully.

On the steps, he kissed her again, but it was a gentle, undemanding kiss, and she returned it in kind. "Sleep well, darling Lori."

Lori felt like she was walking in a maze. Just when she thought she could see the light at the end of the tunnel, another obstacle popped into her path. She had longed to hear him say he cared for her. Now that he had, why was she dragging her feet?

In the quiet solitude of her room, she read a few passages from her Bible. That always helped calm her nerves and put her perspectives in order. She dressed for bed and darkened the room so she could pretend to be asleep when Nicole came in. She didn't feel like answering Nicky's questions tonight. She had to find some answers to her own questions first.

CHAPTER ELEVEN

"Wake up, Nicky." Lori stood over Nicole's bed and gave her back a gentle push. "The sun is out, and it's going to be another beautiful day."

"Go away," Nicole muttered. She pulled her sheet over her head and sank her face into the pillow.

"Okay, if you want to waste the day sleeping, go right ahead, but we don't have many more days left."

Lori moved to the closet to select a pair of shoes, and Nicky pushed back her sheet to satisfy her awakening curiosity. "What are you doing? My goodness, you're already dressed. Where are you going?"

"Don't you remember? Today is Sunday. You know where I'm going. I was hoping I could get you to come with me."

"You're going to church today? But we're on vacation."

"Yes. It's great, isn't it? Throw on a dress and come with me."

"Maybe one of these days I'll go along, but not while we're on vacation."

"Nicky, when we're at home you say you can't go because

you're so busy, and now you say it's because we're on vacation. If you don't want to go, you don't need to invent an excuse for me, but I really wish you'd give it a try. I think you might be pleasantly surprised at what you find."

"I've already been baptized, and you know I'm a Christian, Lori, just like you are. I just don't go around making a big production out of it."

"Going to Sunday services isn't making a big production of anything. It's more like getting your priorities in line. But I'm not going to argue the point, Nicky. We've been through all this many times before. I just know how much my faith means to me, and I wish I could share it with my best friend. Don't be annoyed with me for that."

"I'm not. Of course I'm not. And I know you're right, Lori. I'm going to give it some serious thought, honestly I am. But today I promised to help George get things set up for the new scuba classes that begin tomorrow. Are you taking a taxi to church?"

"No, the man at the front desk told me where there's a small church just a few blocks south of here on Sea Grape Drive. I'll just walk."

"What about breakfast? Want to have something sent up?"

"No, you just turn over and go back to sleep. I'll get some toast and coffee in the dining room before I leave."

Lori enjoyed the short walk through the quiet neighborhood surrounding the church. Couples and families with young children paraded down the sidewalk toward the small wooden building with its tall steeple towering above the trees. Bells chimed strains of *He Leadeth Me,* and Lori felt a familiar warmth fill her heart as she climbed the stone steps. Here in this sacred place, although she was not likely to know a single soul, she would not feel strange or alone.

She accepted a program from an usher and found a seat near the back. While the organ played hymns, she lifted a pew Bible from its rack and began to read and meditate. Here was one place where she could lay all her cares aside and feel surrounded by complete peace. *He leadeth me beside the still waters.* She read the familiar words and felt her heart warm to them.

When she stood to sing the first hymn, her eyes scanned the congregation and stopped suddenly to focus on a man in the third row. It looked just like— but no, it couldn't be! From the back, it certainly looked like Kevin's blond head, but what would he be doing here?

Then she realized the absurdity of her thoughts. What, indeed? He would be here for the same purpose as she. Hadn't he told her he was a Christian? Where else would she expect him to be on Sunday morning? She was ashamed to realize she had doubted his sincerity. She smiled and raised her voice with the others as she sang the familiar verses of *My Faith Looks Up To Thee.*

The young minister gave an inspiring sermon on the second commandment to love thy neighbor as thyself. "Who is thy neighbor?" The age-old question resounded through the sanctuary.

At the close of his message, the pastor stepped from his pulpit and walked toward the chancel rail. "Before I pronounce the benediction this morning, I have an announcement to make. We have just contemplated the question, 'Who is my neighbor?' Folks, today one of our neighbors is in need of help."

A hush fell over the congregation, and even the smallest children focused their attention on the minister's words. "Yesterday I had a visit from a young woman who came to the Keys by bus all the way from Michigan to check on her father. Her family hadn't heard from him in some time, and she feared something terrible might have happened to him. As it turns out, she was correct, because Hector Fonseca fell from a ladder while he was painting his house. Too proud to ask for help, he has been confined to a bed in his small home for the past two weeks. His daughter found him in need of food and attention.

"My wife and I helped this lady with her immediate needs, and tomorrow we will go with her to see what kind of social services she and her father might be eligible to receive to help them over this hump. But sometimes the wheels turn slowly, and this man needs help now. If you feel you can contribute any kind of help, please see me after the service, and we'll try to get something organized. I'll come back into the sanctuary here after I shake hands with the departing members of the congregation, and we'll see what kind of assistance we can put together."

He raised his arms and delivered the benediction before walking down the aisle to the narthex. The organ played as the people filed out to shake his hand.

Lori lingered in the sanctuary. She had little to offer the man who needed help, but she would stay around to see if there was something she could do. How alone and helpless the poor man must feel.

She saw Kevin pushing his way toward her through the throng of people. He seemed as amazed to see her, as she had been when she first spotted him. "Lori! What a pleasant surprise."

As the crowd began to dwindle, Lori and Kevin, along with the remainder of the congregation, drifted toward the front pews and waited for the minister to return.

"I thought I might offer my help," Kevin told her. "I can't do much about his meals or his medical care, but I wondered how far along he was with his house painting before he fell. I have a little experience along those lines."

"I never even thought of that," Lori admitted. "Hey, I'm pretty good with a paint brush myself."

When the minister addressed the handful of people who gathered to offer help, he listened to all their suggestions and ideas, and it became evident that Hector Fonseca would not be without help for long. Some of the women volunteered to set up a schedule to deliver daily meals. A landscaper offered to mow the grass and check on the grounds. Several people offered to drive the daughter to the various places she would need to go for help, and Kevin and Lori's offer to paint was met with warm enthusiasm.

"I must say I'm pleased but not surprised at your response," the Reverend told his crew of helpers. "It's clear to me that you all understand the meaning of the word neighbor." He gave each of them a copy of a map to the Fonseca property and thanked them for their offers of help.

Kevin followed Lori outside the church. "How did you get here? In a taxi?"

"No, I walked. It's only a few blocks back to my hotel."

"I have the red bullet. Come on. Let's drive by the Fonseca house and see what we're letting ourselves in for."

Kevin opened the door for her before circling the car to climb into the driver's seat. Following the map given him by the pastor, he drove through a modest residential area to the outskirts of Marathon and turned off on a dirt drive that seemed to lead into an isolated swamp. Kevin followed the road through cypress and pine trees, past all signs of civilization. At last they reached a clearing, and here the road came to an abrupt end. On their right, a split-rail fence surrounded a small rustic cabin with a tin roof. The yard was overgrown with weeds.

"This must be Hector's place, Kevin decided.

"Yes, and look. He's only painted a few feet of the siding near the roofline. He must have fallen almost as soon as he began his job. I don't see any cars. How do you suppose his daughter got out here?"

"I have no idea. Want to knock on the door and find out?"

Lori hesitated. These were people she had never even met. How would they react to two strangers knocking on their door? "Do you really think we should?"

But Kevin had already bounded out of the car and was coming

around to help her. "We're their neighbors, remember?" He smiled and gripped her arm. "Come on. Let's get acquainted."

They walked up the steps onto a small porch whose rotting wooden planks were worn through in several places. "Be careful where you step," he cautioned her, keeping a firm hold on her arm. "This porch looks like it could sure use some repair."

The door opened even before Kevin had time to knock. An olive-skinned young woman peered through the patched screen door. "Yes? Can I help you? Are you lost?"

"No, I don't think so. Is this Hector Fonseca's house?"

"Yes." Her voice was edged with suspicion. "What do you want."

"My name is Kevin Collins, and this is my friend, Lori Cramer. We've come to see if we can be of some help."

"Who sent you?" She made no move to unlatch the screen door.

"We've just come from church. Our minister said he talked with you yesterday, and he's organizing a drive to get you some help."

She pushed the door open. "You must excuse me. I am Rosa Fonseca. Please come in, but I hope you'll overlook the mess."

Lori hung back. "We aren't going to come in today, Rosa, but we'll be back tomorrow. Does your father still have the paint he was using on the outside of his house?"

"Yes. Oh, yes!" Her petite features lost their wariness and took on a glowing countenance. "You are so kind to help. I don't know people here in Florida, and I didn't know how I could help my father. He came here because he heard there was construction work in the area, and he hoped to find employment. He used his small savings to buy this little place, intending to fix it up himself. Our family has followed the crops for many years, but he has always dreamed of finding a place where we could settle down to stay."

"Where is the rest of your family now?"

"They're in Michigan picking apples. We were just so worried when we didn't get any letters from my father. He is always very good about writing or calling us. My mother gave me money to ride the bus down here to find him."

"Do you have food in the house now?"

"Yes. Your pastor and his wife have been very kind. I didn't know where else to turn, but when I saw the tall steeple with the cross on top, I knew I could find someone there who would advise me.

"Reverend Stanfield and his wife brought food for our cupboards and told us we would hear from them again. My father is a very proud man, and he does not like to accept charity. But he cannot do anything about it right now. When he is strong again, he will insist on repaying the kind people who have helped us."

"We'll leave you alone for now, Rosa," Kevin said, "but as Lori told you, we'll be back tomorrow to help."

As Kevin and Lori trampled through the weeds to their car, another car pulled up in front of the house and a couple emerged carrying dishes covered with aluminum foil. It hadn't taken long for the congregation to respond to the minister's call for help.

"Let's have lunch before I take you back to your hotel," Kevin suggested. "I didn't have much for breakfast."

"Neither did I," Lori admitted. "Lunch sounds great, but it doesn't have to be anything fancy. I passed a fast-food place on my way to church this morning that has a nice salad bar."

Lori went first in the line and paid for her own meal over Kevin's protest. "Hey, I invited you, remember?"

But Lori was insistent. After all, this was not a date. It was mre like a business arrangement. She wanted to preserve that premise.

Over lunch, they planned for their work the following day. "I don't know about paint brushes," Kevin said. "He probably has at least one, but I'll pick up a couple before we go, just in case we get others who volunteer to help. Be sure to wear old clothes."

"I didn't bring any." She hadn't counted on needing any, and most of her things were new for the trip. "I'll just have to be extra careful."

"Ha! I never saw a painter who could keep the stuff off his clothes. Maybe you'd better just plan to work inside."

"Not on your life! Just wait until you see me showing off. I wield a wicked paint brush!"

Kevin gave her a long, pensive look. "There's so much about you I don't know yet, Lori, but I intend to learn it all. Last night was special, and I hope it was only the beginning of our special times together."

Lori pulled her eyes away from his and glanced at her watch. "We'd better go, Kevin. I need to get back to the hotel. Nicky will begin to wonder what's keeping me."

"What's with Nicky? Are you accountable to her for your time and actions?"

"No, not exactly. We're just good friends, that's all."

"What's she doing this morning? Does she attend a different church?"

"She—I—Actually, she doesn't attend any church very often. Just at Christmas or Easter, or for things like weddings and funerals."

"You and your best friend don't seem to have a lot in common, do you?"

"Yes, we do, more than you would imagine. We work together every day, and we agree on more things than we disagree on. Nicky's a good person underneath all her fluffy exterior. One of these days she'll wake up and realize what's important to her."

Kevin drove beneath the portico of *La Hacienda* and leaned across to open the door for her. "I'll get the paint brushes, and I'll swing by and pick you up in the morning. What time can you be ready?"

"What about eight-thirty? That would put us out there by nine, and we could put in a whole day's work. Some of the church ladies are going to bring sandwiches out for the workers."

"I'll be right here in this spot at spot at eight-thirty," he promised.

"Thanks, Kevin. This has been a nice morning." She stood outside the double glass doors and watched him drive away. Her Sunday morning had taken some surprising turns, but somehow everything seemed to be right within her world. *He Leadeth Me*, the bells had chimed. She would put her trust in God and see where he chose to lead her.

CHAPTER TWELVE

Nicole awoke before the alarm sounded, anxious to begin her first day of work at George's scuba diving school. She wore one of her new bikinis beneath a pair of hot pink shorts and a white silk shirt. She used the bathroom mirror to apply her make-up carefully, using the waterproof kind she usually saved for mermaid performances.

She was surprised to hear Lori opening bureau drawers, selecting clothes for the day. "I'm sorry I woke you," she called. "I tried to be quiet so you could sleep late this morning."

"Don't worry, Nicky. I didn't want to sleep late today. Sleeping late seems such a waste of our limited vacation time."

"I guess that's one viewpoint, but some people think that's what vacations are for. Anyway, I still feel guilty about going off and leaving you alone. I hope you won't be too bored or lonely."

"I promise I'll be neither," Lori answered with a sly smile.

Nicole's suspicions were immediately aroused. "You're up to something, Lorelei Cramer. You're not meeting Mike for tennis, are you?"

"Who knows what happens while the cat's away?" Lori knew

just how to pique Nicole's curiosity. She hummed mysteriously as she changed from her pajamas into a pair of cut-offs and one of the tee shirts she had purchased in Key West.

Nicky watched her until she felt satisfied that the clothes Lori chose were not selected for tennis competition. "Come on, Lori, tell me what you're planing to do today."

"You wouldn't believe me if I told you."

"Try me."

"I'm going to paint a house."

"Lori, get serious. Why won't you tell me?"

"Just as I thought. I knew you wouldn't believe me." Lori continued to hum while she brushed her hair and applied her make-up with a light hand.

"You're impossible! Just wait until the next time you try to get a straight answer from me." Nicole's attitude was fast changing from amused curiosity to genuine irritation.

"Simmer down, Nicky. I told you I was going to paint a house, and that's exactly what I'm going to do. Yesterday the preacher told about a man who's down on his luck. He fell while painting his house, and now he needs a little help to get the job finished."

"Lori, I can't believe what I'm hearing! You work yourself silly all year long and finally get a two-week vacation, and you're going to spend it painting a house for a man you don't even know! That's the craziest idea you've come up with yet."

"To each his own, Nicky. You choose to help George, and I choose to help another man. I don't see a big difference."

"Well, there's an ocean of difference, Lori, and if you can't see it, then you're blind as well as crazy. Just please be careful. No wonder weird things keep happening to you. You go off on these wild adventures around people you don't even know, and then you expect everything to fall into place in a normal manner. Mr. Porter is counting on me to take care of you. I just hope I can get you back home in one piece."

"Did Mr. Porter delegate that job to you?"

"Well, not exactly," Nicky admitted, "but he is depending on both of us to come back rested and ready to perform in peak condition."

"Then don't over-extend yourself on those scuba lessons, Nicky. I'll see you tonight." Lori stuffed a bottle of sunscreen into her beach bag, grabbed a wide-brimmed straw hat, and hurried out the door. Wide-eyed, Nicole watched in disbelief, shook her head, and muttered under her breath, "I'll never understand that girl!"

"I'll do the top boards, Lori," Kevin shouted down at her as he climbed up the ladder. "You do the bottom. That way you won't have to worry about falling."

"No, but I'll have to worry about all the paint you'll be dripping down into my hair," she chided.

"This cream color should look real good in your black hair. What is it they call that? Frosted?"

"Don't forget who's standing on the ground near your ladder. Just one good push and you'd be down to my level in a hurry."

Lori dipped her brush into the gallon can of Sherwin-Williams paint and began to give the old house's wood siding a fresh coat of outdoor enamel. Even the first few strokes made an immediate difference as the weathered boards soaked up their new, creamy color. Lori painted for several minutes, then stood back to view her handiwork. "Wow! Look at that!"

"Can't look yet," Kevin said. "I'm too busy."

When Lori looked up, she saw that Kevin had already covered twice as many boards as she, and his weathered surfaces were as smooth and even as the work of a professional painter. But maybe he was a professional. "Kevin, are you a painter by trade?"

He laughed. "Hardly. But if I were, I might consider docking my assistant's pay if she doesn't get back to work."

He still hadn't divulged his occupation, although she had given him the perfect opportunity to do so. He could be so infuriating! With her temper rising, Lori painted twice as fast. She began to slap the paintbrush against the house with a vengeance.

"That's better," Kevin called down, raising Lori's ire several notches.

She made no more attempts at conversation, but continued to work until the sun was midway in the sky. Promptly at noon, a station wagon drove up to the fence, and two elderly couples piled out. The men unfolded a steel picnic table and situated it under the shade of a large oak tree. The two ladies unloaded several plastic containers from the back of the car and set them on the table. "Lunch time!"

Emerging from the house, Rosa Fonseca and two other ladies emptied pails of dirty water onto the ground. Kevin and Lori covered their paint cans and walked to the pump to wash their brushes. "I think I've worked up an appetite," Kevin confessed.

"Me, too," Lori agreed, rubbing her hands together in the clear water, while Kevin worked the pump. "Now let me." She took a turn pushing the pump handle up and down so Kevin could wash his hands and splash some of the cool water on his face.

Rosa spread an old quilt over the ground for the workers to sit on while they wolfed down sandwiches, deviled eggs, and grapes, and cold lemonade from paper cups.

Rosa put some of the sandwiches on a paper plate to take indoors for her father. "I will never be able to tell you how much we appreciate what you're doing for us," she said. "I may not see you again before you leave, because Reverend and Mrs. Stanfield are taking me to town this afternoon to meet the people at Division of Family Services. My father wishes he could come out here and personally thank each one of you, but he isn't able to move around easily yet. A doctor from your church came out to see him this morning and ordered him to stay in bed. He's making arrangements to get my father into the local hospital to make sure he has no broken bones. The doctor says he feels certain the injuries aren't permanent. He thinks my father will soon be up again and able to work."

"Do whatever you need to do, and don't worry about a thing here, Rosa," one of the women told her. "We have another group of volunteers coming out after lunch, and we'll have this place spruced up so you won't recognize it."

"I'm sorry you found things here in such a mess," Rosa apologized. "My father is a very clean, tidy man when he is well. He's embarrassed you found him in this condition."

"Rosa," one of the women said, "let's get the rest of this food into your dad's refrigerator. We need to clear out of here and let these people get back to work."

All day long, as people left, others arrived to take their places, some carrying equipment to clean and make repairs indoors and out. Two men brought lumber to replace the rotten boards of the porch. One man and two women joined Kevin and Lori on the painting crew, and just before sunset, they painted the last board.

"I know Hector will want to put on a second coat when he's able," Kevin speculated, "but this should hold him for a while."

"And just look at the yard! Doesn't it look nice since they've mowed all those weeds?"

"Everything inside is spotless," one of the ladies reported. "We even hung fresh curtains someone had donated to the church rummage sale. They look so nice."

"And Hector is so happy," another woman said. She looked at Kevin and Lori standing together by the gate. "My goodness, I'll bet you two are on your honeymoon! How nice of you to take time to come out and help today. You're a fine Christian couple. God bless you both."

Lori was too astonished to answer, and her blush only seemed to strengthen the lady's mistaken impression. "We'll say a prayer for you at our morning Bible study group," she continued cheerily. "We'll pray you two will have many years of happiness together, and that God will bless you with healthy, happy children."

Lori's head reeled at the woman's suggestion, and unbidden pictures crowded her thoughts. In her mind's eye, a group of tow-headed children clustered around her, pulling at her skirt, their bronze bodies glistening in the noonday sun. *Marriage? Children?* Things were moving at a much faster pace than Lori could match.

Kevin gripped her arm and propelled her through the open gate. "Thank you," he called over his shoulder, as he helped Lori into his car. "We deeply appreciate your prayers."

"Kevin!" Lori admonished as they drove away. "How could you be so deceitful?"

"Deceitful? *Me?* What did I say?" He pursed his lips to prevent a grin.

"It's more what you failed to say," Lori replied. That was the trouble with this relationship; not so much what Kevin said as what he failed to say.

Could she ever be happy in a relationship with a man who kept so much of his life apart from her? Would life with Kevin be a life filled with infinite footprints of secrets and deception? Surely this was not the path God wanted her to follow. Why, then, was she so incapable of resisting his magnetism and charm? *Dear Lord, I need a clearer sense of your direction in all of this. My head seems to be pointing in one direction, my heart in another. Please help me to understand your plan for my life.*

She was quiet for the rest of the ride back to the hotel, and Kevin kept cutting his eyes in her direction. "You're not really angry with me, are you? I just didn't think it necessary to elaborate on our marital status for those ladies we don't even know." When a smile curved her lips, he found the courage to add, "And if they choose to pray for us, who knows what ways God might find to answer their prayers?"

Lori turned her head to the window to hide her broadening smile.

"Let's go back and get cleaned up, and then go out for a nice, relaxing dinner somewhere."

"Not tonight, Kevin. I'm very tired."

He stopped the car several yards short of the lighted portico, and with the engine still running, he leaned over and kissed her on the lips, kindling a flame that made her yearn to put her arms around him and respond with every ounce of emotion within her. All of the doubts that had assailed her only minutes before washed away like the morning tide, and she knew without a doubt that she was in love with him, for better or for worse, forever. "I—I'd better go in."

"This has been a very special day for me, Lori; one I'll never forget. I'll call you tomorrow," he promised before coasting the short distance to the entrance.

The concierge stepped out to open her door. "Good evening, Miss Cramer." If he noticed her strange paint-splattered attire, he was too proper to mention it.

Lori thanked him and hurried up to her room. She needed to get out of her stained and sweaty clothes and into a nice, warm shower where she could let go of her tension and get her head together.

She was tired to the bone, but she was also aware of a gnawing hunger growing stronger by the moment. She almost regretted refusing Kevin's dinner invitation.

She was so confused about that man! Part of her, the cautious part, wanted to distance herself from Kevin Collins and forget she ever met him. But it was too late for that now. No matter what turn her life might take, she would never ever forget him. That was the other part of her— the rash, reckless part that loved him and wanted to be with him forever.

The warm shower did little to calm her confusion. Perhaps

what she really needed was a hot, nourishing meal. It was hard to think on an empty stomach. She chose a lavender jumpsuit she thought suitable to wear to the dining room.

When the phone rang, she assumed it would be Nicole telling her not to wait up. Lori certainly wouldn't expect her to be in early. "Hello?"

"Hello yourself."

At the sound of his voice, Lori sank down onto the side of her bed. Just when she thought she was getting him out of her thoughts, he popped up like a jack-in-the-box. But she had to admit she wasn't unhappy to hear his voice. "Kevin! What's this about? Did you forget to tell me something?"

"As a matter of fact, I do have some things to tell you, Lori. When I came back to my room tonight, I showered and got ready to go out for a bite to eat, but I couldn't rid my mind of a certain green-eyed mermaid who keeps invading my thoughts."

Lori's alarm system went into gear, but her heart chose to ignore it. She tried to sound trite. "I'll bet you tell that to all the mermaids you meet."

"Just one. I know you said you're tired, and no wonder. Lady, you are some mean painter! I'm quite impressed. But even painters have to eat to keep up their strength, so I decided to twist your arm a little and see if you might change your mind about dinner. I could come over to your dining room— you wouldn't even have to leave the hotel, and I promise to go home early."

He sounded like a little boy pleading for a lollipop. She found him impossible to resist. "Don't twist my arm too far, because I have a feeling that arm's going to be pretty sore tomorrow anyway. It's not accustomed to painting for eight straight hours."

"Was that a yes?"

She laughed. "I guess it wasn't a no."

"That's good enough for me. I'll meet you in the lobby in fifteen minutes—ten if my car will go that fast."

"Please. Fifteen is fine."

Once again Lori sat facing Kevin across the table, and again her heart was winning the battle waged with her mind.

When dinner was over, he tried to keep his promise. "I said I'd go home early. Does that mean we can't go for a quick spin along the beach? I know where there's a neat little drive-in that sells the most delectable ice cream sodas you ever encountered."

"Now that I've eaten, I don't feel nearly so tired, and I do love ice cream sodas."

"Then let's go."

He led her to the parking lot and opened the passenger door for her. She slid into the seat and let her head fall back against its back. When he climbed in beside her and started the engine, they followed the highway north along the ocean until he turned in at a fifties-style diner.

"This doesn't look like much from the outside, but just wait 'til you sample those sodas!"

I haven't had one since I was in high school, and then I had to share one soda with two straws."

"Well, tonight you're out with a big spender. Tonight you get your own private soda with two straws both for you."

"You really know how to treat a girl," she demurred.

They passed up the curbside service in favor of savoring the atmosphere of the diner. Kevin put a dollar in the jukebox, and they listened to melodies older than either of them.

On the drive back to the hotel, Kevin put a CD into the stereo and filled the car with a soft, romantic melody. He put his arm around her shoulder and pulled her close. "Sit by me, Lori. I like the feel of your head against my shoulder."

When she didn't protest, he drove a short distance farther and pulled the car onto a small strip of pavement near the water's edge. "Lori, I don't want to rush you into decisions you aren't ready to make, but our time together is about to run out. I can't let you walk out of my life without telling you how I feel."

"There are a lot of things I'd like you to tell me, Kevin. How you feel is one of them, but there are other things I'd like to hear first. Sometimes I feel I've known you all my life, and other times I feel I don't really know you at all."

"Some things take time, Lori, and time is the commodity we're about to run out of. It's true we haven't known each other long, but I know beyond a shadow of a doubt that I love you, and that I'll always love you if you'll give me the chance. Maybe it's too soon to expect you to make a commitment to me, but I can't let you go without telling you how I feel."

"Kevin, I do—" No, she must not tell him she loved him. Not until he trusted her enough to tell her all the things she wanted to know. "I do— think very highly of you," she finished lamely. "Maybe in time things will work out for us, but there are just too many loose ends right now."

"I understand your reluctance, and I know a lot of it's my fault, but if you can find it in your heart to trust me for just a little while, I promise I'll give you every answer you want and a whole lot more."

"I don't know what it is you want from me. I've already told you I'm not like Nicole."

"You're not like any other woman in the world. That's why I can't let you get away from me." He drew her into his arms and kissed her.

Lori felt her body tremble from the emotional impact of his kiss and his words.

"Darling, You're trembling. Are you cold?"

She didn't want to admit her tremors weren't due to the weather. "Yes, I guess I am. The night air is chilly."

"Here." He reached into the back seat and pulled up his nylon windbreaker. "Put this on. It may not look like much, but at least you'll be warm."

She slipped her arms into the sleeves and pushed the cuffs up to her wrists.

"Is that better?"

"Um hmm."

They exchanged few words on the drive back to the hotel, with only the radio's romantic music filling the silence of the night. Lori sat near the door; her eyes turned to the sparkling sea. She wanted to believe Kevin's words, to know that he loved her the same way she loved him. But how could she trust a man who kept so much of himself hidden from her? She wasn't ready to commit to a halfway relationship. She wouldn't do it!

Kevin parked in the hotel parking lot, and in the darkness of the car, he kissed her again. "Keep the jacket until tomorrow. You're still shivering. I'll call you in the morning. Sleep well, darling Lori."

Kevin walked her to the lobby and left her by the elevator door. Lori felt more confused than ever. Every time she jumped one hurdle, another appeared in front of her. Tonight he had told her he loved her. Weren't those the words she had longed to hear? Why then was she so reluctant to let him know she loved him too?

When she opened the door to her room, she was relieved to see that Nicole was still out. She wasn't ready to face another barrage of questions. She slipped out of the silky windbreaker and rubbed it against her cheek. Something fell from the pocket. Stooping to pick it up, she saw a letter stamped and addressed for mailing. And there was something else! A business card.

She moved closer to the lamp and read the card. *Kevin R. Collins, Private Investigator.* Kevin was a private investigator? Was she some kind of assignment for him? She sank into the chair and looked at the envelope she held in her other hand. It was addressed to Mrs. Kevin Collins, Ames, Iowa. *Mrs. Kevin Collins?* Lori felt faint. No wonder he hadn't wanted her to know all about him. Well, now at last she knew all she needed to know. He was a private investigator, and he was married. What more was there to ask?

As her tears flowed, she dressed for bed and darkened the room. When Nicole came in, Lori pretended to be asleep— she didn't want Nicky to see her red, swollen eyes. She muffled her sobs into her pillow until she fell into an exhausted sleep, but her dreams were of a blond, bronze hunk named Kevin.

CHAPTER THIRTEEN

"Whose jacket is this?" Nicole stood at the foot of Lori's bed, turning Kevin's windbreaker in her hands.

Lori didn't want to see or talk about that wretched jacket. What a fool she'd been! She pulled the sheet over her head and mumbled, "When the phone rings, you answer it. Just tell Kevin he can pick up his jacket at the front desk. Tell him I'm not here. Tell him anything you want. I'm not talking to him." She buried her face into her pillow and pretended to go back to sleep.

"Lorelei Cramer, get up this minute and tell me what's going on!" Nicole pulled at the pillow, but Lori held fast.

"Go away. Let me sleep."

"Not until you tell me what happened last night. Did you and Kevin have a fight? It must have been something major."

Lori sat up in bed and slumped in resignation. She might as well tell Nicky enough to get her off her back. There'd be no peace until she did. "No, we did not have a fight. My goodness, Nicky, not everyone falls in and out of love the way you do." She was hitting below the belt, but with Nicky, sometimes that was the only way to get the message across. "I've just decided things were getting a little too serious with Kevin, and I want to nip it in the bud."

Nicole fumed. She stood over Lori with her hands on her hips. "Well, you sure do miss out on a lot of fun being so prim and proper all the time. If you'd just relax a little, you might find yourself having a much better time."

"I'm having a very fine time, thank you, if I could just get people to let up on me. And how am I supposed to relax? I was trying to sleep, but you couldn't be happy until you got me all stirred up."

"Well, *excuse me!*"

The shrill ring of the bedside phone broke into their bickering, and although Lori was closest to it, she looked to Nicole to answer it. "Remember what I said, Nicky. I meant it."

"Hello? Good morning, Kevin. Oh, well, she can't come to the phone right now. Yes, you can try again in a few minutes if you want. Right. Okay, then. So long, Kevin." She hung up and glared at Lori. "I refuse to get in the middle of this, Lori. If you want to tell him anything about the jacket, you'd better talk to him yourself."

"Please, Nicky. I'm sorry I was so sharp a minute ago."

"Apology accepted. But it doesn't change anything. I'm still not doing your dirty work for you."

"After all the times I've come through for you?"

"This is different. I like you, and I like Kevin. If there's a problem between you two, I'm not going to add to it. In fact, I'm on my way to the beach. Bye now." Lori watched her flounce out of the room, barefoot and bikini clad, towel in hand.

Lori got out of bed and picked up the jacket, holding it at arm's length as though it contained lethal germs. So Kevin Collins was a private investigator! Then their frequent meetings were not just coincidental. She was under surveillance. Who was he working for?

And that letter to Mrs. Kevin Collins. She had really fallen for his line in a big way. He was very convincing when he spoke those words of love in the moonlight. She'd been fool enough to believe they might share a lifetime together. Uninvited tears began to stream down her cheeks again. She thought her tear ducts must be dry by now. Somewhere in Iowa, there was a sweet little wife just waiting for his return.

She looked again at his business card. It did give a Jacksonville address. Perhaps his wife was on a trip. The letter was clearly addressed to Iowa. It even had a stamp on it. Well, she wouldn't mail it for him. She tucked it back into the inside pocket of his jacket along with his card.

The phone rang again. She was sure it was Kevin. She would just let it ring. She didn't want to talk to him— not now or ever again. But the ringing persisted. Wasn't he ever going to give up? She might as well bite the bullet— get this over and done with. "Hello."

"Lorelei?" Just hearing his voice again made her knees turn to oatmeal, and she sank down onto the bed.

"Yes."

"You sound different this morning. I hope you didn't catch a cold last night."

"No, I'm fine."

"I didn't sleep much last night. Kept thinking about us and where we're headed. Lori, I've told you how I feel about you, but you haven't given me very much reason to hope you feel the same way too. I know part of that is my fault. I haven't meant to be evasive with you. I owe it to you to be more open, and I want to do that. May I come over this morning?"

Every fiber in her body screamed *yes!* But she steeled herself for her icy reply. "You might drop by and pick up your jacket. I'll leave it at the front desk. I have some errands to run."

She listened for a response, but heard only a long silence on the other end of the line. At last he said, "Right, Lori. I understand. I'll pick up my jacket on my way to the airport. See you around."

On his way to the airport? Lori sat on the bed with the receiver in her hands several minutes after he hung up. He wasn't due to leave until the weekend. Well, this is what she wanted, wasn't it? She wouldn't have to keep finding excuses not to see him.

Lori had never felt more desolate. She still hadn't resolved the problems she came down here to escape. Now, in addition to all of that, Nicky was mad at her and Kevin was leaving. Probably going to see his wife.

She dressed slowly. A pair of black shorts and a gray tee shirt seemed to fit her mood. She reached beneath the bed for her sandals. She'd have to buy a new pair of sneakers to replace the ones she'd left somewhere at the bottom of the Gulf of Mexico. Maybe she'd walk to the shops today and look for a pair.

She found a bag to hold Kevin's jacket. The bag said *Belinda's Boutique* and brought a sad smile to her face as she remembered that eventful day in Key West. Had Madame Zenobia perceived she was being misled by the man at her side that day? Was that why she refused to project the future for her?

Lori folded the garment carefully, making sure the contents of the pocket were still intact. She rode the elevator down to the lobby and took the bag to the front desk. "Mr. Collins will come by to pick this up," she told the desk clerk.

"Fine, Miss Cramer. We'll make sure he gets it."

Mike passed her in the lobby. He was probably there to meet his friends. "Hi, Lori. Have you had your breakfast yet?"

"No, Mike. I'm skipping breakfast today, thanks."

"Say, you do look a little under the weather. Hope those crabs didn't disagree with you."

"No, they didn't. In fact, I don't know when I've enjoyed anything so much. You were very nice to include us."

"We all had a good time that night," Mike agreed. "We'll

have to try it again. The crabs are still lining the shores after dark. Think your boyfriend would like to join us again? Kevin seemed to really enjoy himself. He's a nice guy."

"Yes. Yes, he is. But he has to leave soon."

"That's too bad. We all liked him. Well if you and Nicky want to try your hands at it again some evening, just let us know. And say, you'd better get something for that cold. I can see it in your eyes, and your voice sounds a little rusty too. Drink lots of orange juice and get plenty of rest."

"Thanks, Mike. I'll do that. Bye."

Lori returned to her room and picked up her book. She had been so anxious to start it, but somehow she just couldn't get interested in it. Her mind kept wandering away from the story line, and she had to reread some of the pages in order to follow the plot.

Maybe there was some plausible explanation for Kevin's elusive behavior. She wanted to believe there might be, but it was hard to see what reason he could have for keeping his work a secret. Why not just tell her he was a private eye on vacation? She could have readily accepted that. Why act so mysteriously unless his actions involved her in some way? It all came back to the unavoidable conclusion that he had come here to watch her. But why? There were too many *whys* and not enough answers.

Then there was that letter to his wife. True, he could be divorced or separated. But most divorcees wouldn't continue to use their married name, at least not in that manner. If it had read "Mrs. Mary Collins or something like that, she could have believed they were estranged. And even if they were separated, didn't he owe it to Lori to tell her before feeding her that line about being in love with her?

When Nicole came in, Lori was still holding the book in her lap, staring out into space.

"Hi, Lori. It's great out there today. The surf's up and there's a group trying to organize a volleyball game for this afternoon. I came upstairs to bury the hatchet and get you to join us." She threw her towel in the chair and came closer. "Hey, you look terrible. Are you coming down with something? I should have suspected as much this morning. You usually wake up so cheerful."

"No, Nicky, I'm fine. Honestly. I guess I'm just tired. I'll be okay, though. I'm sorry I was so grouchy this morning."

"I know what you need— some lunch. Let's go down and see what they're serving today."

"No, you go on ahead, Nicky. I-I'm really not very hungry."

"Lori Cramer, you *are* sick." She put the palm of her hand on Lori's forehead to see if she detected fever. "Your head feels cool, but you look real pale."

Nicky would never let go of anything. She might as well go down to the dining room just to convince her she wasn't sick. "You're right. Maybe I just need some food in my stomach."

Over bowls of seafood chowder, Nicole continued to probe. "Did Kevin pick up his jacket yet?"

"I don't know. He said he would get it on his way to the airport."

"Airport? But he's not leaving until next Friday, is he?"

"I don't know what his schedule is. Perhaps he was called home on business." Anything to get Nicky on some other subject. "What's George doing today?"

"He's checking out all the equipment for another big day tomorrow."

"Nicky, are you really teaching a class?"

"No, I'm not certified, but I do have a beginner group for orientation. And I'm handling a lot of George's paper work. You know, the registration forms and things like that."

"Well, if you're sure that's what you want to do. But remember this is your vacation. We only have a few more days."

"Don't remind me! We have to check out before noon on Friday, and our plane doesn't leave until three in the afternoon."

"It's going to seem good to get home. Good to see Fluffy and

Mr. Porter and all the girls. And I want to give my mother a call first thing when we get home. I keep getting this uneasy feeling that she needs me."

"Well, for goodness sake, Lori. Call her today if it will make you feel any better. That silly promise we made about keeping our destination secret was all for your sake anyway. I couldn't care less who knows."

"You're right. I'm going to call her tonight. I guess I'm just being silly again. It's probably just as you said. She and Andy are probably off on some kind of exotic vacation. Anyway, I'll give her a call and ease my mind."

"You know, Lori, you never used to be this way, worrying all the time. I hope after we get back home you'll be that happy, carefree girl I've roomed with for the past few years."

"I will, Nicky. I promise. You've been great to put up with me these last few months. When we get back, you'll see a return of the lighthearted, happy-go-lucky Lorelei you used to know."

"That's the spirit. Now let's go lend our expertise to that volleyball game."

They were in the middle of their highly competitive game when Lori saw Kevin trudge up to the steps of the hotel and disappear through the entry doors. Even at this distance, there was no mistaking that cottony hair above the broad, erect shoulders that had felt so comforting to lean on.

"Watch it, Lori. That ball came right at you, and you didn't even swing at it. We're behind already, so let's shape up over there." The good-natured chiding came from the self appointed captain of her team.

"Sorry, Herb. I think maybe I need a break."

"She hasn't been feeling well." She heard Nicole making excuses for her as she left the group.

Sitting under the shade of a coconut palm, she watched until she saw him leave, carrying the bag from *Belinda's Boutique*. Did he feel the dejection that she felt? Probably not. To him, it was probably just a romantic interlude to break the monotony of his work. Or worse yet, perhaps she was part of his assignment. Well, he was gone now. Out of her life forever. Like the other things that had happened to her lately, she'd just have to write it off to experience and try to forget. That would be much easier said than done, but Kevin had given her no choice.

For the rest of the afternoon, Lori set about resolutely clearing her mind of all the disturbing thoughts that had been crowding it of late, and especially thoughts of Kevin Collins. End of chapter. Period. Case closed.

Nicole was going out to dinner with George again, and Lori welcomed the chance to have the evening alone. She loved Nicky, but she got so tired of her endless probing. "Have fun," she told her when as she was leaving. "Don't do anything I wouldn't do."

As soon as she was alone, Lori placed the call to her mother. She made a mistake by not choosing to make it person-to-person. She had no desire to talk to Andy, especially in her present low mood. But of course, it was Andy who answered the phone.

"Hello, Andy. It's Lorelei. I'm glad I caught you at home. I didn't know if you and mother were there, or off on a trip somewhere."

"No, baby we're right here." *Baby? She wasn't all that much younger than he was!* "Your mother will be glad to hear your voice. She's been under the weather lately."

"What's wrong with her?"

"Oh, nothing really. Here, I'll let you talk to her."

"Mother? I can barely hear you. Are you ill?"

"No, dear. I'm fine. Just a little tired, that's all. Where are you?"

"I'm in south Florida, just having a little vacation. Listen, when I get back, why don't you plan to come down some weekend for a little visit? It's been a long time."

"Wouldn't that crowd you and Nicole? Your apartment is pretty small."

"I'll sleep on the couch and give you my room, and you'll be quite comfortable. You can come watch the show, too. Mr. Porter's made a few changes. He always likes to add new things every year to keep people coming back."

"I don't know, dear. I'll have to discuss it with Andy. Perhaps if I get my strength built back up a little."

"Mother, have you seen a doctor?"

"Oh, no, darling. It's nothing that serious. Andy says we've just been on the go too much. He's taking good care of me, pouring nutritional milkshakes down me and making me rest a lot. I'll probably be fit as a fiddle in a few days. I'll let you know what he thinks about my visit."

"Please try. It's been a very long time since we've had some time together, just the two of us. We'll go shopping, treat ourselves to a beauty parlor make-over, and, oh, you know— do all the girlie things."

"Darling, it sounds like fun. Thanks for calling, Lorelei. It's good to hear your voice."

"Goodbye, Mother."

It was not a completely satisfying conversation. Lori was certain Andy had been hovering over her mother the whole time. Was she just being petty and jealous? After all, her mother was an intelligent, mature woman capable of making her own decisions, and if Andy was her choice, then Lori had no business interfering. If and when her mother came for a visit, she'd make a real effort to think and talk positively about Andy, and perhaps she could rekindle some of that closeness she and her mother used to share.

She turned her attention to her mystery novel. This book certainly didn't measure up to the standards of Jared Jones's other books. In fact, it didn't seem to hold her interest at all. After a few pages, she closed the book and stood to stretch.

She remembered then that she hadn't eaten anything since

lunch. She'd go down to the dining room for a snack. Then after supper, she'd take a short walk on the beach and breathe some of the clean salt air into her lungs, hoping it would help her sleep better tonight.

But later, walking on the beach in the moonlight only served to remind her. There were no children playing outside this late, and all the beachcombers seemed to come in pairs. She gazed at the moon that was growing bigger each night. Was it only last night when she had surrendered to Kevin's arms by the light of this same moon? Where was he tonight? Maybe back in Jacksonville, or maybe even way up in Iowa. If he saw that waxing moon, would it trigger his memory as it had hers? Or was he holding someone else in his arms this very moment, whispering those same sweet words she had savored in the moonlight only a few short hours before?

Lori had no way of knowing Kevin Collins was, at that precise moment, standing on the shores of Jacksonville Beach. Quite alone, he was watching the same brilliant moon play across the ripples of the same Atlantic Ocean. Although they were miles apart in body, they were inseparably joined in heart and mind.

Shuffling along the shoreline, Kevin picked up a small shell, threw it out, and watched it skip across the water. Far out in the ocean, he could see the twinkling lights of distant boats flickering like fireflies on a summer night. Everything only served to remind him of Lorelei, his precious little mermaid, for whom he had taken the risk and lost.

The breeze had picked up, and coming in off the water, it felt brisk and cold. Kevin pulled his nylon windbreaker closer around his chest. Even the jacket was a reminder of Lori. He crossed his arms over his chest, remembering how big and sweetly comical his coat had looked on her slender frame.

Something crisp and starchy scratched his chest. He reached his hand into the inside pocket of his jacket and pulled out his letter. *Darn!* He thought he had mailed that thing a week ago. Yesterday was his mother's sixtieth birthday, and he hadn't even mailed her a card. That's what female distraction could do to a man!

There was something else there in his pocket too. Just one of his business cards. He changed the letter and the card to his outside pocket and zipped his jacket closed. The same jacket Lori had worn only the night before.

Zing! A light exploded in his mind as stark realization set in. Lori must have seen his business card. The letter, too. What must she have thought? No wonder she backed off so suddenly. He sure had a lot of explaining to do. He only hoped he could convince Lori to listen.

CHAPTER FOURTEEN

Lorelei's bare legs drank in the heat of the weathered planks, as she lay stretched across the old wooden pier, her left arm shielding her eyes from the afternoon glare. Today was the first time she had returned to this beautiful, isolated cove since that memorable day when Kevin had scared her out of her wits by pulling her from the deep water.

With Nicky working at the scuba school and Kevin gone, the morning had stretched long and lonely. Lori wandered back to the secluded cove this afternoon almost without thinking, but once there, she decided to take advantage of an opportunity to practice her mermaid routine among the beautiful coral reefs. These living underwater formations renewed her respect for the artificial ones so skillfully created in the tanks of Weeki Wachee Spring, and reminded her of her good fortune in being associated with a genius like Mr. Porter.

In just a few more days, she'd be returning to her daily performances, so it seemed wise to put in a few hours of serious practice before vacation's end. Over and over again, she'd gone through the difficult maneuvers of her routine.

The wooden dock, warm from the afternoon sun, felt soothing to her muscles, as she lay exhausted from the exertion of her strenuous workout. She closed her eyes and let her thoughts wander.

It was on this very spot where she had first laid eyes on Kevin Collins. Even then, as mad and as frightened as she had been, she knew he held some special magnetism for her. And later that same morning, under the strange power of his unexpected nearness as he knelt in the sand and tenderly held her hand, she had unwillingly lost her heart forever.

From the beginning she realized the relationship was unwise. She had resisted it with ever fiber of her being. Indeed, she had denied her feelings even to herself. Now, alone here at the spot of their first meeting, she knew without a doubt there would never be another man she could love the way she loved Kevin Collins.

There was only one thing left for her to do. She would drown herself in her work. She smiled at the thought of that word. What was it she had told Kevin? *Mermaids never drown!* And here she lay, drowning in misery and self pity. She must find a way to shake it, to prove to the world and to herself that, although she might be swimming upstream against a strong current for a time, she was a mermaid and mermaids never drown!

"Somehow I knew I'd find you here." His voice floated over her like a soft summer breeze. Was she dreaming? She didn't want to open her eyes for fear she'd wake up and find it was only her imagination playing tricks again.

"Lorelei? Are you asleep?" She felt a gentle pressure on her shoulder.

"Kevin!" Her eyes popped wide in astonishment. "What are you doing here? I thought you'd gone back to Jacksonville."

"I did. I caught the first plane out of here on Tuesday, and I caught the first plane back on Wednesday. You've made me take leave of all my senses. Lori, we have to talk."

"*You're* telling *me* we have to talk? Kevin, I've been talking since the moment I laid eyes on you. I've told you just about everything there is to know about me. But *you,* you've been evading and avoiding my questions from the start. I know absolutely nothing about you. Now you kneel here beside me and tell me we have to talk? I find that a little incongruous. Well, start talking. I'm listening."

Kevin's face glowed with renewed hope. "You're absolutely right," he told her. "I made a big mistake by not telling you everything from the beginning. I see that now."

Lori raised herself to a sitting position, careful to maintain a safe distance between them. She knew her own weakness and vulnerability, and she wasn't taking any chances. She'd been hurt enough already. "Go ahead, Kevin. Say whatever it is you came to say, then leave."

"I don't even know where to start. First, let me tell you why I didn't want to reveal in the beginning that I'm a detective."

"That might be a good place for starters."

"Lori, when we first met, I'd come down here to forget all about my work and anything related to it. I felt I needed a real change of pace for a few days. Then, after I heard about all the bizarre things that happened to you recently, my training as an investigator just couldn't casually brush them off. I'm not saying the unfortunate sequence of events in your life lately couldn't be coincidental. Probably they were. But in my business, I can never afford to assume that."

So, he hadn't scoffed at her anxieties. Well, he was the only one who had taken them seriously. That in itself was encouraging. "You believe someone is really out to kill me?"

"Not so fast. I didn't say that. But I wanted to get all the facts. Lori, in spite of what you may believe, I've never lied to you about anything. I came down here for a vacation, and I certainly didn't plan on investigating anything. But when I met you and learned what you'd been going through, well, I just couldn't ignore it."

"Then why didn't you just tell me all that at the start?" She was still skeptical, but she wanted so badly to believe him.

"I guess I should have. I realize that now. But at the time, you were so nervous about the situation and so suspicious of me, I didn't want to add to your fears without deciding they were something to be concerned about."

"And now have you decided there is reason for concern?"

"No, you keep putting words in my mouth. I don't have all the facts yet, but I have some work in the mill that should give me some answers soon. Believe me, Lori, when I know anything at all, you'll be the first to share that information."

While he kept easing his body closer to her, she kept sliding away. They were almost at the end of the pier now, and she realized uneasily that if she slid any farther, she'd go over the edge. "I still don't see why you couldn't just tell me you were a private investigator and let it go at that."

"Think back, Lori. You were so sure I was out to harm you in some way, remember? If you had known I was a detective, you'd have thought I was sent here to trail you."

Truthfully, that's exactly what she'd first thought when she found his card, and even before that. What he was saying made sense, but it still didn't explain that other thing she'd discovered in his jacket pocket and she was too proud to ask. She didn't want him to think it mattered. But finally she could no longer resist. "Tell me about your family." She hoped that her request reflected only a casual interest. It certainly sounded better than saying, "Tell me about your wife."

He saw through her efforts at once— she could tell by the mischievous little-boy grin he fought to suppress. "I come from a small family. Only one brother, no sisters."

She didn't move a muscle. Just maintained their eye contact without flinching. "And?"

"I grew up on a small farm in the Midwest," he continued. "My father is a farmer and my mother is a typical farmer's wife. Loves to bake pies and cakes, and always wins a few ribbons at the county fair. Her name is Katherine. My father's name is Kevin. Like mine," he added, watching her closely. "They still live in the same farmhouse in Iowa where I was born."

She sat in silence for a few moments while the truth seeped through the shield of her resistance. "Your parents live in Iowa?"

"Yes."

Lori's breath came faster, and her head whirled. "If your father's name is Kevin, then your mother must be Mrs. Kevin Collins, and you must be a junior."

By now Kevin's grin spread all the way across his face. "No, my father is Kevin Robert, and I'm Kevin David. My mother just had a birthday, and I almost slipped up. I almost forgot to mail her a card. I had it stamped and addressed and everything." He spoke the words deliberately, as though to make sure she lost none of their meaning. His face came close to hers, and he reached to embrace her with arms that had ached with yearning since the moment he saw her. "Lorelei, my adorable little mermaid..."

SPLASH!

They were over the edge, turning in the crystal clear currents, looking at each other through bubbles of underwater laughter.

They surfaced simultaneously, embracing as their legs churned to keep them afloat in the salty sea. They dove, turned, and resurfaced like two playful otters, jubilant to be united in understanding at last.

Kevin climbed up on the pier first and stretched his hand down to pull her up beside him. "This is the second time you've caused me to go overboard and drench my freshly laundered clothes. And look at these shoes." He pulled them off and poured water from them.

Lori giggled. He looked so funny, standing there grinning, with his clothes clinging to his dripping frame and his bare feet surrounded by an ever enlarging puddle. "At least you kept your shoes. I wonder how many pairs of shoes are hiding out there on the ocean floor keeping company with mine." They sat on the edge of the dock and let their feet dangle over the edge.

The mood turned suddenly sober as Kevin held her hand and looked deep into her eyes. "We've only scratched the tip of the iceberg, Lori. There's so much more we have to say to each other."

"I know, Kevin. This is only the beginning, but from here on out, words between us will be much easier." At that moment, her heart felt so filled with love for him she thought it would surely burst. "We've crossed our first big hurdle."

"Let's go make ourselves presentable so we can go somewhere special for dinner tonight. Afterwards, maybe we can continue that talk on the beach— the one we didn't quite finish the other night."

He carried his dripping shoes in one hand as they walked, fingers linked, up the beach together toward the hotel.

"It's over a mile to the hotel. You must have been pretty confident to come this far on foot."

"Desperate would be a better word for it." He squeezed her fingers. "Where would you like to go for dinner?"

"Why don't we just get some crabs from the deli downtown and take a picnic basket down to the beach?" There was a time when she shied away from being alone with him. Now she searched for a way. There was so much more she wanted to hear from him and so much she wanted to say. They had a lot of catching up to do.

"You leave everything to me. But first I have to find myself a room and get out of these wet clothes."

"Oh, that's right. I forgot you checked out of your hotel room yesterday. I know *La Hacienda* is full. I heard the desk clerk turning down reservations this morning. You may have a problem finding a room on such short notice."

"At least it's not the weekend. I'll make some inquiries. They'll probably take one look at me, though, and turn me away."

"Kevin, why don't you get some dry clothes out of your suitcase and come up to my room to change? You can't go out searching for a hotel room looking like that!"

It did seem like a logical solution. He found his big, black rental car in the shade where he had parked it. Lori was disappointed to see that he no longer had the little red bullet they had all enjoyed so much. "This was the only car available," he explained, unlocking the trunk. "It's a big gas-guzzler."

She watched him riffle through his suitcase, pulling out a pair of navy blue shorts, a white cotton knit golf shirt, socks and underwear, and a pair of tennis shoes.

Like errant children, they sneaked furtively through the back door of the hotel and hurried down the back hall to the elevator.

"I'll unlock the door and let you in, and I can just wait for you in the lobby."

"In your wet bathing suit? I must admit it looks great to me, but I think the management would frown on it. I'll change in your bathroom, and everything will be right and proper, ma'am." His dimpled smile revealed his amusement. "I need to wash this saltwater out of my hair. Mind if I use your shampoo?"

"Not if you don't mind smelling like lilacs." It was her turn to tease. She was pleased to see his momentary look of dismay before he realized he was being ridiculed. Lori felt no pity— he deserved it all and more.

She gave him her shampoo and a towel and a fresh bar of soap and busied herself selecting her own dry clothes to wear after her shower. She could hear him singing to the accompaniment of the running water, and she decided it was a very nice sound.

Not wanting to sit on any of the furniture until she changed into dry clothes, Lori was standing when Kevin stepped out of the steaming bathroom, combed and groomed and smiling. "I feel like a new man."

A key turned in the lock, and they both turned toward the opening door.

"Oh, excuse me!" Nicole gave them a wicked smile as she backed out of the room, pulling the door closed behind her.

"No, wait, Nicky. Come back. It's not like you think." Lori ran into the hall in time to catch a glimpse of Nicole's shadow disappearing behind the closing elevator doors.

Kevin was apologetic, but he could scarcely conceal his amusement. "I'm sorry if I've caused you any embarrassment, Lori. I'll run along and let you get changed. When I find a room, I'll call you to make arrangements for this evening."

Lori was flustered. "If you see Nicky in the lobby on your way out, will you try to explain this to her?"

"Of course. But knowing Nicole, I don't think she'd give it a second thought."

"That's just it," Lori agreed. "Knowing Nicole, I know she wouldn't. That's the whole point. I'm the one who lays down all the ground rules, both here and at home. And I've just broken one of my own rules."

"Then I'll make it a point to look for her. Don't worry about it. Set your mind on more important matters, and wait for me to call."

He gave her a light, chaste kiss.

She had showered and dressed before Nicole returned, smirking like the cat that just swallowed the canary. "So Kevin has returned."

"Yes. Did he find you and tell you what happened?"

"Yes, he did. I must admit I was a wee bit disappointed. I thought you had begun to thaw into a real girl after all."

Now, *that* made her mad! "Just because I'm not—"

"Oh, simmer down, Lori. Don't say something you'll end up having to apologize for. I'm the one who usually does that. Anyway, we agreed not to quarrel anymore, remember?" It was unusual for Lorelei to be the first to take offense. More often, it was Nicole whose temper flamed. "I was only teasing you. Come sit down and tell me all about everything."

"First tell me about your day at the scuba school." Lori was stalling until she could sort out what she wanted to share with Nicole and what she wanted to keep privately to herself.

"Fantastic!" Nicky's eyes sparked with excitement as she began to relate the adventures of her day with George. "I only wish I had more time so I could become a certified scuba instructor. You should see George He's really something with those kids."

The two friends shared the experiences of an eventful day and confided their plans to each other until the sun was low in the sky. Lorelei was careful, though, to hold back the depth of her feelings when she talked about Kevin. She had only just begun to admit them to herself. She wasn't ready yet to share them with anyone else— at least not until she and Kevin reached some kind of an understanding.

When the phone rang, both girls jumped up at once and nearly collided in their race to answer it. Nicole managed to reach it first.

"Hello. Oh, Kevin, how nice that you were able to come back. Were you called home on business, or was there a personal emergency?"

"Give me the phone, Nicky." Lori tried to wrest it from her grasp.

"Just a minute, Lori. I only wanted to be sociable." She held one hand over the mouthpiece while she talked.

"Well, quit giving him the third degree. Just be sociable and get on with it."

"You don't have to be so cross about it. Hello, Kevin? Yes, I'm still here. Sure, hold on. I'll get her."

Again with her hand covering the mouthpiece, she said, "Really, Lori, it's not like you to be so eager." With an impish smile, she handed over the phone.

Lori gave her a reproving glare before she smiled into the

telephone. "Were you successful? Did you find a room? Great. Yes, I know *The Commodore*. It's just down the road from us. Of course. Seven will be fine."

"Are you going to wear your new party dress?" Nicole asked after she hung up.

"Not tonight. Nicky, can I borrow your sneakers? I lost mine."

"Sneakers? You're going out for dinner with Kevin, and you want to wear my sneakers? Lori, I hate to tell you this, but nobody wears sneakers to dinner at *The Commodore*."

There was no way of keeping anything private around Nicole. "Nicky, we're just going on a sort of picnic."

"Well, that sounds different. It might be fun after all. Give me the phone, and I'll see if George wants to come along."

"Wait a minute, Nicky. Have you been invited?"

For a moment, Nicole looked as though she had been slapped in the face, but Lori saw that she recovered quickly when she sensed this might be the nucleus of a nice, juicy story. "Just *what* is on tap tonight, Lori? Something special?"

"If you call a picnic something special, then I guess so." She tried to look nonchalant. "It's just that Kevin planned this, and I don't think it would be very polite for me to invite anyone else unless he suggested it."

"And he didn't." Nicole gave her a skeptical appraisal, apparently sensing there was more here than she had been told.

"Right. He didn't. I'm sorry, Nicky. Maybe we can do something together tomorrow night, if he's still here. I haven't had a chance to find out what his plans are yet."

Nicole was still in the clothes she had worn all day. "Don't you think you'd better be getting ready yourself?" Lori asked her, anxious to drop the discussion.

"I suppose so." Nicky seemed to sense the futility of further prying just now, but Lori knew there would be more questions after they both came home tonight.

* * *

Lori slid into the red leather seat of Kevin's impressive car. "I feel like Cinderella in the royal coach. I thought we were going to walk down the beach."

"Nothing is too good for my princess. Do you think you'd fit into the glass slippers tonight?"

"I sure hope so. I could use some new footwear. Then maybe I can return Nicky's sneakers." She leaned over the seat and eyed the picnic basket on the back seat. "Is that our dinner?"

"Yes, but I still have a few surprises in store."

Where was he taking her? He was heading out toward the Overseas Highway. It was too late to be starting for Key West. "Isn't that the Seven Mile Bridge ahead?"

"Right you are. Good memory."

She didn't much care where he was taking her. The important thing was being here beside him. And if he meant everything he'd said to her, perhaps there was still a chance for the two of them. Not only that, but he *believed* her. He would help her either overcome her fears or uncover the reason for them— maybe both. At least he wasn't ridiculing them.

She watched people fishing in the twilight from Henry Flagler's famous old railway trestle. Folks seemed to come to the Keys and drop all their cares in the water, letting them be carried away on the tides. Hopefully, she'd soon be able to do that too.

They reached the end of the bridge, and Kevin pulled into an area marked *Bahia Honda State Park*. "This is the largest park in the Keys, and it just might be the prettiest spot." He drove down the curving road until he came to an unoccupied sheltered table.

"Kevin, this is so beautiful!" Banana trees and coconut palms towered over them, and a lush blanket of verdant ferns surrounded them. The idyllic setting was further enhanced by the soothing sound of soft ocean ripples playing a liquid lullaby in the background. "This is much nicer than a hotel dining room."

She helped him spread a cloth over the concrete table and peered into his big wicker basket. "Mmm. I smell them. You really did get crabs."

"Yes, and this time they're already cleaned. All we have to do is eat them." He began removing the tops of several plastic containers. "We have potato salad, coleslaw, baked beans, and an assortment of tropical fruits."

"You've thought of everything!"

"Wait! There's more." He opened the trunk and lifted the lid of a Styrofoam cooler. A gallon jug of tea nestled in a bed of crushed ice, and two tall goblets coated with frost lay on top.

Lori sipped the cool tea and nibbled at the food Kevin passed to her, but nerves were taking their toll on her appetite. She kept thinking ahead, to the serious matters they had yet to discuss.

"You aren't doing justice to these poor crabs who gave up their lives for you," Kevin chided her. "Here. Have some of these beans. They're still warm."

"These Styrofoam containers really do a good job," she agreed as she munched on a slice of fresh, cold pineapple. They were both making small talk, putting on hold the important words that were waiting to be spoken.

"If that's all you're going to eat, we might as well get this stuff packed up." Kevin began to stack the remnants of their supper into the basket, and Lori shook and refolded the cloth. Kevin carried the basket back to the car and disposed of their garbage in a metal oil drum provided by the park service. Then he took Lori's hand and led her toward the beach.

The reflection of the moon over the ocean lighted a golden pathway so vividly marked that it seemed to invite them to walk out on it. The phosphorus in the water sparked like tiny neon lights beneath the ripples of the ebbing tide.

"Lori," Kevin began. "Before we talk about *us,* I want to talk about *you* because there are some barriers we have to cross before we can be free to make the kind of commitments I'm hoping we both want."

"What kind of barriers?"

"First there's this thing about someone wishing you harm. I don't want to alarm you, but my preliminary investigations indicate you should be extremely careful until we get this thing resolved."

Her sharp intake of breath made him hasten to continue. "Now, don't go jumping to conclusions. We haven't reached any yet. But on Friday, we both have to leave and go in opposite directions and I won't be around to help you. All I'm saying is that I want you to be careful. Please stay close to other people, and don't go wandering off on your own like you did this afternoon."

"But when will I see you again?" Just when they had finally come together, she was losing him again.

"You just have to trust me, Lori. I'll be there for you when you need me."

"Oh, Kevin. It's all so confusing and frightening. I'm so tired of the fear and uncertainty. When is it all going to end?"

"Soon, my darling. Together we'll see this thing through." He squeezed her hand reassuringly. "Now, here's what I want you to do. During the next few days, when you're in your room alone, write down names and addresses of all your friends, family, people with whom you work— anyone who comes to mind."

"Goodness, the list would be endless."

"I know. It's a big job, but it's important. Detail any unpleasant encounters, any arguments, and any disagreements you can think of, no matter how trivial they may seem. Don't leave off things you think have been forgiven or forgotten. Sometimes even the most remote detail can be a clue, and if I'm going to help you, I'll need your cooperation."

Lori was pensive for a few moments. "Perhaps Nicole can help me with the list."

"No, Lori. You mustn't confide in anyone, no matter how

much you trust them. Please, Lori will you do as I ask— for me? For *us*?"

"All I can promise is that I'll try. I really can't see how a list like that can help you, but if you're willing to spend time trying to help me, the least I can do is cooperate."

"That's the spirit. Now, let's put that subject on the back burner for now and get on to more important things." He stopped walking and pulled her toward him. He held her close to him, and her arms encircled his neck as she responded to his kiss with a passion she hadn't allowed herself to express before. Yielding herself to him in complete surrender as he held her in his arms and pressed his body hard against her own, she ran her fingers through his pale hair, and he gently stroked her back as he murmured her name between each kiss.

"Lori, I love you."

"I love you, too, Kevin." For Lori, love meant faithfulness and loyalty and marriage. What did it mean to Kevin?

As if reading her thoughts, he took her arms in his hands and pushed her gently away to look into her eyes as he spoke. A slight frown creased his brow. "If you'll have me, Lori, I want to plan my future with you, a future that includes marriage and a Christ-centered family, the two of us growing old together."

Lori felt weak with happiness. These were the words she had wanted to hear from him. Yet, even loving him as she did, she could not help but wonder: *Are we moving along too fast?* Two weeks ago she didn't even know Kevin Collins, and now under the star-studded moonlit sky, she was about to pledge her whole life to him. "That's the kind of future I want too, Kevin. But it's all happening so fast. What if you don't feel the same after you return to your normal daily routine, away from the magic of the tropics? What if we find it was all a romantic summer night's dream? I— I don't want either of us to end up with a broken heart." Tears glistened in her eyes.

"Lori, darling! It's true we haven't known each other long, and I can't explain how I've come to know so quickly that you're the one woman God has chosen to share my life. But I am sure beyond a shadow of a doubt that I will always love you, and I promise to do everything in my power to make you happy."

"I feel that too, Kevin. I've prayed for God to give me a clear direction, and no matter where I turn, He always sends me right back into your arms. I just don't want you to make promises you'll regret at summer's end."

"I've prayed about it too, Lori. I've lain awake nights trying to figure how we can mesh our two careers into a marriage that won't separate us, yet allows us both the freedom to grow. I know you've reached the pinnacle in your career, and I don't want to jeopardize that. I'd never ask you to give that up. On the other hand, I've just begun to turn a profit in my own agency. It took me several years to become established there. And unfortunately there aren't any mermaid springs in the Jacksonville area."

"But Kevin, being a mermaid isn't a lifetime vocation. It's more like a beautiful interlude."

"And what do you have in mind for your life after mermaids?"

"I'd like to finish earning my college degree. Then I think I'd like to try for a job with a large city newspaper. At least, that's what I had in mind when I was in high school." She paused thoughtfully and smiled before adding, "But more than anything else in the world, I'd like to be Mrs. Kevin *David* Collins, and raise a house full of little Collins offspring."

Kevin's expression let her know that her words were sweet music to his ears. "Oh, Lori, even though I've known you for less than two weeks, it seems as though I've waited forever to hear you say that." He kissed her again before continuing to unfold his plan. "There's a very good college in Jacksonville. You could begin there any time you want. But how soon would you be willing to leave the show?"

"Would tomorrow be too soon?" She laughed. "No, of course I don't mean that. I'd want to give Mr. Porter plenty of notice. Besides, I want you to finish your investigation and get all that resolved before we start making wedding plans. I don't want any clouds hanging over us on our wedding day."

"I agree completely. As long as I know you're waiting for me, I can be very patient. But I plan to keep the road hot between Jacksonville and Weeki Wachee Spring. We'll have to get married soon. Otherwise I won't be able to afford the gas bill."

Lori felt as though her heart would explode with happiness. Perhaps she and Kevin could have all their problems worked out by fall. A September wedding would be beautiful. But no matter how long they had to wait, she was certain of one thing at last. She would be with Kevin Collins for the rest of her life. Things just couldn't get any better than that.

CHAPTER FIFTEEN

"Lori, do you have extra room in your suitcases? I can't get everything into mine." Nicole sat on top of her luggage, tugging at the straps in a futile effort to get everything secured. A two-inch gap yawned between the edges of the suitcase zipper.

"No, Nicky, I don't. I barely have enough room for my own things." Every time the two of them had gone shopping, Lori had reminded Nicole of the impending problem of getting it all home. But impulsive Nicky had failed to listen. "We'll have to hurry, too. We have to check out by noon."

"I'm going down to the gift shop to get one of those jumbo shopping bags to use for my carry-on. I think I can cram everything else into that."

"Nicole, you already have two carry-on bags, and they're both packed full. What do you plan on doing with those?"

"I guess I'll just have to check one of them and pay the extra fee. I can't leave any of this neat stuff behind."

Lori shook her head as Nicole hurried out the door in search of a shopping bag. She just hoped Nicky wouldn't find some handsome guy in the gift shop. If she did, Lori would be left with the job of checking out all alone.

Where had the time gone? It seemed only yesterday when Kevin found her beneath the coral reefs, and yet it seemed that every important facet of her entire life had happened in these last two weeks.

For the first time in months, Lori felt a sense of peace and security. Kevin promised she would be safe, and she believed him. Someday perhaps they would both look back and laugh at the strange sequence of events that nearly made an emotional cripple of her.

Yet even in the midst of all her newfound joy, she felt a bittersweet sadness in leaving the magical, romantic Keys, especially since it would begin a painful separation from the man she loved more than life itself. But that separation would only be temporary. One day soon their lives would be inextricably joined together for a lifetime!

Last night on the beach, they had made plans for that day. They would begin their life together with a trip back to the Keys. They'd spend a few days in Key West to see all the things they missed on their first trip. She might even drop in and pay a little visit to Madame Zenobia, just to gloat a little and show that old prophet of doom how wrong she had been.

She had not told Nicole any of her plans. Although she felt like shouting the news from the rooftop, Kevin insisted she wait until after he completed his investigation. She had agreed, but it was a hard edict to follow. Nicky was so darn nosy, and she had such sneaky ways of prying information when her curiosity was aroused. Thankfully, Nicky had been so busy with George and the scuba school this past week that there had been little time for them to be together to pursue their customary little confidential chats.

Where was Nicky, anyway? Lorelei was all packed and ready to call the bellboy to come for the luggage, and Nicole was gone, her belongings scattered across the bed. Honestly!

Lori set her suitcases by the door and went downstairs to look for her. She found her in the lobby, enjoying the male companionship of the cook from their crab boil.

"Lori, you remember Herb. Can you believe it? We're both from Louisiana. It's a small world, isn't it?"

This was their last day. If Lori could only hold her cool for a few more hours! She took Herb's extended hand and shook it politely. "Of course I remember Herb. Nicole, I'm going to the desk and ask them to send up a bellboy for our bags. We have to check out now. If there's anything you've neglected to pack, we'll just have to leave it here." She smiled sweetly behind clenched teeth.

"Lorelei Cramer, don't you dare!" Nicole remembered to smile at Herb before she turned and ran for the elevator. "Don't forget to write, Herb."

Lori had to laugh. Nicole, who was only six months younger than she, seemed destined to remain a child forever. Would she ever change? Dear, sweet Nicky. Would anyone even want her to?

They were scheduled to meet Kevin and George in the dining room for lunch. Afterwards, Kevin planned to drive them to the airport. Since his plane didn't leave until nine, he'd have plenty of time to get them to their concourse, check in his car, and catch his own flight to Jacksonville.

Even though she would miss Kevin like crazy, in some ways Lori looked forward to getting home. She hoped Helga hadn't forgotten to feed Fluffy. And she wanted to call her mother again, to insist that she come for a visit, especially now with so much exciting news to share.

In spite of Lori's heavy daily work schedule, there would be ample time for the two of them to drive to Tampa to shop and browse. Maybe they would drive to Silver Springs for lunch one day and ride in the glass-bottomed boats. Her mother would enjoy that. Lori would see that she had plenty of opportunity to rest, too, while Lori was working. Even though a wide chasm had grown between them in recent months, Lori felt confident they could begin to build some bridges.

The clock in the lobby had just started striking twelve when Lori saw Nicole hurrying across the marble floor, the faithful bellboy following in her footsteps. His cart was piled high with all of their luggage, plus a gigantic, bulging shopping bag, its contents spilling over the top.

"I'm not sure they'll let you on the plane with those," Lori cautioned her.

"Don't worry. I'll think of something. Here's my key, if you want to go ahead and check us out."

Lori took the keys to the desk, reviewed the bill, and signed her name on the credit card slip.

"It's been a pleasure having you here, Miss Cramer. We hope you enjoyed your stay." That had to be the understatement of the year!

Turning from the counter, she saw Kevin coming toward her. "My car is in the drive," he told her. "Let's go ahead and load it before we have lunch."

His eyes widened when he looked at the cart being rolled out to his car. He lifted the lid to the spacious trunk and opened the back door of the car to make room for everything. "I'll park the car and meet you in the dining room," he told her.

"No, I'll come with you. George is coming over on his lunch break, and I'm sure he and Nicky will save places for us at the table." She hopped in beside him, not willing to forfeit a minute of their last few hours together.

Kevin pulled into a spot beneath a shady oak tree. "I'll leave the car here, and perhaps it will stay moderately cool."

Lori reached for the door handle, but Kevin stretched across and laid a restraining hand on her arm. Her free arm wound around his neck as her lips lifted to meet his kiss, and she discovered that sunlight could be every bit as romantic as moonlight when the setting was right. "Oh, Kevin, I'll miss you so much!"

"It isn't easy to let you go, love, but we both know it won't be for long. Lori, promise me you won't forget all the things we've talked about. Did you make me that list of names?"

"Yes, I have it right here." She untangled herself from his embrace and rummaged in her pocketbook, extracting several sheets of *La Hacienda* stationery covered with names and addresses of almost everyone she could think of. "I feel a little foolish about this," she confessed. "Some of these are people I hardly know, and not one of them is capable of the kind of action you're investigating."

Kevin tucked the papers into his inside coat pocket. "I know. You're just satisfying a silly whim of mine, but I thank you." He kissed the tip of her nose. "Come on, now. Let's go have lunch with our friends."

Nicole, Lorelei, and Kevin hurried toward Gate Seven, only to find that their plane would be forty minutes late for take-off.

"You can just leave us here, Kevin," Lori told him. "You have your own flight schedule to worry about."

"I have plenty of time. I intend to stay here until I see your plane in the air."

"Watch my bags, you two. I'm going to the news stand for a magazine." Nicky put her cases and the infamous shopping bag on the floor beside them, and clicked her heels down the concourse toward the shops.

"Darling, this is probably the last time we'll be alone together for a while," Kevin reminded her, and his words fell on her heart like a lead weight. "But you have my telephone numbers. I carry a beeper so my office can get hold of me on a moment's notice. Now, don't forget your promise to call me at the slightest hint of anything unusual in your life, no matter how insignificant it might seem at the time."

"I promise." She would have promised him anything he asked at that moment. She never realized love could be so all-consuming. She leaned against him, savoring the last few moments of his nearness. How could she bear to leave, not knowing when she would see him again?

Ignoring the stream of people passing them in either direction, he gathered her into his arms for one last kiss. "I love you, Lori. No matter what happens, always remember that." He used a thumb to wipe a tear from her cheek and coaxed a reluctant smile from her lips. "That's my girl. Chin up. I'll call you tonight after I get home."

In actuality, their plane was almost an hour late taking off, and Kevin stayed with them right up until the moment they boarded the big turbo jet. Nicole managed to wheedle her way on board with the two suitcases and her shopping bag. She put the cases in the upper compartment and squeezed the shopping bag under the seat in front of her, pushing the overflowing contents around the sides of Lori's bag under the next seat over.

It was Lori who caught the brunt of the stewardess's displeasure. "Miss, you'll have to contain those things around your case. Can't you put them inside?"

"I'll see what I can do." Lori poked Nicole with her elbow. "You've gotten me in trouble again, Nicky." She bent to rearrange Nicky's erstwhile luggage, forcefully cramming it into her own.

Once they were off the ground, it only took a little over an hour to get into Tampa International Airport. Since a light snack was served on the plane, the time passed quickly.

As prearranged, Helga met them in Lori's blue sports car. "I started to bring Fluffy with me, knowing how much you two probably missed him, but I was afraid the plane would be late, and I didn't want to leave him in the hot car."

"As a matter of fact, it was late," Lori reminded her. "Helga, you've been so sweet to take care of our cat and to come to meet us like this. How are things with the show?"

"Great. For this time of year, the crowds have been surprising. We've all been working hard." She sounded sincere when she said, "I'm glad you two are back."

Lori took the wheel for the short trip home, happy to feel in control of her precious car again. It was barely dark when they pulled into town. "Shall I drop you off at your house, Helga? I know Nicole and I will have to go to the grocery, but we want to get home and see Fluffy first, and unload our bags."

"You can just drop me off at the corner. I don't mind the short walk. I walked over to your place earlier to pick up your car. And listen, I knew you two would be tired when you got in. I didn't know what you'd want, but I picked up some milk and orange juice and put it in your refrigerator, and I left a loaf of bread on the kitchen table. I figured you could at least get through breakfast before you had to think about going to the store."

"Now, wasn't that the sweetest thing to do?" Nicole gushed. "And we didn't forget you either, Helga. As soon as we get unpacked, you must come over and see what we brought back for you."

"But we almost had to drop it out of the plane," Lori told her. "When the stewardess saw all the stuff we were bringing back with us, she almost evicted us in mid-air. Just kidding," she added, seeing Helga's shocked expression. "Seriously, we really do appreciate all the things you've done for us."

In spite of Helga's offer, Lori turned the corner and drove right up to her doorstep. "Now, don't forget to call on us for help when it's your turn for a vacation."

Helga hurried up the walk, while Lori waited to make sure

she got safely inside before driving away. "It'll be nice to get home again."

Lori turned her car onto the familiar oak-lined street and parked in their driveway. It took several trips from the car to the house to bring in all their belongings, and the place looked like a wreck when everything was dumped in the middle of the small living room.

Fluffy literally leaped into her arms the moment Lori entered the door, and she nuzzled her face in his soft yellow fur. "Look, Nicole. He didn't forget us."

Nicky braced herself as Fluffy gave her the same exuberant welcome he had hurtled at Lori. "Goodness, Fluffy, if I didn't know better, I'd think you're glad to see us."

"Let's get all this stuff put away," Lori suggested. "It takes up most of our living room."

"I'm so tired, I'm inclined to wait until tomorrow." Nicole was a first-class procrastinator.

"Come on, Nicky. Dig in and in the morning you'll be glad we have it all done."

"Oh, all right. Slave driver." She opened the biggest bag and watched the contents spill out onto the floor. "There's the tee shirt we got for Helga." She held it up against her chest. "I wish I'd gotten one just like it for myself."

"Well, I'm glad you didn't. I couldn't have crammed another thing into *my* carry-on."

Nicole began to scoop up her belongings from the carpet. "What's this, Lori? Is this yours?" She held up a small gold cuff link. "I don't remember seeing it before."

"Well, it certainly isn't mine," Lori assured her. "Good Old George must have dropped it when he was wrestling with you."

Nicole giggled. "Silly, I don't think it came out of my things. Anyway, I never saw George wearing cuff links. He's more the casual type."

"Let me see that." Lori held the small oval ball of gold at eye level for a better look. Heavy burnished gold glistened in the lamplight, and Lori had a strange feeling she'd seen it before. But where? She tried to remember. "I don't know, Nicky. Put it on the mantle and we'll ask Helga about it when we see her. Whoever lost it must be upset. It looks expensive."

By the time they had everything unpacked and put away, it was nearly ten o'clock and both girls were exhausted. "Let's hit the sack. We can shop for groceries in the morning." Lori didn't feel energetic enough to go anywhere else tonight.

They were both asleep when the phone rang. Lori fumbled for the receiver in the dark and answered groggily. "Hello."

"I'm glad you're the one who answered." Lori melted at the familiar sweet sound of his voice. "I didn't want to wait this late to call, but my plane just landed and I wanted to make sure you arrived home safely. Next time I promise to call earlier."

"Kevin , you can call me anytime you please. I'll always be glad to hear your voice." She clutched the receiver with both hands, eager to hold him close.

"Is everything there normal?"

"Perfectly. We put everything away tonight, and we're going to the grocery store tomorrow."

"Well, I'll let you get back to your dreams. I just needed to hear your voice. Good night, darling. I'll see you just as soon as I can. I love you, Lori."

"And I love you," she answered. She sat on the bed, holding the receiver long after it was silent, as though it contained a little piece of him, until finally she replaced it on its base and closed her eyes to dream.

When the first rays of early morning sunlight coaxed her into consciousness, Lori thought she was still in Marathon. She listened for the rolling murmur of the ocean waves, but all she heard was the blare of a horn sounded by an impatient driver on her street.

Fluffy, seeing her stretch, jumped from his chair onto the foot of her bed.

"You silly! I do believe you missed us." She ruffled his fur affectionately. "Let's go put the coffee on. She slipped into an old pair of cut-offs and a tee shirt, and slid her feet into satin bedroom slippers.

Moments later, the percolator began to pulse its rhythmic sounds, while Lori got out the cups and cereal bowls. Nicole was still sleeping, but she'd be hungry when she woke up. Lori hummed as she worked.

"Meow!"

"Oh, don't worry. I haven't forgotten you." She filled Fluffy's bowl with the dry cat food the vet had recommended. Fluffy sniffed once, then looked up to see if anything else was forthcoming.

"Has Helga been spoiling you with other treats?"

The new cereal box in the cupboard was Lori's favorite kind. Helga had been so thoughtful in bringing in the groceries for them. It made Lori ashamed of the thoughts she had harbored about Helga's jealousy. Things were much more pleasant now that they were friends. She poured two glasses of orange juice and filled her cereal bowl.

Surprisingly, the milk carton was already open. Helga must have opened it for the cat. She lightly sugared her cereal and covered it with the cold milk.

"Meow!"

"Just as I thought. She has been spoiling you. Just the sight of that milk carton set you off." Lori laughed and poured some in a bowl and set it on the floor. "Now, will you just let me eat my breakfast in peace, please?" She scratched the fur behind the cat's neck as he eagerly lapped the milk.

The automatic percolator was silent now, and a red light signaled that fresh, hot coffee was ready. She filled her cup and carried it to the table.

"Mmm! Smells wonderful!" Nicole stood in the doorway with her short red nylon robe wrapped around her. "Pour me a cup so I can pry my eyes open."

Lori filled the second cup with the dark brew. "Come sit down, and we'll have our breakfast. I already poured your juice."

"What's wrong with Fluffy?" Nicole asked.

Following the direction of Nicole's startled look, Lori watched in horror, as the big orange cat staggered toward them and collapsed in the middle of the kitchen floor.

"Fluffy!" They screamed in unison, rushing over and dropping to the floor beside him.

"What's wrong with him, Lori?"

"I don't know. He was perfectly fine when he woke up. All he's had is his regular cat food and a little milk. That couldn't have hurt him."

"I'll call Dr. Peterson. He'll tell us what to do."

Minutes later, Fluffy was gently wrapped in a big, soft beach towel. Nicky cradled him in her lap while Lori drove as fast as she dared. "Dr. Peterson said he'd meet us at the animal clinic."

Both girls were crying. Neither had spoken the words or dared to admit it to themselves, but instinctively both knew this was a futile journey.

They reached the clinic at the same moment Dr. Peterson pulled into his drive. He unlocked the door, and all three of them rushed inside. Nicky was still wearing her short pajamas and robe, and Lori had on her bedroom slippers. There had been no time to change.

It didn't take long for the kindly veterinarian to give them his grim report. "I'm sorry, ladies. He's gone."

"No!" Lori's mind refused to accept the inevitable truth. She had grown to love Fluffy like a member of the family. Tears streamed down her cheeks as she grabbed Nicole and asked, "What will we do? How can we learn to live without him?"

Hugging and moaning, the two women sobbed on each other's shoulders. Finally, Lori broke free and pulled a tissue from her pocket. She wiped her eyes and blew her nose. "What was the cause of death, Dr. Peterson?"

"I can't be sure without an autopsy. On the surface, it looks like poisoning. Have you put out any rat poison, or do you have any neighbors who hate cats?"

"No, neither. How could anyone hate Fluffy? Everyone who ever saw him loved him on sight. I suppose it doesn't matter why, anyway. But please, do an autopsy. We won't rest until we know the cause of his death."

"I won't have the results until tomorrow. Meanwhile, put away and save the rest of the cat food. We may need to look at it. That and anything else you know of that he's eaten."

Sorrowfully, the girls drove home. In their haste, they had forgotten to unplug the coffeepot. "I'm glad we didn't burn the place down." Lori pulled the plug from the wall and emptied her bowl of soggy cereal down the garbage disposal. There was no appetite for food. Lori and Nicky moved like silent robots, washing the few dishes and cleaning up the small kitchen.

When the phone rang, it was Mr. Porter. "It's good to have you back. We've been busier than usual for this time of the year. Do you feel like running through your routines this afternoon?"

"Not really, Mr. Porter," Lori told him, and Nicky confirmed the answer from the extension phone in her room.

"What's wrong? You both sound sick. Maybe I made a mistake sending you two off together on a vacation. Sounds like too much partying to me."

"Oh, no, Mr. Porter, it's nothing like that," Nicole said with a sob. "It's our cat. He died this morning."

"I'm sorry to hear that. Well, with pets, those things happen. Getting back to work is probably the best medicine to get your minds off it. Come on over this afternoon. We won't work out too long. Just enough to get those muscles tuned and get your timing right. Remember, you both have performances tomorrow."

After they hung up, Nicky came out into the living room. "Well, he certainly didn't display much sympathy, did he?"

"That's Mr. Porter for you. Heart of gold, but all business. But he's right, you know. We can't just sit around here and mope. Let's go over to the spring and have a work-out."

Grocery shopping could wait. Food was low on the priority list right now.

Mr. Porter was waiting for them when they drove up. "Glad you decided to come over. You made the right decision."

He had made a few minor changes in some of the routines while they were gone, and Mr. Porter explained them carefully. "We won't rehearse them in costume today. Just your bathing suits this time." That meant they could swim without the bulky mermaid tails that made swimming difficult, yet added authenticity to the acts.

As their director predicted, their strenuous workout served to take the edge off their grief, but the somber mood remained as they started for home.

The grocery store was on the route home and, although neither of them was enthusiastic about it, they stopped and filled a cart with things they would need to get them through the week.

"If you put the groceries away, I'll fix something for supper," Lorelei offered when they unlocked the back door.

"Don't fix much. I'm not very hungry."

"How about some soup and crackers? I'm not hungry either."

Lori poured the contents of a can of mushroom soup into a small saucepan and opened the refrigerator to get the milk. She was just about to fill the empty can with the milk when she remembered Dr. Peterson's words. Save the cat food. And anything else you know of that he may have eaten. She'd given him some of the milk.

"Nicole, don't use any of this milk until we hear from Dr. Peterson. He told us to save everything Fluffy had eaten."

"That's silly. It's the kind of milk we use all the time. How are you going to fix the soup without milk?"

"I'll use canned milk. It may be silly, but we have to do as he says. He'll call us tomorrow. I suspect Fluffy had some kind of virus or something, don't you?"

"Don't talk about it, Lori." Nicole's eyes filled with tears.

It was while they were eating the hot soup that Lori remembered her promise to call Kevin if anything unusual happened. This hardly seemed to qualify as the kind of news he'd want to hear, but because she had promised she dialed the number he'd given her. Anyway, it gave her a good excuse to hear his voice again.

"Lori, what a nice surprise. Is everything okay?"

"No, not really." She proceeded to tell him all the details of the day's events.

Kevin was silent for so long that she feared the connection had been broken. Then at last she heard, "Tell me the name and number of your veterinarian, Lori. And remember what I told you about staying with people and exercising caution."

"Kevin, you don't think—"

"I don't think anything yet. Like I told you, when I know something, you'll be the first to find out."

"Oh, by the way, Kevin, do you own a pair of gold cuff links?"

"No, I don't, but I have some silver ones. Do you want to borrow them? What's the occasion?"

"No, I just— I was trying to remember where— never mind. It's not important."

Their conversation ended with endearments, constrained by Nicole's presence in the room.

"Yes, Kevin. I do, too. Yes, I will. Bye."

Lorelei was brushing her teeth for bed when she heard

the phone ring again. Nicole was talking to someone. Perhaps George had called her. That would be nice for Nicky. It would bring a little sunshine into an otherwise gloomy day. But Nicole's voice didn't seem to be conveying much sunshine.

"What? No, that can't be. Yes, all right, we'll do that. The police? Do you really think it's necessary to bring them into this? You have? All right, Dr. Peterson. Thank you for your help. Yes, we'll call you later. Good night." She stood by the phone in shocked silence.

"Nicky, what is it? What did Dr. Peterson say?"

"Arsenic. It was arsenic poisoning. He said Fluffy had ingested enough to kill a healthy adult. Oh, Lori, he said— I don't remember everything he said— oh, yes. He said he had called the police."

This was like a nightmare! When the police arrived, the girls had to relive the whole grisly scene. There were questions on top of questions, all about their neighbors, about Fluffy's activities, about his diets, and even about their friends and acquaintances. It was late, and Lori was tired. She just wished they'd finish whatever they needed to do and leave.

The police were still there when Kevin called, and he insisted on talking with one of them. When Lori reclaimed the phone, it was to ask, "How did you know to call?"

"I don't need any reason to call my future wife. Just hang in there, Lori. We're going to get to the bottom of this. Be careful, and remember, I love you very much."

"Me too, Kevin," was all she felt free to say with Nicole and two policemen wandering through the room.

While she was on the phone, the police had confiscated the bag of cat food and the carton of milk. "Are you sure this is all he had to eat?"

"That's all we know of. We've only been home twenty-four hours. Helga was feeding him while we were gone."

"Who's Helga?"

That opened up a whole new line of questioning, and Lori wished she had never mentioned it. The officer recorded Helga's name and address, and queried Lori extensively about their relationship.

"She's just a co-worker and a very good friend, and that's about all I can tell you." She wasn't about to tell them that the two of them had just recently ironed out some differences between themselves. She valued Helga's newly won friendship too much for that.

"What about your neighbors? Any of them have a grudge against you?"

"No, of course not. This is a quiet neighborhood. Very little excitement. And Nicky and I have never caused any kind of trouble."

"How do they feel about pets? Cats, in particular?"

"We don't know many of them that well," Lori admitted. "But we've never had any complaints about our cat. We pretty much kept him inside."

"Well, we'll make a routine check of the neighborhood and talk to the residents to see if we can come up with anything. If you think of anything you've forgotten to tell us, be sure to call and let us know."

Harry circled the block three times. He had an idea, and he hoped this one worked out better for him than his last two.

The blond and her friend had returned to their pad yesterday. He'd watched them lug in their suitcases. Now he could finally begin to put his brilliant new plan into action.

True he'd been promised nothing for accomplishing this mission, but surely if he carried off his plan without a hitch, a bonus would not be too much to expect for his success.

Even though he had been told to drop the case, what did he have to lose by trying once more? He had to relocate anyway. His life was not worth a plugged nickel if he stayed at his old address. He'd seen what loan sharks were capable of doing to guys who crossed them. He had cleared out of his rooming house last week owing two weeks' back rent, with no place to go and no money to put down on a new place. He couldn't go on sleeping in his junk heap of a car forever. His latest plan was the last straw, and he was grasping for it like a drowning man.

The apartment house across the street from the blond dame's digs had a sign on the porch. VACANCY. INQUIRE WITHIN. Well, he had no intentions of inquiring within. Instead, he waited until nightfall so he could determine which apartment was empty. Fortunately, he discovered it was in the front of the house where he could hide to get an excellent view of the activities across the street, and it was on the ground floor where breaking in through a window had proved to be a snap. It seemed to Harry that things were beginning to turn his way at last!

He had slept quite comfortably in the vacant apartment last night, curled up in a corner on top of his few belongings. Just his luck that the place was unfurnished, denying him a bed with a nice, soft mattress. But if he could pull off this deal and collect a nice cash bonus he'd be out of here and as far away as he could get, with a new name and a whole new life stretching in front of him. Yes, sir, Harry's luck was beginning to turn!

As soon as it was dark, he parked his car near the bus station where it was not likely to draw attention and walked the few blocks back to the apartment he'd already begun to think of as his. He'd been careful to leave the window unlocked before he left this morning, so that getting inside was even easier this time.

Once inside, he took off his shoes and stumbled around in the dark until he could get his bearings. He found his way to the kitchen to check on his rifle. Before leaving the house this morning, he had pushed all his things behind the refrigerator to keep them out of sight, just in case some nosy landlord came in to show the apartment. The rifle was harder to hide. He had simply stood it behind a broom and a mop in the corner of a pantry and hoped no one would notice it.

He picked it up and ran his hands over the barrel. Luckily, he had not pawned his rifle. His car and his rifle were the last two things he owned, and once they were gone, so was he!

In his stocking feet, he moved to the front window and braced the barrel of his rifle against the window frame. A light burned on the porch across the street, illuminating the area with a soft glow that would make his job a piece of cake once his target stepped outside. All he needed to do now was wait.

There were several cars parked in her driveway. If the dame was entertaining guests, there was a good possibility she'd follow them onto the porch when they left, and he could finish his job and move out of here. Patience, he reminded himself. Just be patient and don't botch the job this time!

Harry's knees were beginning to ache. It seemed to him that he had crouched in this position for hours, but in reality, he knew that quite possibly he had only begun his long night's vigil. His fingers grew numb clutching the cold handle of his gun.

His eyes never left the front door of the apartment across the street. Harry knew the dames were still in there, and had already gone to bed. He could tell because of the intermittent shadows that played across the windows from time to time. He even considered drawing a bead on one of them. He was a top-notch marksman. But how could he tell which one was the proper target? If he messed up this one last chance, he felt sure there would never be another. No, he'd just have to wait for the right moment. It might take several nights of watching and waiting, but eventually he'd get his chance and this time he wouldn't miss! Then he could move forward into his new life.

His throat was parched. He craved a drink, even water, but he did not dare to run water through the pipes for fear the upstairs tenants might hear it and report him for trespassing. He hadn't committed any major crime here yet, but if his presence was discovered it would put an abrupt end to his present clever plan.

Wallowing in his own self-misery, his attention had momentarily lagged when the front door across the street swung open. Harry jerked to attention, took careful aim, and waited. His big opportunity was almost at hand! His breath came rapidly, and his palms grew sweaty, but his eyes never left their focus. His finger tensed, and he almost pulled the trigger when a figure stepped through the doorway and onto the porch, but Harry stifled his impulsive action just in time. That wasn't the blond. It wasn't even her friend. It was the last person in the world Harry wanted to see. *A cop!*

This changed everything. What were the police doing there tonight? Were they still investigating the tampering of her car brakes and the hit-and-run accident? And if so, how much did they know? Were they on his trail? There was only one person whose accusations could have incriminated him. If he found out that tongue had wagged, he had ways of getting even— and they weren't pretty.

He'd have to come up with a new plan, but for now he needed to back off and lay low until he could figure out what was cooking with the police. At least he had a temporary roof over his head and a place to sleep until someone came in to rent this apartment. He'd keep his eyes open and his mouth shut, and wait to see what happened.

CHAPTER SIXTEEN

Lori woke from a sound sleep to an insistent pounding on the front door. Her heart lurched in alarm. Who would be banging on their door before daylight? She looked at her bedside clock and saw it was not quite five. She reached for her terry robe as her feet probed the floor for slippers. "Who is it?"

"Kevin. It's Kevin, Lori. Open the door."

It couldn't possibly be Kevin. Was this someone's idea of a joke? She had talked with Kevin just before she went to sleep, and he was in Jacksonville. Warily, she pulled aside the window blind to get a view of the porch.

"Kevin!" Flinging open the door, she threw herself into his outstretched arms. "You're supposed to be in Jacksonville! How did you get here?"

"In my own car, for a change." He grinned down at her. "Aren't you going to invite me in?"

Sitting beside him on the living room sofa, she noticed he had not shaved, and his face looked lined and tired.

"What's this all about, Kevin?"

"The poison was in the milk, Lori. I've been with the police ever since I got here, and they traced the arsenic to the milk you poured for the cat. They're pulling every carton of that brand out of the grocery stores before they open this morning."

"Someone contaminated the milk supply?"

"That's one theory, but since there haven't been any other reports of poisoning, it's beginning to look like an isolated incident. They'll know more after they confiscate all the milk and test it."

"Kevin, what does this mean?"

"It means I want to get you away from here, Lori. How would you like to spend a week or two on a farm in Iowa until we can unravel some information? You'd love my parents— especially my mother. She's always fussing at me for not bringing any girls home. The two of you would have a fine time getting acquainted."

"Oh, Kevin, that's sweet, but I just couldn't. Mr. Porter depends on me for the show, and I've already been away for two weeks."

"Lori, I can't force you to go, but I'm asking you. Think about it for a few minutes before you say no. There's something rotten going on around here, and like it or not, I'm afraid you're right in the middle of it. Don't give me your answer yet. Just consider the possible consequences if you insist on staying here. Meanwhile, I want you to tell me everything you can remember about your relationship with Ken."

"Ken?" She was horrified. That was the last subject she wished to discuss with Kevin. "Why do you want to hear about that? It's over between us, and that's all you need to know."

"Not quite. You see, Lori, I traced the call you received that night at *La Hacienda* when the caller failed to identify himself. I've talked to Ken—"

"You called Ken?"

"Yes, and he admitted he called you that night. He said he was in Key West on business. He thought he saw you as he passed through Marathon, so he stopped and looked through the Yellow Pages and called every hotel in Marathon until he found the one where you were registered. When he got to his own hotel in Key West, he placed a call to your room at the hotel just to make sure you were there."

"Then why didn't he talk to me?"

"That's just what I asked him. He felt sure you'd refuse to see him if he asked, so he decided to try for an accidental meeting instead. He hit pay dirt when he found you in the hotel dining room that day."

"Are you saying that near accident in the boat wasn't an accident at all?"

"You're always trying to second guess me, darling. I only said I want to check him out. I already have a plane reservation out of Tampa to Chicago later this morning. Now, are you going to tell me what I asked? I don't have a lot of time. Have you changed your mind about getting out of the state until we find some answers?"

"You have to understand, Kevin. I would if I could. I'd love nothing better than to spend a few days with your parents and see the farm where you grew up. But it's just not possible right now."

He was obviously disappointed, but he couldn't force her to go. "All right, then. Let's talk about Ken. Start at the very beginning."

"Well, I certainly don't like wasting our precious time together discussing Ken Talbot, but I'll tell you whatever it is you want to know."

But there wasn't a lot to tell. She answered all his questions and talked freely about her relationship, the breakup, and the angry words that followed. "Ken turned out to be a real jerk, but I'm sure he's no murderer."

"Don't rule out anyone until the case is closed," he told her. "May I try one more time to convince you to go away for a few days?"

"Let me talk to Mr. Porter first. Helga has a day off today, so I really have to work. If he thinks she can take my place for a little longer, I'll think about it."

Kevin had kissed her goodbye and left the apartment before Nicole ever came out of her room. "Were you talking to someone on the phone?" she asked. "I thought I heard your voice."

Lori busied herself in the kitchen, putting on the coffee and making cinnamon toast to avoid giving an explanation. "We need to get ourselves organized here this morning. We're due at the spring in an hour."

Nicole munched her toast thoughtfully, washing it down with the freshly perked coffee. "I don't know anyone who'd wish Fluffy any harm unless it's that cranky old man next door. He's always chasing neighborhood pets off his property. But Fluffy stayed inside most of the time, so I don't see why he'd pick on him, unless he just hates animals in general. Anyway, he couldn't have gotten into our refrigerator."

"Nicky, let's not talk about it anymore. Just leave it in the hands of the police. Right now, we have to think about work."

The parking lot was already beginning to fill with cars. Nicky parked her little blue car near the back entrance in the spot reserved for employees. As the girls stepped out of the car, flash bulbs popped in their faces. "Excuse me, miss. Would you give us a statement?"

"About what?" Nicole beamed a pretty smile. She didn't know what all the fuss was about, but she was always happy to smile for a camera.

"Are you the ladies whose cat was poisoned?"

"Where did you buy the milk?"

"Did it look strange when you poured it?"

The questions came at them from all directions until Mr. Porter stepped on the scene. "Get off my property, all of you.

This is a private parking lot. Don't you see the 'reserved' signs?" His face was contorted with anger. To the girls, he said, "Get inside to your dressing room. I'll be in there to talk with you in a few minutes."

As Lorelei and Nicole slid quickly through the back entry, they could hear him shouting at the reporters. "All this fuss over one dead cat?"

Mr. Porter cornered them in the dressing room. "Now, you look here." He shook his forefinger to give emphasis to his words. "I've heard just about enough of this. I'm sorry about your cat and all, but I don't need this kind of publicity at the spring. We've never furnished fodder for the tabloids, and I don't intend to start now."

"We're sorry, Mr. Porter. We didn't expect the reporters here either. Thank you for sending them away." Lori understood how Mr. Porter must feel. He always prided himself on featuring wholesome family entertainment. The mermaids were expected to act accordingly, even when they weren't performing.

"Well, just don't talk to them or encourage them in any way. The less of this that gets into the papers, the better." He left them to dress for their act.

"See you after the show," Nicky called to Lori, hurrying away to the upstairs dressing room.

Already Lori could hear the music beginning to entertain the audience. It seemed good to get back into the performances. She thought again what a lucky girl she was to have a job she enjoyed so much.

Lori was always the last mermaid to enter the water. The others entered the upper tank from side doors concealed by fake vegetation and coral reefs. Lori made her entrance from below, where she swam upward through a maze of realistic looking underwater scenery, directly into the center of a circle of mermaids in the tank above.

She checked her oxygen supply and listened for her musical cue. Exactly when the drums started to roll, she began her ascent. The fins of the other mermaids weren't visible until she passed the largest reef, and then she saw the colorful, iridescent circle of giant fishtails. Just as the cymbals sounded, her glittering body appeared to the audience, who applauded wildly in appreciation of the difficult choreography and magnificent costumes.

At the end of the show, the girls gathered in the upstairs dressing room. "It's great to have you back."

"How was Key West?"

"Did you meet any cute guys?"

Everyone chattered at once. Lori and Nicky were so busy hugging and answering questions that Lori forgot all about speaking to Mr. Porter about leaving the show for a few days.

On the ride home, she thought of it. "Why don't we swing by Helga's house to make sure she wouldn't mind taking my place a little longer."

"Are you kidding? She'd give her eye teeth to have that spot permanently."

Helga met them at her front door with eyes red from crying and a face that looked like her best boyfriend had just dumped her.

"What's wrong, Helga?"

"Maybe you can tell me. All I did was try to help out some friends, and look where it landed me!"

"What do you mean?" Lori sensed this was in some way connected to the poison milk, but she wasn't sure just how.

"I've been down at the police station the entire morning. They're treating me like some kind of criminal. Oh, Lori, Nicky, you don't think I'd deliberately hurt Fluffy, do you? I loved him too!" She sobbed into her hands.

"Of course we don't think that. We know you were kind to Fluffy." Lori put a comforting arm around her shoulder. "What have the police been saying to you?"

"Mostly they want to know where I bought the milk, and what time I was in the store, which clerk checked me out, that sort of thing. They wanted to know if the carton looked like it had been opened. Now, do they think I'd be stupid enough to buy a carton of milk that was already open?" She began to cry anew.

"Helga, we know it wasn't your fault. But we need to help the police get to the bottom of it. Are you sure the milk wasn't opened before you left our apartment?" Lori remembered the carton was already open when she removed it from the refrigerator.

"No, of course not. I just put the milk and juice in your refrigerator and the cereal in the cabinet. Then I fed Fluffy his dried food and left. I had to hurry because I was driving to Tampa to pick you up, don't you remember?"

Lorelei knew she had uncovered a key piece of information, but this was not the place to discuss it. She'd call the police as soon as she got home.

The police were skeptical. "If that's true, then it means someone else entered your apartment between the time Helga took the groceries in and the time you got home from the airport. We've looked for signs of forcible entry, and you've assured me no one else has a key. We've checked with all your neighbors, too. No one other than Helga was seen entering your apartment or even prowling around the grounds. By the way, where is that boyfriend of yours who was down here all night trying to get information?"

Did the police actually suspect Kevin? "He had to go out of town on business."

"Well, next time you hear from him, tell him we want to talk to him some more."

"I'll tell him." If they thought Kevin had anything to do with this, they were way off base. What an idiotic idea!

She hadn't found the nerve to ask Helga to fill in for her again.

Not after all she'd been through. When Kevin called, she'd just have to tell him she couldn't leave town until some of this blew over. She had caused enough trouble for Mr. Porter and all the others. The least she could do was stay around where she was needed.

After lunch, she telephoned her mother in Pensacola. "Have you set the date for your visit?"

"Not yet, dear. I'm not quite up to it, but it does sound like a lot of fun."

"Are you getting any stronger, Mother?"

"Oh, yes, I think so. I don't know. Andy says I'm beginning to look better."

"Could I speak with Andy, please?"

"Certainly, Lori. I hope this means you two are finally becoming friends. It's been a long time in the making."

Lori didn't comment. She waited until she heard Andy's voice. "Andy, what's wrong with my mother? Is she improving?"

"Yes, I'm happy to say she is. Her color is beginning to come back. I think she had the flu or something, and then she wouldn't slow down and take care of herself. She'll be getting back in the swing of things soon, though, and she's looking forward to visiting you."

"Andy, I could take her to a good doctor I know in Tampa and get him to give her a complete physical. Don't you think that would be a good idea?"

"Lorelei, we have some of the best doctors in the world right here in Pensacola and I'm giving her excellent care. You always were a worrier, weren't you? Relax, honey. Your mother is going to be just fine."

"Andy, I have to go. I have another performance in thirty minutes. Tell my mother I'll call her again, because I really do want her to come soon. I'll make arrangements to come out there and pick her up if I need to."

"That won't be necessary, Lorelei. We have several cars and if she wants me to drive her there, I'll be happy to. But please don't pester her about it. She'll come as soon as she feels up to it."

Pestering her? Her own mother? Who does he think he is, the little twerp?

Lori had three more performances that day, and when she finished, she was tired both physically and mentally. That night, she was happy to fall into bed. Still, exhausted as she was, sleep eluded her. Troubles and worries always had a way of becoming magnified late at night.

Was her mother really getting better, or was she more seriously ill than she and Andy were letting her know? Lorelei wanted to help, but Andy always took offense at what he considered interference from her. Well, he could just take offense! She had only one mother, and she was going to satisfy herself that her mother received the proper care.

And where was Kevin tonight? He'd promised to be there for her when she needed him. Well, she certainly did need him now. She couldn't understand why he had chosen to go off on some wild goose chase to Chicago at a time like this.

Unable to sleep, she decided on a cup of soothing herbal tea. On her way to the kitchen she saw that Nicole had fallen asleep on the living room couch, oblivious to the swashbuckling actors battling it out on the television screen.

Lori sat in the living room, balancing her cup and saucer on her knees as she flicked the remote control over to the nightly late news. She didn't have to worry that Fluffy would jump up in her lap and upset her dishes the way he used to. She would welcome the intrusion, even if it meant a broken cup and stained carpet. Oh, how she missed that funny little ball of fluff!

Her thoughts were on Fluffy when a familiar face flashed on the screen before her. Her scream brought Nicole to full attention.

"That's Helga! It can't be true! They're holding her as a suspect in what they're calling *the poison milk case*. That's ridiculous!"

Lorelei was horrified too. "Anyone who knows Helga knows she's not capable of anything like that. We have to help her."

She went straight to the phone and dialed the police. "But we're the only ones affected, and we're not pressing any charges, so how can you hold her?" she argued. "I see. Well I can tell you right now, you're wasting your time. Helga had nothing to do with it. Mr. Porter? He's there at the police station now? May I speak to him?"

Mr. Porter's voice came over the wire. "I'm posting a bond for her, Lorelei. She'll be able to go home tonight. Yes, I know it's ridiculous. I agree. But the fact remains that she's the only person who had a key to your apartment. You'd better start remembering if you gave one to anyone else."

Nicole listened as Lorelei related the conversation verbatim. "It's all so awful. I feel like we're living in a nightmare."

Prophetically, all week long, they moved and worked as though they were existing in that nightmare. The two of them seemed to be cut off from the rest of the world. Helga gave them a wide berth except during performances, and Mr. Porter remained cool and aloof. Kevin hadn't called, and neither had George. Andy was barely civil to Lori when she called, and her mother always seemed to be sleeping— or so Andy said.

"If only we'd never gone away," Nicole lamented. "All of these things might never have happened."

Was Nicky indirectly blaming her for all the trouble? After all, the only reason they had left was because of what Nicole called Lori's silly fears. Lori didn't have the courage to ask Nicky if she still felt those fears were silly. No one had voiced the concern that either Nicole or Lorelei might have been a target for the poison in the milk, but the unspoken undercurrent of suspicion ran deep in all the ongoing investigations.

The police questioned them together and separately, over and over again. Lorelei felt she had answered the same questions phrased differently at least a hundred times. There were questions about people she barely knew. And of course there were always a myriad of questions about her relationship with Helga, her role in the show, and how she had achieved the coveted role of the mermaid queen.

There were questions about Kevin, too— how they met, what they talked about, what their plans were for the future. They hadn't questioned her again about his absence. Did they know where he was? She hadn't divulged that bit of information, but their lack of curiosity led her to believe they might know his whereabouts.

Except for performances and practices, the two girls went out as little as possible. Wherever they went, they were conscious of stares and whispers. Mr. Porter, hating the publicity, now sent someone to pick them up and drive them right up to the stage door each day.

Even between the two of them, conversation was scarce as they went about their daily routine, trying to keep everything as normal as possible. Lori had never felt so lonely in her life. Where was Kevin, and why hadn't he called her? Her only real peace came from her nightly Bible reading, prayer, and meditation. She had placed herself in God's hands, and now she must trust Him to see her through.

The ringing of the phone jerked her out of her reverie. She was sure it would be Kevin.

"Hello." She was breathless from excitement. "Oh, George. How nice of you to call." She hoped her disappointment didn't carry over the wire. "Hold on. I'll call Nicole."

Even from the next room she could hear Nicky filling him in on all the odious details of their ordeal. She tried to close out the sound of their conversation by turning on her radio, but even drowning out the words couldn't blot the thoughts from her troubled mind.

She could see at once that the call had been a wonderful nostrum for Nicole's broken spirit. She came into the room smiling.

"Whatever possessed George to call you at this late hour?" Lori asked her.

"He was watching the news and heard our names. He said he had heard and read about the poison milk case, but hadn't realized we were the victims."

"Victims! What an ugly word!"

"Intended victims? Is that better?"

"Nicky, do you really think we were?" It was a sobering question.

"What else can we think? They didn't find any other milk cartons that had been altered. Besides, how can we explain the fact that Helga said the carton wasn't open when she left it?"

"She could have been mistaken."

"Are you absolutely certain it was open when you found it?"

"Nicole, if one more person asks me that same question, I think I'll scream. Let's turn out the lights and go to sleep."

Lorelei was sure she wouldn't be able to sleep, but her dark hair had scarcely spread across her pillow before she was swept away into a troubled, confusing dream. As her body drifted into a graceful glissando, deep among the iridescent coral reefs, menacing tentacles seemed to reach toward her from every direction. In panic, she darted among the reefs in a vain attempt to elude their murderous grasp. Then the bubbles! Always the air bubbles, followed by a myriad of lights—a repeat of the dream that had haunted her for all these months. Was there some cryptic meaning to it all?

When daylight broke and sun rays sliced across her silky percale sheets, she lay in a cold, clammy sweat, completely drained and devoid of the energy she would need to carry her through the day ahead. *Kevin, Kevin. I need you so!*

Mechanically, she performed her morning routine. While the coffee perked, she brushed her teeth and laid out clothes for the day.

Her hopes soared when the phone rang. Nicole reached it first. Lori had thought Nicky was still asleep, but a phone call was more effective than an alarm clock in snapping her to attention.

"Hello. Yes. No, we're not listening to the radio right now. What was that question again?"

Lori stood in the doorway trying to decide what this strange conversation was about.

"Let's see. I think it was the City Slickers who made that recording. I'm right? And what did you say I've won?"

Nicky let out an ear-piercing scream of delight. Now Lori was really curious. "What is it, Nicky?"

Nicole's eyes were shining as she turned to face her. "You'll never believe this, Lori. We've just won two tickets to see the City Slickers in concert in Tampa tomorrow night. That was radio station WXYZ, and just because I answered one of their silly questions, they're going to treat us to dinner on the town and a chance to meet the Slickers in person! I'm so excited!"

Lori stood beside the table laughing at her, thinking how good it felt to have something to laugh about again. "That's great. But does that mean we have to drive to Tampa tomorrow night?" In normal times, a drive into the city would have seemed a lark, but with all the recent turn of events, it seemed to Lori like a lot of trouble.

"No, that's the best part. They're going to send a limo for us! Oh, Lori, this is the most exciting thing that has ever happened to me! I've never won anything in my life, and I've never even ridden in a limousine. We have to be ready by five o'clock, so we'll have to hurry home after our last afternoon performance." Nicole rattled on in excitement, while Lori watched her thoughtfully.

"I don't mean to be a wet blanket, Nicky. Of course it's wonderful. It's just that I can't seem to get in a festive mood in view of all our recent troubles."

"All the more reason why it's going to be so wonderful. Don't you see, Lori, this is just what we need. A whole change of scenery. At least for one evening, we can push our troubles under the table and forget about them. Imagine meeting the City Slickers in person!"

Nicole's enthusiasm was contagious, and Lori had to smile. "Take that new CD cover with their picture on it, so you can get it autographed, Nicky."

"Oh, I will. What should we wear? How will I ever be able to work tomorrow? This is just about the luckiest day of my entire life!"

"You're going to have to calm down, Nicky. If you keep on like this until tomorrow night, you'll be too tired to go out."

Of course it would be exciting to meet their favorite recording artists. Just to attend their concert would have been enough to thrill her under normal circumstances, but her heavy heart put a damper on everything these last few days. She'd have to muster some enthusiasm, though. It wasn't fair to Nicky to keep dashing cold water on all her plans. Lori felt all the troubles that had been heaped on them lately were indirectly her own fault, and she owed it to Nicky to try to ease the tension if she could. Trying to match Nicole's enthusiasm, she followed her into the kitchen. "I've never ridden in a limousine either, Nicky. We'll have a grand time."

"Let's get to work early so we can tell all the girls about it." Nicole was riding on a cloud of euphoria.

"Maybe we should wait until after we get back to tell them, just in case it doesn't work out like we think."

"Well, how could it not work out? I mean, the man at the radio station plainly told me I won."

"I'm not trying to rain on your parade, Nicky. It just seems strange to me that a disk jockey would call you. I thought you usually had to be listening to the station and call in with the answer. Suppose it was just someone playing a prank? Don't you think you should call the station just to make sure the call was legitimate?"

Nicky pursed her lips to suppress her temper. "I know it was the radio station, Lori, because I could hear their music playing in the background." As if to lend credence to her statement, Nicole snapped on the kitchen radio and tuned it to WXYZ. "See, they're playing one of the Slickers' songs now."

Lori regretted sharing her skepticism; Nicky had been so happy only moments before, and now she looked like she had just been caught up in a black cloud of doom. "I'm sorry, Nicky. I need to develop more of your optimism. I think the coffee's ready. Let's have some."

Sitting at the table, they listened to the music and made plans about what to wear. "I wonder where they'll take us to dinner?" Lori mused. "I suppose we should put on something dressy, don't you?"

"Definitely. You could wear that new green thing you bought for our vacation, and I can wear my new hot pink outfit. Should I wear my gold pumps, or will they look too dressy at the concert?"

The disc jockey on the radio was waxing passionately about the newest hits of the City Slickers, reminding everyone that tickets for tomorrow's concert were still available— yet there was no mention of the tickets they'd supposedly just given away.

Lori had a hard time getting caught up in the fervor of Nicole's elation. "I'd still like to wait until after tomorrow to tell everyone about it. By then we'll have lots of details to share with them. If we tell them ahead, they'll all come over to watch us leave in the limo, and that would be embarrassing."

"Okay, if you think that's best," Nicole conceded. "But it'll be hard not to talk about it among our friends."

And it was hard, especially for Nicole. Her gregarious nature made it next to impossible to resist sharing the news of their good fortune. For two days Lori helped by steering the conversation in other directions. She was afraid the whole thing would blow wide open when she overhead two of the girls in the cast wistfully voicing their yearnings to go to Tampa to attend the big City Slickers concert. Nicole's eyes lit up at once, and Lori had to literally pull her from the group before she let the cat out of the bag.

"Remember," she admonished. "You promised."

Once the mermaid show began, the girls were too busy to socialize, and the temptation to share their secret disappeared.

After the seemingly endless afternoon preceding the special night of the concert, the two friends were finally back at their apartment busily laying out their clothes for the big event, selecting shoes and sharing jewelry.

"Wear my jade bracelet," Nicole offered generously. "It would be a perfect match for your dress."

"Thanks. What time did you say the limo would be here?"

"Five o'clock, I think. Or did I say five-thirty?"

"Oh, Nicky, in all that excitement, I don't know what you said. We'll just go ahead and get ready anyway."

"I could call the radio station, just to be sure, but why don't we go ahead and be ready by five anyway. That way we'll be sure to be on time."

Lorelei thought about that for a minute. "You know, Nicky, I don't think it would be a bad idea to call the station anyway, just in case there's any glitch in this whole scenario."

"Oh, Lori! You and your skepticism! But if it will make you feel any better, I'll call them."

A male voice answered on the fourth ring. "Station WXYZ. Do you have a song request?"

"No, this is Nicole Drake."

"Yes? Well, what can I do for you, Miss Drake?"

"Don't you remember me? I'm the winner of the City Slickers concert tickets for tonight. I just wanted to check on the time of the limousine arrival."

Lori could tell by the sudden change of expression that what Nicole was hearing was not good news.

"You must be mistaken. Are you sure? I was told— no, I don't know the name of the person I talked to, but it had to be someone at your station. Well, because— I could hear music, and— I don't know. I'm just sure, that's all. You were? You didn't? All right. Thank you very much."

Nicole stood there in her slip, her hand still resting on the phone, with tears slipping down her cheeks. "Lori, I was such a fool. Evidently this was someone's idea of a joke. There weren't any tickets given away, and there sure isn't going to be any limousine coming to pick us up."

Lorelei's disappointment was small in comparison, but she felt sorry for Nicole, who had counted so much on this night. "It's okay, Nicky. Since we're all dressed up with no place to go, let's just go out on the town by ourselves."

"It's not just the concert or the limousine. It's that I was dumb enough to be taken in so easily. I should have checked it out. The man at the radio station said this sort of thing happens all the time."

"It wasn't dumb, Nicky. We were both fooled, but at least we didn't tell anyone about it, so there's no need to be embarrassed. We'll just go out for dinner at that fancy steakhouse on the edge of town. Let's really blow our paycheck. We won't hear the City Slickers, but I understand the band there is quite good. If we leave right now, we could catch an early movie first and then go feast on a choice T-bone steak."

"Lori, you're such a good sport. Who else would put up with me?" Nicole was finally able to manage a smile as she took her dress from the hanger and pulled it over her head.

At half past four, Lori backed her car out of their driveway. "Did you have any trouble making reservations at the steakhouse? I hear they're always crowded."

"I called, but the man told me they don't take reservations. I guess we'll just have to take our chances. If the line is too long, we'll just have to go someplace else."

"Well, I heard the steaks there are worth the wait, and we have nothing else planned this evening. We can catch the early movie at five and be at the restaurant by seven-thirty. Just don't eat too much popcorn; I want to be able to sample several things on their menu besides the steak. Denise says their 'bloomin' onion' is a meal in itself."

"Mmm. I can hardly wait to sink my teeth into one."

The movie was light and entertaining, a musical comedy, and in the quiet solitude of the theater, Lori almost went to sleep. It just felt so good to push all her worries aside and let her mind drift aimlessly along with the simple plot.

When the movie ended and the lights came on, Nicky nudged her. "Come on, Lori. Were you napping?"

"Not really. Just relaxing."

"Well, come on. Let's get over to the steakhouse and get our names on the list."

As they expected, the line stretched all the way to the parking lot. Lori let Nicky out before she parked the car; in order to get their names registered as quickly as possible.

"The man says we have a forty-five minute wait," Nicky reported, joining Lori at the end of the line. "What do you think? Do you want to go somewhere else?"

"By the time we went anywhere else, parked the car, and went in to get a table, we'd probably use up that much time anyway. Let's just wait."

"I'm glad you said that. I've been dying to try this place. Look, up there at the front of the line. Isn't that Denise Connerly and her husband?"

"I believe it is," Lori agreed. "Let's go say hello. We don't have to stand in this line. Since you've already registered our names, they'll call us when our table is ready."

Denise was a mermaid, too. Since her husband was a successful real estate broker, dining out was a more frequent occurrence in her life than it was for Lori and Nicky.

"Hi, Denise!"

"Hi, Lori! Nicky! Have you met my husband Bill?" After Denise made the introductions, she gave her friends a puzzled look. "You gals live pretty high for mermaids, don't you?"

"High? Well, I guess so, if you consider an occasional movie and dinner out as high living."

"No, but riding in a limousine? I consider that pretty extravagant, unless you're getting married or something." Denise cast her eyes around. "You're not, are you? I don't see any fellows with you. What's the occasion?"

Lori couldn't imagine where Denise got such a foolish idea. "I'm afraid you have the wrong mermaids, Denise. Nicky and I came in my little blue sports car. Unless Nicky's been holding out on me, neither of us has ever even seen the inside of a limousine."

Now Denise did look confused. "But I thought— yes, I'm sure that was your driveway, unless you've moved recently."

"What?" Nicky prodded. "What about our driveway? We've lived in the same apartment we've shared for the last few years."

"When Bill and I passed your place, there was a limousine parked in your drive, and a uniformed driver ringing your doorbell. I made Bill slow down so I could see you come out, but the man stood there ringing your bell for a long time and we finally had to move on. Maybe he had the wrong address."

While Denise babbled on about mermaids and limousines, Lorelei and Nicole looked at each other with wide eyes and parted lips, neither of them able to put words to their thoughts.

"Lori, you don't suppose—"

"Nicky, could it have been—"

"Are you ladies all right?" Bill asked. "You both look like you've been hit in the belly with a football."

"We're fine," Lori finally managed to say. "We've just realized we must have made a terrible mistake."

"Come on, Lori," Nicky said. "Let's go home. It seems I've suddenly lost my appetite for steak."

All the way home, Nicky sulked in the corner of the front seat while Lori drove in silence. Once inside, Nicky let go of the reins to her temper. "If you just hadn't been so dog-gone skeptical, Lori Cramer! If you hadn't made me call that radio station, we'd be sitting in the Tampa Bay Center listening to the City Slickers at this very moment. I wish you'd quit suspecting everyone of ulterior motives and learn to trust the people you meet."

Lori couldn't argue. The things Nicky said were true. "I'm sorry, Nicky. I really am. Why do you suppose the radio announcer didn't know about the contest?"

"Probably some new disc jockey. He told me he was on duty the night we received the call, but obviously he was wrong. I'm going to call that station and give them a piece of my mind!"

"What good will that do? Tonight is the last night for the City Slickers anyway. I'll try to make this up to you, Nicky, but I'm not sure how."

Sipping coffee at the kitchen table next morning, Nicky was still cool and aloof. She munched a piece of cinnamon toast and read the funnies.

Seated across from her, Lori studied the front page of the local paper. Suddenly she shrieked, "Nicky! Look at this!"

Startled by her friend's outburst, Nicky raced around the table and tried to read the article Lori pointed to by looking over her shoulder. The newspaper shook so badly she could hardly read the words. "Hold it still, Lori. I can't tell what it says."

"The limousine!"

"Limousine? Here, let me see that." Nicky snatched the paper from Lori's hands and began to read. "Oh, no! How horrible."

Police are investigating a mysterious explosion that demolished a white stretch limousine on the outskirts of town, claiming the life of the driver. The name of the driver has not been released pending notification of the family. Tampa Travel Services is cooperating with the police in an effort to determine the cause of the explosion.

"How terrible," Nicky repeated. "I wonder who—oh, Lori. You don't suppose..."

"I don't know, Nicole. I can only guess. I think we'd better call the police and tell them what we know."

CHAPTER SEVENTEEN

"I know you're right, Lori, but I can't bear the thought of getting involved with the police any more than we already are," Nicky complained. "Mr. Porter is about to boot us both out of the show as it is. He said he wouldn't put up with this kind of publicity much longer. Let's wait and see what the papers say about it tomorrow. Maybe the driver got a cigarette mixed up with his gas tank or some explosive he was carrying."

"I guess that's a possibility. Perhaps the whole thing was some kind of a freak accident, but we don't know for sure do we? And even if it was an accident, I still think we have an obligation to report what little we know to the police. We have no choice, Nicky. This is serious business. A man has been killed!"

"We don't even know for sure if that was the same limo that came to our driveway."

"No, but let's face it— we don't see many limousines running around town."

"Let's just try not to think about it until tomorrow, Lori. It's not like we really know anything factual. It's just going to make us sound foolish."

"We'll leave it to the police to decide whether our experience was related to the case or not. Give me the phone."

"We don't have time now, Lori. Look at the clock. In just half an hour, Mr. Porter's car will be here for us, and we aren't even dressed. If you call the police, we'll miss our matinee performance, and that will be the last straw for us in Mr. Porter's book. You can call them as soon as we get back tonight."

"I think I should call them right away."

"Okay, but don't involve me. If you call them, you'll be tied up with them for hours. If they let you loose by tomorrow; you can spend the day looking for another job. You do what you like, but I'm getting ready for work."

Lori watched Nicky flounce out of the room before she picked up the phone. She dialed the police station, but the line was busy. She waited several minutes before dialing again, but the line still rang busy. She might as well get dressed for work. She'd try them again before she left.

"Hurry, Lori. I see Mr. Porter's driver out front. Are you ready?"

"No, Nicky. You go on ahead. I'll just have to come in my own car. I'll park on the side and slip in without being seen. I'm not quite dressed, and I still have that telephone call to make."

"Forget it, Lori. That call can wait a few hours. I'll go on to the theater now and try to cover for you if Mr. Porter asks why you're late; but please hurry. You can't afford any more black marks on your record."

"Thanks, Nicky."

Nicky dashed out the door, letting it slam behind her.

Lori finished dressing and ran a brush through her hair. She felt an obligation to make that call, although time was running out. She reached for the phone, but heard its shrill ring before she had time to lift the receiver. She was tempted not to answer, but then, if she let it continue to ring, she'd surely not be able to make her call to the police. "Hello?"

"Lorelei?"

"Andy! Is anything wrong?"

"Now, why do you always expect the worst? I'm just calling to see how things are going with you and the show. Do you have a performance today?"

"Yes, as a matter of fact, I'm running late. I don't want to be rude, Andy, but let me call you back tonight. Will you be home?"

"Sure, I'll be right here, but hold on. I won't keep you long. I just want to ask you about the show."

"I may not even be in the show if I don't get in gear, Andy. I'm sorry, but I'm going to be in trouble with the director if I don't get to the amphitheater within ten minutes."

"What time is your performance today?"

"One-thirty. Really, Andy. I have to ring off. It's one o'clock already."

"So it is! I hear my clock chiming the hour."

In the background, Lori could hear the single chime of his clock. She didn't even wait to say goodbye. She slammed down the receiver, grabbed her car keys, and hurried out the door. Her call to the police would have to wait a few hours. She'd have a hard time now just getting to the theater and into her costume and make-up in time to come in on cue. Her tires squealed around the corner.

Andy had some nerve! It always made her mad to visualize him standing at the other end of the line. He was probably grinning into the phone, wearing one of her father's ties, and perhaps his solid gold cuff links. *Cufflinks!* That rang a bell! The little gold oval she had found on the carpet when she and Nicole returned from the Keys! Now she remembered why that cufflink had looked so familiar. It was exactly like one of the cufflinks her father always wore! But that was impossible. How could it have gotten there? Andy had never been in her apartment. Or had he? Her mother did have a key made the last time she visited Lori, but that was over a year ago. Andy? Suddenly a lot of things began to make sense.

She shuddered, but took comfort in the thought that even if Andy did have some malicious intent; she wouldn't have to worry about him today. She had just talked to him on the telephone. At least for today, he was hundreds of miles away in Pensacola.

What should she do? She would call Kevin's office when she got home to tell his secretary she had an extreme emergency and ask her to get in touch with him at once. Kevin had told her his office would always know how to reach him. She wished she had called them sooner.

As soon as Kevin returned, and she was sure he would waste no time in coming once he received her urgent message, she would tell him everything she now knew, and together they would contact the proper authorities. How comforting to have Kevin standing with her through what was sure to be a terrible revelation. Meanwhile there was the show, and she was definitely running late.

Something else kept gnawing at the back of her mind. There was something strange about that phone call; something she couldn't quite pinpoint. She'd have to think about it later; she didn't have time now. She was nearing the parking lot, and she had only minutes before her cue.

Her brakes squealed as she rounded the building and brought her car to a halt.

CHAPTER EIGHTEEN

Mr. Porter stood at the back door with his hands on his hips. "Lorelei, I want to speak to you in my office as soon as this performance ends. Right now, we don't have time for words. Just get to your dressing room and get ready. The other girls are already in their places."

Lori didn't try to explain. She took the stairs two at a time that went below to her dressing room, and Mr. Porter followed her. "I've already checked your costume and props. Everything seems to be in order. We have a record crowd today, Lorelei. I hope you aren't letting all this crazy stuff about a cat get you down. You look a little peaked."

"No, I'm fine, Mr. Porter. I'm sorry about being so late, and about all the publicity."

"Yes, well, the media exploitation can't be helped, I suppose. Even though it's not the sort of image I want to promote, it does seem to be bringing in the crowds. Just be sure you use plenty of that waterproof make-up. You really do look pale today."

He left her alone to dress. She couldn't allow herself to think of the new knowledge she possessed. She would have to get through this performance some way, and then she would get in touch with Kevin. Together they would move ahead and do what must be done.

Lori always felt nervous before show time, even after so many performances. But once she entered the water, all traces of her butterflies disappeared as the cool currents carried them away.

The giant fishtail that would cover the lower part of her body lay by the entry to the lower tank. Once she squirmed into that costume, her movement was limited, and she could only push through the rubberized door into the tank and swim away. Mermaids couldn't walk on dry land, even in this land of make believe.

She'd better use the bathroom now before she finished dressing. She had enough time. There were several acts before she made her own climactic entrance.

Coming out of the bathroom, she noticed her dressing room door was slightly ajar. Funny she hadn't noticed it before. Mr. Porter must not have closed it well before he left. She pulled it shut but didn't turn the latch. The girls weren't allowed to lock dressing room doors, in case an emergency arose and help was needed.

She took her time and carefully applied the special waterproof make-up Mr. Porter provided for all the mermaids. She listened to the music to be sure she recognized her entrance cue. Remembering Mr. Porter's words, she dabbed a little extra color on her cheeks.

Her thoughts kept returning to that phone call. It seemed strange that Andy would call her in the middle of the day, and especially with nothing to talk about but her performance. She'd call him again tonight to see if there was some other reason for his call.

How thoughtless of him to keep her on the phone after she told him her performance was scheduled to begin at one-thirty.

He was certainly aware of the time as they talked. She had heard his clock chiming the hour. *Clock! That's it! The piece of her puzzle that was missing. His clock had only struck once, but it should have chimed twelve bells if he was calling from home! Pensacola was on Central Standard Time, not Eastern Standard Time. One o'clock in Weeki Wachee was twelve o'clock in Pensacola, so Andy couldn't have been in Pensacola as he claimed to be. Instead, he was much closer! Now the big question: where was Andy?*

She heard the change of tempo and saw the yellow light above her entry begin to flash its ten-minute warning. Better begin to squirm into that awkward fishtail. The costume makers had labored for weeks getting the perfect fit for the foundation before covering it with thousands of jewels and sequins. Nowhere in the world was there a match for this opulent costume.

It was because of their similarity of stature that Helga had been chosen to replace Lorelei during her absence. If Lorelei left the show, Helga would almost certainly be placed in the leading role. Of course, she was an accomplished swimmer too, as all the mermaids were. Helga would certainly welcome the news of Lori's marriage plans.

The yellow light blinked faster now, and Lori recognized the musical cue that meant her entry time was at hand. She positioned her body so her head would push through first, into the narrow rubber passage. One, two, three.. *now.*

The surrounding water, with its cool familiarity, soothed her nerves even in the darkness of the entryway. She moved her arms and gave a strong flip of the glistening tail, propelling her body up into the immense overhead tank.

She looked upward. She couldn't see the other girls yet, but she knew they were circling just above the vegetation and coral that separated them from her view. Real living fish, red and blue and shimmering gold, swam around her. They accepted her presence in their underwater world with as much nonchalance as she accepted theirs.

She could feel the vibrations of the drums as they began their roll. Her spectacular entrance bursting through the circle of mermaids was imminent. She forced her body into a smooth glide over to the oxygen tube to fill her lungs with fresh air before her mighty upward surge.

What was going on? Where were the air bubbles that signaled oxygen coming through the pipe? Was there a malfunction in the system? A chill swept through her body. Such a thing had never occurred before! She still had her emergency air supply hidden within her costume, but she wanted to save that in case she needed it during her performance above.

There was another pipe just beside the door where she had entered the lower tank. There was no time to turn back, but she had no choice. She knew the band would cover for her by stretching their drum rolls, and although the other girls would wonder at her delay, they would continue to smile at the audience from their watery stage as they had been coached to do, and the spectators would never be aware of a problem.

Her lungs felt ready to burst by the time she reached the pipe by the entry. There it was! Just one more stroke and she'd have it. *There!*

Complete panic seized Lori when she detected no air bubbles rising from the hose. That could mean only one thing. The oxygen was turned off. Jerking the small emergency supply secreted in her bathing suit, it came as little surprise that it, too, was empty! Now her only choice was to exit the tank the same way she entered. Time had run out for her. A woozy sickness enveloped her as she pushed against the rubber entryway.

She had used this special opening many times in the past when Mr. Porter directed their practices. The flexible door had always yielded to the pressure of her body, allowing her to squeeze through to the world of fresh, oxygen-filled air. Today it did not.

But now it was too late anyway. *Oh, Kevin, Kevin. I'm so sorry. All those beautiful plans we made for our future together. Dear Lord, have mercy on me. I can't breathe!* And then suddenly she didn't even want to. Red and yellow, purple and green. A whole spectrum of beautiful colors danced around her, just as they had done in her recurring dream. She gave herself over to the swirling waters that swept her away on wings of comforting warmth. No more worries; no more cares. *Kevin, my darling, I'm sorry. I didn't want to leave you!*

CHAPTER NINETEEN

"Stand back everybody!"

"Somebody call an ambulance!"

"Is there a pulse?"

"Who was that guy who crashed through the side tank entrance?"

"I don't know, but it was like something out of a movie, the way he dove down to the bottom tank with all his clothes on and pulled her out."

Everyone who was crowded into the dressing room seemed to be talking at once, while medics worked over the limp and lifeless form on the floor.

"Please get back. Give them some room." Kevin barked orders from where he stood in his wet clothes, a puddle widening around his feet. A siren sounded in the distance and grew louder as it approached.

"Over here!" A path cleared for the attendants who crashed into the room. Lori's wet, motionless body was gently lifted onto a gurney and wheeled toward the door.

The hospital was only three miles away, but Kevin thought

the journey would never end. Holding Lori's cold, still hand in both of his, he wept silently while the medics continued relentless administrations to their patient.

Kevin shook his head. He'd finally found the answers he'd sought, answers that would assure her a world of peace and security, but was he too late? He prayed openly and without embarrassment. "Please, God. Don't take her away from me now. Please let her live."

It was two hours before the nurses and doctors finally had her stabilized and rolled into the Intensive Care Unit. Her chalky face framed by the mass of black hair looked startling against the background of the hospital pillow. Through the plastic covering of the oxygen tent, Kevin could see her chest rise and fall with each breath. At least she was still alive!

No one could tell him yet what her condition would be when she regained consciousness. Whatever it was, whatever *she* was, he vowed he would spend the rest of his life protecting her. He blamed himself for leaving her in the first place. If only he could go back and start all over. He'd never leave her again. Never.

He sat in a chair beside her door. Except for five minutes every two hours, that was as close as the nurses would allow him to come.

For two days and nights he sat riveted to the chair. Lori's mother Jean and Nicole had both been there and talked with him. So had Mr. Porter and a couple of the girls from the show; he didn't know their names. When he refused to leave his chair outside Lori's room, they had brought him hot coffee that he accepted gratefully, and food that he usually declined.

Nurse Carter found him there and tapped him on the shoulder, rousing him from a light and troubled sleep. "It's time for your visit, Mr. Collins. You can go in for five minutes now."

"Has there been any change?" His question was always the same, and so was her answer.

"No, no change.

Nurse Carter hated having to answer him. He was such a kind, gentle man, and his hurt was so immense. She wished she could hold out some ray of hope for him, but she had seen too many of these cases. Even when the patient came out of the coma, the end result was far from a happy one. This one was so pretty. She hoped it would be a different story this time.

Kevin stood beside her bed and softly called her name. "Lorelei?" Was it his imagination playing tricks on him, or did he see her eyelids flutter beneath the plastic tent that separated them? "Lori? Nurse, come quickly! She's opening her eyes. How do I get into this contraption?" He fumbled with the transparent wall between them.

Lori could hear a voice calling her name. Not just any voice; she was certain it was *his* voice! If only she could answer. She was tired. So tired! She wanted to sleep, but Kevin was calling her. He needed her. She had to answer him.

Her eyelids fluttered, and she saw movement all around. People in white. Where was Kevin? That big, blond guy leaning over her face *looked* like Kevin, but his eyes were red and swollen, and his face was covered with an unruly blanket of stubbley hair. Kevin was always so neat and clean-shaven. But, yes, it *was* Kevin. No mistake about it. Why did he look like that? Where was she? She wanted to know all the answers to her questions, but asking them took too much effort. She closed her eyes and drifted off into sweet oblivion.

The next time she opened her eyes, she was sure she was in a different place. That odd plastic tent was gone, and so were all those people in white. "Kevin?"

"I'm right here, darling." He jumped up from his chair and leaned over her bed, a broad smile covering his unkempt face.

"Kevin, you need a shave!"

His laugh was so loud that it prompted a nurse to poke her head in the door and frown at him. "Shhh!"

"After all we've been through these last two days, and your first concern is my whiskers?" He subdued his laughter to a decorous chuckle.

"Where are we, Kevin? I know this must be a hospital, but I don't remember how I got here. The last thing I remember is my entrance into the performance tank. Did I blow it? I don't remember the show at all."

"No, you didn't blow it. It nearly blew you. But you don't have anything to worry about any more, I promise you. I have all the answers to your questions, and we're going to be married and live happily and securely for whatever years the good Lord grants us together."

"Oh, Kevin." Her happiness spilled out in her smile.

"I'll tell you everything when you're strong again. Your only job now is to get well and get out of here."

Footsteps sounded outside her door. "Come in, Jean. I know Lori will be glad to see you."

"Mother! She had never seen her mother look so thin and pale. Her illness had certainly taken its toll. "Where's Andy?" As soon as her lips formed his name, small, ugly drops of memory began to trickle into her brain. Something terrible, but she couldn't remember what.

Jean looked at Kevin, and he offered her his chair. "I haven't told her anything yet, Jean."

"Told me what, Kevin? Don't talk over my head. I'm not a little child. What's going on?"

Tears welled in Jean's eyes and trickled down her cheeks. "My darling child, I'm so sorry. You tell her, Kevin. I can't seem to find the words."

"Lori, Andy's in jail." Yes, that was it! Scraps and pieces of information began to fit together in her mind like a crazy quilt. It had been Andy all along. Now she was gathering the lost remnants of her thoughts in horrifying chunks. The cufflinks, the phone call, the time differential. It was all coming back to her now, but she still could not imagine a reason for Andy's malevolent actions. She tried to raise herself on her elbows.

"Please, Lori. Try to calm down and restrain your emotions. It isn't good for you to get upset this way, and besides, they're already threatening to throw me out of this place."

Andy was in jail, her mother looked like a waif from a third world country, she was in the hospital without knowing why, and Kevin expected her to be calm and collected? She supposed she'd better try, though, or she never would get to the bottom of this to find out what was happening. She let her head sink into her pillow and took a deep breath. "Kevin, I knew Andy was responsible for the poison milk, and I suspected he was somehow connected to the other crimes."

"You knew? You never told me! When did you find out?"

"Andy phoned me just as I was leaving for the follies matinee on Friday, and I couldn't quite understand the reason for his call. But after we hung up, I began to put things together enough to realize he had lied to me during our conversation, and that he was not as far away as he pretended to be. I also learned he'd been inside our apartment while Nicky and I were out. But I still don't understand why Andy would do anything like this. Does he really hate me so much?"

"Lori, your mother is a wealthy woman. Your father left her in a very enviable financial position. Andy stood to inherit that money at Jean's death, but only if you were out of the picture first. Now do you understand?"

"No, not really. What are you saying?" The obvious was so unthinkable that Lori didn't want to believe it.

"I'm saying that Jean's recent illness has been the result of slow cyanide poisoning."

"Mother!" Lori raised her torso in alarm.

"Now, Lori, remember what you promised. Please calm yourself. Honey, would you rather save the details for later?"

Lori drew a deep breath and forced herself to lean back on her pillows. "Go ahead, please, Kevin. You can't stop now."

"I know all this is bound to be very upsetting for you, Lori, but you have nothing to fear any longer. Your mother is fine now. She just needs time to regain her strength. That's something the two of you will enjoy working on together."

Jean gave Lori a reassuring smile. "Yes, we will, and we'll begin just as soon as Lorelei can leave the hospital. I'm finally going to come for that visit you've been urging me to make, and this time I may stay so long you'll have to turn me out to get rid of me."

"I'll never do that. Now, Kevin, please start at the beginning and tell me everything."

"At the beginning? Well, Andy paid someone to get rid of you, Lori. It's as simple as that. First, he had someone mess with your car in an effort to create an accident, and when that didn't work, he had someone try to run you down, but you were too quick for him.

"When the first two attempts on your life failed, Andy finally decided to take matters into his own hands. Apparently he had a key made from one you gave your mother last time she visited your apartment. While you were away, he slipped into your kitchen and laced your milk with poison. I guess he figured you'd be the one to drink the milk, so in a manner of speaking, poor little Fluffy saved your life, and maybe Nicole's as well. I guess it didn't concern Andy that there might be two victims instead of just one."

"Oh, poor Nicky. What a lot of trouble I've caused for her. And Helga, too."

"Yes, Andy felt confident Helga would catch the blame for

his crimes. She almost did, too. And this story gets even worse. We've only recently learned about the death of a limousine driver who was one of Andy's innocent victims."

Lori shuddered. "Oh, that limousine! I know now that Nicky and I were meant to ride in it!"

"Well, when that crime came to light, Andy was charged with first-degree murder on top of all his other charges."

"But there's still something you haven't explained to me, Kevin. Why am I here in this hospital?"

"I'm coming to that part. Andy made a real study of the performances and the tanks and all the technology. He masqueraded as a tourist and watched a number of the shows. Mr. Porter remembered him because he asked so many questions about the workings of the tanks and props.

"Evidently he broke into the lower dressing room and tampered with the equipment, causing it to malfunction during your act. Jean says he's an electronic genius, but I guess he just used his expertise for all the wrong, evil purposes. Anyway, it's over now. The police have him in custody, and it's a sure bet he won't ever be around to bother you or your mother again."

"But you still haven't told me what landed me in the hospital."

"You don't remember the dry oxygen pipes?"

"No, I only remember entering the tank. The rest is really hazy. When I try to think of it, all I see is a profusion of beautiful colored lights like the ones in my dream."

"I hope that's the way it will stay in your memory forever, darling. You don't need to remember the rest."

"But how did I get out of the tank?"

She would always remember his sheepish grin when she asked him that question. She could tell he'd been up to something, but she couldn't imagine what part he could have played in this horrible scenario. "Tell me, Kevin."

"I was sitting in the audience waiting for you to pop into the act.

When you didn't enter on your cue, I knew something had gone wrong. I'd already uncovered enough information to know I didn't have time to waste asking questions, so I just dashed into the tank through the side entrance and dove to the bottom to find you. I grabbed your hair and pulled you up and out."

"Déjà vu!" In spite of her weakened condition and the seriousness of the situation, Lori couldn't hide her amusement. She remembered how she had kicked and struggled against him the first time he had pulled her from the water by her hair. How long ago that all seemed now.

"The crowd went wild," he continued, ignoring her innuendo. "They all thought it was part of a comedy routine. I got more applause than the mermaids."

Lori laughed as she pictured Kevin, fully dressed, coming to her rescue again. "Did you get your shoes off first?"

"No, of course not. There wasn't time. You've caused me to ruin yet another pair, and I'm not forgiving that easily." He smiled and kissed her gently on the cheek. "You'll owe me a lot when you get out of this place."

"Kevin, I wish I could have seen your performance. If only I had a picture of that!" Even with his two-day growth of beard, he still looked wonderful to her at this moment.

"You'll have enough pictures to fill a scrapbook. The papers have been full of it, including pictures of me in my underwater attire. Nicole has been saving all the clippings for you. She'll give them to you as soon as you get home."Lori's memory of the past few weeks had finally ebbed back into her consciousness. She remembered the gold cufflink that had given her the first inkling of Andy's involvement. And then there was that telephone call when he told her he was in Pensacola, but the chiming of the clock had given him away. She could remember everything now, including where Kevin had gone before all the events of the past two days. "Did you find Ken Talbot?""Yes, I did. And I found out Ken's really a nice guy. He felt terrible about the boating accident and all the trouble he caused for you. He admitted giving you up had been a real struggle for him, but he's finally accepted your decision, and he's moving on with his life. He helped me put together a profile on several suspects, and we were able to help the police pin down the hired hit man. You'll never believe where he was hiding out when the police nabbed him, but that's a whole story in itself, one we'll save for another day."

"No, please. I want to know everything now."

Kevin wondered if it might be too much to pile on Lori's plate if he told her that Harry had taken up residence only a few hundred yards from her front door. "Can't we save some of this for tomorrow?"

"Not a chance. I'm beginning to remember some frightening details, and I won't be able to rest until I know the whole story. There are parts of this I haven't even had a chance to tell you about yet."

Kevin was puzzled by her comment, but he would save his questions for later. Now he would try to fill in just enough information to ease her anxieties and allow her to concentrate on regaining her strength. "The police made a routine call on every house and apartment in your neighborhood. They became suspicious of a unit that was supposedly vacant, and they got the owner's permission to search it." He decided to skip the part about the rifle that was loaded with ammunition intended for her. Perhaps he would tell her about this later, or perhaps he would never tell her at all. "They found the man Andy had hired to perform his devious deeds, and they placed him under arrest. After that, the rest was easy. Harry was only too happy to spill the beans on Andy in order to try and save his own skin. In fact, he seemed oddly relieved to be taken into police custody. He seemed to have an idea that someone was after him, and that jail would be a safe haven where he could get food and shelter without fear. I don't know just what that was all about, but I'm grateful for his help that cinched the case against Andy."

"And Helga. What happened to her? Is she starring in the show?"

"Helga's fine, but she's been quite concerned about you—all the mermaids have been. Mr. Porter closed the show for a few days, but I think they're going to reopen tomorrow. And yes, Helga is going to have the lead until you are well and strong again."

Jean moved closer to her daughter's bedside. "Don't you think we've tired her enough for now, Kevin?"

Kevin looked at Jean and decided she looked as though she could use some rest herself. "You're right, Jean. Now that we know Lori's going to be all right, I'd like to go and get a shower and shave. Then you and I will go out on the town for a nice, relaxing dinner."

"Can't I go too?" Lori pleaded. "I'm not sick and I really want to go with you."

Kevin leaned over and kissed her gently on the lips. "No, you can't go, but I'll come back to see you after we get something to eat, I promise."

"Lorelei, Kevin needs some rest himself. He's been sitting outside your door for two days without a break. I hope you'll send him home to get some sleep tonight."

"Of course he must go home and sleep," Lori agreed. "I don't know why he was worried about me anyway," she added with a chuckle. "I don't know how many times I'm going to have to explain to him, *MERMAIDS NEVER DROWN*."

EPILOGUE

Two years later...

George and Nicole waited in the terminal of the Marathon airport and watched the big turbo-jet land and taxi up to the unloading ramp. "There they are," Nicky squealed as soon as she spotted them.

Lori ran into Nicky's open arms, while Kevin and George pumped hands and greeted each other with warm words of friendship.

"We have our car in the parking garage. Is this all you brought?" Nicky eyed their two carry-on cases skeptically.

"No, we'll have to go down to baggage claim and get the rest of our things," Kevin said. "Want to come along?"

"Of course we do! I'm not going to miss a single minute of your visit," Nicky said with her usual enthusiasm. "Oh, we're just so glad you decided to spend your second anniversary with us, aren't we, George."

"Indeed we are," her husband agreed. "Let's get those suitcases and get out of this place."

After their luggage had been loaded into George and Nicky's waiting car, Kevin and Lori climbed into the back seat. "This is just like old times," Kevin reminisced. "Just like the time we all went to Key West."

"No, you were the driver that day," Nicky reminded him. "George and I had the back seat. I remember every minute of that day. Wasn't it great?"

"Great!" Lori agreed, although at the time, she would have given a less enthusiastic response.

"Are you sure you won't reconsider and stay at our house?" George asked as he steered the car along the coastal drive. "We have plenty of room, and you know you're always welcome. In fact, Nicky was a little miffed when you told her you'd made reservations at *La Hacienda*."

"Don't think we didn't appreciate your invitation, Nicky," Kevin said. "Anyway, don't be miffed at Lori. I'm afraid you'll have to put all the blame on me. But since this is our anniversary celebration, I wanted to recreate as many of our memories as possible."

Nicky looked over the seat and smiled. "I understand. Really I do. Lori knows I'm the most romantic person alive, and that is certainly one romantic idea!"

"Well then, if you're sure—" George pulled under the portico of the hotel and got out to help unload their baggage. "We'll give you just a few minutes to get settled into your room, and then we're going fishing, unless you're too tired."

"All of us?" Lori exclaimed. She had hoped to have some time alone with Nicky. "Why don't you two men go fishing and leave us here to catch up on girl talk?"

"That's exactly what I told him, Lori," Nicky agreed. "Anyway, I think he was just being polite until he knew you didn't mind being left behind. They don't really want us tagging along."

"Not unless you've learned to bait your own hook," George

agreed, giving Lori a big grin. "Aw, you women would probably just get your lines tangled again. Come on, Kevin. We'll leave them here to catch up on their gossip while we do some serious fishing."

Noting Lori's look of relief and pure pleasure, Kevin said, "Give me ten minutes, George, and then I'm your man."

"It's incredible how little this place has changed in two years." Lorelei and Nicole sat under the striped cabana, sipping cool drinks from tall, frosted glasses. "Even the volleyball game is the same. Only the players are different."

"George and I were so happy when you wrote to tell us you and Kevin were planning to celebrate your second anniversary here in Marathon. We've planned a surf crab party for tonight, and George has managed to line up several from our old crowd. Remember Mike and Herb? They're both planning to come."

"We told you not to go to any trouble, Nicky. We just wanted to see the two of you again." Lori studied her friend thoughtfully. "Nicky, are you really happy settled down as a housewife?" It was difficult for Lori to envision Nicole doing the domestic scene.

"Lori, I didn't even know it was possible to be this happy. I have so much to tell you. But I'm not a housewife in the fullest sense of the word. I work at the scuba diving school every day, and I have help with the cooking and housework. You know I never was any good at either of those. I have full certification now to give scuba diving lessons, and I've learned to love it. Now, what about you? What has your life with Kevin been like? I feel so bad that we haven't kept in closer touch."

"I finally got that journalism degree I always talked about, and I'm working full time for *The Jacksonville Journal*. I write a weekly column, and I even have my own byline. It's a lot different from being a mermaid, but I really do enjoy it. And Kevin is so sweet and thoughtful. He helps me keep everything going in the right direction. I've truly been richly blessed, Nicole."

Nicky lowered her eyes and softened her voice. "I've suffered a lot of guilt over not supporting you through your fears during the time when you really needed me."

"You mustn't. You only acted in what you thought were my best interests. Who could have guessed my own stepfather wanted to kill me, and my mother, too!"

"How is your mother? She had such a rough experience."

"She came through it all like a trooper. She was under a doctor's care for almost a year, coaxing her body back to health, and she had to undergo a lot of therapy too, but now she seems to be getting along fine. Of course, she has some emotional scars that will never heal, but she leads a normal life.

"She lives in Jacksonville, just a few miles from our house, as a matter of fact. Lately she's been attending a small church in her neighborhood, and I see signs she's growing closer to making a full Christian commitment, but I can't push her. I can only encourage. It has to be her own decision.

"She puts in a great many hours of volunteer work at the local hospital, and she's made lots of friends in the condominium association where she lives. Kevin and I see her from time to time, but she's still not easy to find when I try to call her."

"What about Kevin? Is he getting along well?"

"Judge for yourself. Here come the fishermen now." Kevin and George came walking toward them through the sand, fishing rods in hand, but no fish in sight.

"Any luck, guys?"

"Sure. Look what I caught." Kevin held up an old sea-soaked tennis shoe. "Does this belong to anyone you know?"

Lori laughed. "You idiot! Mine has probably long since been digested by a shark. Throw that old thing away."

He stooped to kiss her. Even after two years, Lori still felt a thrill from each kiss, almost like those first ones here under the palm trees in this very same place. "I missed you," he whispered. "I wish you had come along."

"Nicky and I had so much news to catch up on. It's been two years since we've been together, and lots of things have changed."

"You bet they have." George sat on the edge of Nicole's beach chaise. That same old look of adoration remained in his eyes when he was by her side.

"Well, hurry and catch up on everything, because as soon as we wash the fish smell off our bodies and get into some clean clothes, we're going to take our best girls out for lunch."

Left alone again, their conversation continued. "Nicky, do you remember our trip to Key West?"

"How could I ever forget that? Remember Madame Zenobia? Lori, did you really believe she could see into our future?"

Lori hesitated. "Of course, I didn't really believe it, but I have to confess she did upset me that day. But I was already upset about a lot of other things, and—"

"Ooh, Lori, look! Isn't he gorgeous?" Nicole's eyes were caught by something in the area of the volleyball game, and she tried to turn Lori's attention in that direction.

Lorelei tried not to let her disappointment show. She used to think it was amusing the way Nicky always had an eye out for the hunks, as she used to call them, and flirted outrageously with all of them. But now that Nicky was married to George, Lori no longer found her behavior amusing. She guessed Nicole would never change after all. "Nicky, what's the matter with you. Won't you ever grow up?"

"But look, Lori. He's so adorable."

Reluctantly, Lori's eyes followed the direction of Nicky's pointing finger, and what she saw surprised her. A toddler with a sand pail and shovel was experimenting with his first steps across the bumpy terrain, and yes, he *was* adorable. Although he fell with each few steps, he determinedly rose and tried again. His chubby cheeks were flushed, and his dark, tousled curls were damp with perspiration.

"That child?" Lori queried. "Is that where you're looking ?"

"Of course. What did you think? No, don't tell me. I can guess." Nicky chuckled. "I still look for the cute ones, Lori, but I've changed my focus on what I define as cute these days. I'm definitely eyeing the sandbox set."

"I plead guilty. I did misjudge the object of your admiration. And yes, he is adorable. What fortitude!"

"No wonder he caught my eye. Look at those dark curls. I'll bet mine will look just like that."

Lori turned to stare at her. "Nicole! Are you trying to tell me something? Are you…?"

Nicole giggled. "Yes, Lori. I wanted to wait for Kevin and George, so we could both tell you when we were all together, but somehow I just couldn't keep my secret a minute longer. Besides, we might have a few more surprises to spring before your visit ends."

Now, what did she mean by that? "Nicky, that's wonderful news. When is the happy event going to take place?"

"In November. We think it's pretty great, too. George has already increased his inventory of pint-sized snorkeling gear. He'll have him in the water before he learns to crawl."

"Or her."

"Whatever."

Lori leaned over and gave Nicole a hug. Some things had changed, all right, but Nicole was still the dearest friend she would ever have. "I see the guys coming. Let's meet them and go for some lunch."

Over lunch they talked about their plans for the evening. "We're going crabbing at the same cove where we went before," George told them. "If we're lucky, we'll eat our fill of crabs."

"It will really seem like we're rolling back the calendar, won't it?" Lori said.

"But we won't keep you out late," George promised. "We know you're on your second honeymoon, and besides, Nicky and I have to get up early in the morning."

"I was going to tell them about that, honey. In fact, I'm hoping maybe they'd like to come along with us."

"Of course, you know we'd like to spend lots of time with you and George while we're down here, Nicky, but tomorrow is Sunday, and you remember what Kevin and I do on Sunday. Maybe we can get together later in the afternoon."

Nicky laughed. "You can't get used to the new Nicole, can you, Lori?"

"I'm trying, Nicky, but you're moving pretty fast for me. Tell me what you're referring to this time."

"George and I were hoping you'd go to church with us tomorrow. We have to leave pretty early, because we lead a youth group that meets before the regular service."

"You and George...?"

George was amused at her surprise. "Did you think we were heathens, Lori?"

"Well, no, of course not, but I didn't know— that is, we hadn't—"

"Never mind, Lori," Nicole said. "It's all right. I don't blame you for being surprised, but this is the something special I've been saving to share with you."

Lori could feel her heart growing warm with joy. "Tell me all about it, Nicky."

"I always told you I was a Christian, but I never understood what it meant to give my whole heart to the Lord. When George and I were first married, even though we were in love, we had some unsteady times, and our marriage was kind of like that house built on sand. You know, the one that washed away when the rains came down." Her voice dropped to a lower pitch as she continued. "We talked about you and Kevin and the kind of relationship you two had. We always knew you had something special that seemed to be missing in ours, but we didn't recognize what it was until almost too late. Our minister helped us a lot, and when we finally got our priorities in the right order, we began to build our house on a rock. I don't need to tell you what rock that was."

Tears rolled down Lori's cheeks as she listened to her friend's testimony. "I'm just so happy for you both. God has truly answered my prayers in a wonderful way."

"We couldn't be more pleased," Kevin agreed. "This is something Lori and I have prayed about together."

"Well, that's why we're working with the youth group now," George explained. "Nicky has said so many times it was the seeds Lori planted for all those years that finally took root and grew, and we hope to plant some seeds ourselves— sort of a pay-back, I guess you could call it."

"But Nicky, you never let on that you listened to any of the things I said," Lori protested.

"I didn't really know it myself back then. That's what George means about the seeds. We never know when a seed hits fertile ground, do we? Have you ever heard that song, *Pass It On*?"

"Yes, it's one of our favorites, and I see what you're getting at. It begins, *It only takes a spark to get a fire glowing, and soon all those around are warmed up to its glowing.*"

"Exactly! You were the spark for me, Lori, and I hope George and I can light a few sparks here in Marathon. Say, by the way, do you remember Hector Fonseca, the man whose house you painted?"

"Of course," Kevin and Lori chorused. "Is he still in this area?"

"Yes, he certainly is, and you'll be interested to know that one of Hector's sons is in our youth group. He's a fine boy. The family has settled permanently on their little farm outside of town, and Hector has a job with a local construction company. Rosa works in a local florist shop, and the two younger children are enrolled in school here. They were a little behind when they first came here because they'd moved around so much, but they're both bright children and managed to catch up to their age group quickly."

"Is Reverend Stanfield still at the little church?"

"Yes, and the church is growing. You'll have a chance to see for yourselves tomorrow—that is, if you agree to come with us."

"On our vacation?" Lori teased, mimicking Nicky's response two years earlier. But when Nicole raised her eyebrows, Lori laughed. "Of course we'll come. We wouldn't miss it."

The crab boil was almost an exact repeat of the one they enjoyed on their first visit to Marathon. Just as Nicole promised, Mike and Herb were both there, and while many of the faces were new, the same jovial spirit remained.

Later, singing songs in the moonlight, George had a special request. "Do y'all know *Pass It On*?"

The sweet strains of the hymn drifted across the warm sands and hung in the evening air, and Lori and Nicole both dabbed at the tears that ran down their cheeks.

"*It only takes a spark...*"

The evening ended on a quiet note as the guests gathered their belongings and headed down the beach toward their cars. Hugs and promises to keep in touch were exchanged, and everyone agreed the party was a huge success.

* * *

Riding in the elevator up to the sixth floor, Kevin took advantage of the privacy of the small cubicle and pulled Lorelei into his arms. "It was a great beach party, and the crabs tasted just as delicious as I remembered them, but I thought it would never end. I was ready to bring you back to the hotel hours ago."

"Me too," she sighed happily. "I was ready to come back."

The elevator stopped, and the heavy doors slid open with a clang. "After you, my pretty little mermaid."

"Ex-mermaid," she corrected.

At the door of Room 641, Kevin fumbled with the key. "Are you going to let me inside this room with less hassle than you gave me last time?"

"It's against ground rules. Remember?" she teased.

He swept her up in his arms and carried her across the threshold. Laying her down on the big king-sized bed, he sprawled beside her. "I'm making the ground rules tonight, Miss Mermaid."

She smiled as he reached over and turned off the bedside light.

~THE END~

About the Author

Muncy Chapman, along with raising a family and pursuing a career in nursery management, has won numerous awards for her poetry, stories, and articles for newspapers and magazines, and was a regular columnist for a local newspaper. She has served as the president of Martin County Writers' Association and is a member of National League of American Pen Women.

Her first adult novel was published in 1998. *What Love Remembers* is a contemporary romance set on one of the beautiful Barrier Islands off Florida's west coast. *Margaret's Quest*, an inspirational novel set in Apalachicola in 1836, was released by Barbour Publishing Company in early 1999, followed by *The Name Game* in February 2000 and *Condo-Mania!* in March 2001.

Along with her husband, Florida historian Herb Chapman, Muncy co-authored *Wiregrass Country*, a historical novel set in the Florida Territory in 1835. This first in a series of Florida pioneer stories was released by Pineapple Press in the fall of 1998.